"Don't fall for me, Carly," Gary said

His voice was low, despondent. He tried to push her hand away from his face, but to his dismay he found himself leaning closer. "Good God, lady, it's bad enough that my own life is in tatters. Don't let me bring you down with me."

"To me it's not a matter of bringing each other up or down, Gary." Her thumb swept over his jaw and across his chin, teasing the corner of his lower lip. "It's a matter of walking hand in hand, and—"

"Don't!" The word was no more than a desperate croak as he caught her thumb. "It would never work, never in ten thousand years." But even as he said it he felt the iron wall he'd worked so hard to erect between them collapsing....

ABOUT THE AUTHOR

Suzanne Ellison, an accomplished Superromance writer, is not one to run from challenges. And writing a realistic romance with a prison setting was a challenge with a capital C. Suzanne lives in California with her husband Scott, her daughter Tara, and a large menagerie of beloved pets. Be on the lookout for books about dog lovers and camel jockeys!

HARLEQUIN SUPERROMANCE
165–WINGS OF GOLD
258–PINECONES AND ORCHIDS
283–FOR ALL THE RIGHT REASONS
308–WORDS UNSPOKEN
315–FAIR PLAY

HARLEQUIN INTRIGUE
46–NOWHERE TO RUN

Don't miss any of our special offers. Write to us at the following address for information on our newest releases.

Harlequin Reader Service
901 Fuhrmann Blvd., P.O. Box 1397, Buffalo, NY 14240
Canadian address: P.O. Box 603,
Fort Erie, Ont. L2A 5X3

Candle in the Window

SUZANNE ELLISON

Harlequin Books

TORONTO • NEW YORK • LONDON
AMSTERDAM • PARIS • SYDNEY • HAMBURG
STOCKHOLM • ATHENS • TOKYO • MILAN

FORTY YEARS OF Romance

Published August 1989

First printing June 1989

ISBN 0-373-70369-4

Copyright © 1989 by Suzanne Pierson Ellison. All rights reserved. Except for use in any review, the reproduction or utilization of this work in whole or in part in any form by any electronic, mechanical or other means, now known or hereafter invented, including xerography, photocopying and recording, or in any information storage or retrieval system, is forbidden without the permission of the publisher, Harlequin Enterprises Limited, 225 Duncan Mill Road, Don Mills, Ontario, Canada M3B 3K9.

All the characters in this book have no existence outside the imagination of the author and have no relation whatsoever to anyone bearing the same name or names. They are not even distantly inspired by any individual known or unknown to the author, and all incidents are pure invention.

® are Trademarks registered in the United States Patent and Trademark Office and in other countries.

Printed in U.S.A.

For Uncle Don and Aunt Wava,
with love

PROLOGUE

"HAS THE JURY reached a verdict?" asked the judge.

Vaguely, as though it were a terrible dream, Gary Reid heard the jury foreman respond in the affirmative, saw him hand a piece of paper to the bailiff, saw the bailiff pass it on to the man in the long black robe. He knew that the words on that paper were vital to his future, to his life. He also knew he should have cared deeply what the jury had decided, but the truth was, he was numb. The scene before him was too surreal to be frightening.

Although he was only thirty-four, Gary's hair was prematurely snowy white, very thick and smooth. He was a tall man, lithe and agile, who'd once worn a ready smile, enhanced by two very deep, boyish dimples. Until last year, his blue eyes had sparkled whenever he laughed, but now they showed no animation whatsoever. Blankly they stared at his long, gentle hands, which had been trained so painstakingly to heal and soothe.

Today he was dressed in the same sharp three-piece suit that Michelle had picked out for him on their eighth anniversary, and—on the outside—he looked about the same as he had then. But inside, Gary was a completely different man. On that faraway golden afternoon, he'd been deliriously happy to get a day off from his demanding schedule as a resident at St. Paul's Hospital, a day to spend at home with his beautiful wife and darling daughters, a day to bask in the sun.

Three weeks later he'd found out that his beloved Michelle was dying; six months later she was dead. And while he'd still been reeling from that agony, clinging to the love of his two precious youngsters to give him the strength to go on, the next blow had struck him with whirlwind force. He was still too stunned to make much sense of it. All he was sure of was that a pair of uniformed policemen had shown up at St. Paul's emergency room one rainy winter night and asked to speak to him alone. He hadn't seen either of his little girls since then.

Pain and shock still made the circumstances hazy in his mind, but one thing remained quite clear to Gary. Somehow, someway, he *would* get his babies back; someday he would rebuild his life. But that someday, he realized with renewed anguish, was going to be a long time in the future, because the judge was gesturing impatiently now, repeating his request for the defendant to please rise.

With a jolt, Gary remembered that *he* was the defendant in this real-life trial. And—incredible as it seemed—the judge was informing the court that after eight years of joyful marriage, four years of proud fatherhood and eleven years of grueling training for a professional career, Dr. Gary Reid had a new role to play.

In the blink of an eye he'd become a convicted felon who was going to serve hard time.

CHAPTER ONE

IT WAS NEARLY 4:00 p.m. when Carly Winston's old black pickup rattled into the new fire camp on the southern edge of Camelback Ridge. She'd made the trip in less than two hours, which wasn't bad considering that she'd been sound asleep when the dispatcher in Goleta had first called to sound the alarm.

"We've got another fire in the Los Padres," he'd informed her briskly, referring to the massive national forest that sprawled down the central coast of California, ending just a few miles from her home. "We need a division supervisor for the night shift. How soon can you get there?"

Carly received such calls at all hours of the day and night, frequently when she was exhausted from putting in a week's worth of sixteen-hour days on a previous blaze, but it never occurred to her to refuse a summons. Fire fighting was her life, her passion, her personal mission. She defended the wildlands of the Los Padres National Forest the way her father had defended his country all of his life; he'd taught her young that one never questioned duty.

Carly didn't blame her dad for choosing a profession that had uprooted her every year of her childhood; he loved what he did and he was very good at it. After Carly's mother had died, however, the Air Force became Colonel Carl Winston's entire life, and although Carly knew that he loved his only daughter dearly, she'd almost been more relieved than lonely when he finally checked her into a boarding school at the age of twelve. She tried to tell herself that she hadn't really been abandoned; it was the lot of any military family to have their menfolk gone a great deal. In fact, the idea of somebody coming home every night seemed so bizarre to Carly that it was entirely natural for her to choose to work in a professional field where unpredictable hours went with the territory....

In less than half an hour she had showered, tugged on a clean T-shirt and a pair of jeans, and grabbed her last letter from her father and her fire bag on her way out the door. She always kept the bag stocked with several changes of clean clothes and life's bare essentials because she never had time to pack anything once she got a call. For the same reason she kept the rest of her gear in her old Chevy truck at all times: a hard hat with a headlamp, her web gear and fire shelter, and a "handy-talky" radio to listen to the Forest Network band on her way to the fire.

"Sorry, Homer," she'd told her huge marmalade tomcat before leaving, tugging gently on his ears and giving him a scratch or two under the chin. Savoring the sound of his contented purr, she'd opened a can of tuna and filled up a huge bucket of dry cat food that she kept for him on the floor of her yellow duck-and-daisy-decorated kitchen. "I know we didn't get much time together this week, but you know how it goes."

Homer, the only roommate Carly's unpredictable hours allowed her, took time to rub her shin a couple of times and squeak out a disapproving meow at Carly's abandonment, but there was nobody else in her small apartment to mourn her absence, nobody to know or care if she was gone for three or four days at a time.

Actually, Carly suspected that Willard Jameson, her landlord, noticed when she was gone, based on the way he affectionately clucked over her whenever she was sick. Her apartment was a converted "mother-in-law" suite that Willard had built over the garage for his mother before her death ten years ago. It wasn't very roomy, but the sitting room, kitchenette and single bedroom were very tastefully furnished. Carly was especially partial to the blend of French provincial maple with the blue-and-yellow floral print on the sofa. So much of her life was spent with rugged men in rough country that she craved feminine ambience in her own home.

There was nothing feminine about the sight that greeted Carly as she pulled into the dusty clearing on Camelback Ridge, where several other trucks were already parked; as usual, she was the only female for miles in all directions. But she didn't have time to dwell on anything so mundane. No matter how many times Carly arrived in a new fire camp, she could never stifle the heart-pounding thrill that seized her. Part of it was the sight and smell of the falling ash, the nearby crackle and pop of the raging fire; another part of it was anticipating the hurrying and scurrying of burly men hauling in trailers that would house every aspect of the camp, right down to the sinks, showers, cots and kitchen supplies. Part of it was simply the sense of knowing that she, Carly Winston, was a component of something so much bigger than herself: man's show of force against the elements, where there was always some question as to which side might win.

It was a lot like going to war.

Less than a month ago, John Campbell, a good friend of Carly's—a professional fire fighter who'd frequently battled blazes by her side—had gotten trapped by a fire during a routine reflagging mission. He was as skilled as any man in the Forest Service, and it was still hard for Carly to believe that he was dead. Among the staff his name was still spoken gingerly and with great respect. Carly knew his tragedy was a reminder that every person who volunteered to fight a fire was putting his or her life on the line. It was also the reason that the courageous people who banded together for these sieges—these exhausting, intense days and nights—forged a bond that was both instantaneous and everlasting.

"Carly!" A brisk masculine voice reached her through the hubbub. "Over here!"

She eased her way around a landing helicopter to join Bill Lundgren, who would be her supervisor for the duration of this fire. He was a man of medium height and maximum integrity. In his mid-forties, he was just beginning to lose some of his sandy brown hair. But he made no attempt to hide his bald spot—one of many reasons he'd earned Carly's respect.

"Glad you could get here so quickly, Carly," he greeted her warmly, shaking her hand. "We've got a lot to do tonight."

That was the understatement of the century; as far as Carly was concerned, executing a fire plan was like mobilizing troops for battle. But she'd worked many previous fires with Bill, and she had a lot of faith in his leadership skills. She followed him to a clearing that had apparently been temporarily designated as headquarters for operations, at least until the trailers arrived. She nodded briefly to the familiar, heavyset man leaning against Bill's truck, but she couldn't quite summon up the same warm smile of greeting for him that she'd flashed at Bill.

Wade Haley was a huge man—not fat, but solid as a rock—with a cultivated, tough expression and an intimidating, macho walk. Not yet forty, he was nonetheless one of the old school, the sort of man who might easily have said, "Now, now, Carly, honey, don't you worry your pretty little head about the big, bad fire." He'd never said those exact words to her, fortunately, but his patronizing attitude had irritated Carly on more than one occasion.

"I want Carly to take Division A tonight," Bill informed the two of them as he rolled out a map on the hood of the truck and began to present the night shift's fire plan. "Wade, you're Division B. Division A has one of our crews, one college crew and three convict crews from the prison at Tejon."

Quickly he rattled off the names of the professional Tejon County fire fighters who would serve as crew bosses for each of Carly's five crews. Previously she had worked with Paul Jeffries, who was supervising one of the convict crews, but the other names were new to her. "The college kids have a lot of guts, but not much sense, so keep an eye on them," Bill continued. "The prisoners are pretty well trained, but as you know, they're not professional fire fighters when they're not behind bars, so they lack the experience of most of our Forest Service men."

"And women," Carly said patiently, as she did every time Bill forgot to include her in his mental calculations of his staff. Actually, Bill was one of her mentors and had only the ghost of chauvinism in his heart. It was Wade Haley who passionately believed that no woman should be allowed to fight forest fires alongside the men, let alone be in a position to give orders to them.

Carly had mixed feelings about serving with Wade on the Camelback Ridge fire. They'd been through a lot together on more than one dangerous mission, and she couldn't deny that he was a crackerjack fire fighter who knew how to lead his crews. But Carly had little patience with the sexual discrimination that ran rampant in her male-dominated profession, and out of all the men she'd worked with, none of them was more narrow-minded about women than Wade.

At the moment he stood on her left, glowering, but it was hard for Carly to tell whether his frown stemmed from his concern about her presence, the prospect of fighting the fire with convict crews, or simply the fact that he was passionately committed to these mountains and considered every fire a personal affront to their dignity. He was never happy when the forest was in flames, and Carly, of course, never saw him at any other time.

"Bill, let me get this straight," Wade drawled, casting a baleful eye at Carly. "You're letting this little gal loose on a two-thousand-foot peak in the middle of the night to fight an inferno with eighty-five kids and criminals?"

Despite his anger, Carly sensed a note of genuine concern in his tone, and she couldn't deny that she was feeling a little bit uneasy about the situation herself. She'd worked with convicts on the line before, and lived with them in fire camp, but she'd never been in the position of giving them commands. Overall, she'd kept her distance from the prisoners, and she felt relieved when she recalled that their guards had kept a pretty close eye on them. Nervously she reminded herself that she'd grown up on Air Force bases all over the world, and was accustomed to handling herself with all kinds of men; surely she could supervise sixty or seventy inmates. All she had to do was establish her authority in a quiet, firm manner and ignore any efforts on their part to make an issue of her gender.

At five foot six, Carly was not a big woman, though she was certainly quite strong and agile for her size, and her success in the U.S. Forest Service had more to do with her knowledge of fire-suppression tactics and her leadership skills than her physical abilities. As far as the terrain was concerned, she had no more concern for her own safety than she usually did. Fire fighting was a dangerous career, but she'd chosen it partly because she'd always had a bit of the daredevil in her.

Carly's degree in biology and her gravitation to the U.S. Forest Service as a resource technician—a summer job in college and full-time one later—had been a natural evolution of her lifelong interest in wildlife. Technically, fire fighting was not a part of her regular job description, merely an "adjunct duty" for which she'd volunteered. Her daily tasks, especially during the winter months, revolved around wildlife research, maintenance of trails and some paper-pushing. But, as a valued member of the firefighting crew, she had her immediate supervisor's directions to drop everything the instant she received word of a new fire—no matter how involved she might be in any other assignment—only to return after the blaze receded.

After nearly a decade in the Forest Service, Carly had broadened her field of expertise—fire ecology—and steadily moved up the ladder. She didn't think her sleek black hair and emerald green eyes were assets to her career-wise, but they weren't handicaps, either. Fortunately, her shapely figure was usually buried by a thick layer of Nomex and her round, perky face was often masked by fire goggles. More than once she'd worked on a hot line for hours beside a new crewman who'd been astonished to discover her sex when the goggles and heavy clothes had come off. Wade Haley was one of the few who'd never gotten over the shock.

"I can handle the prisoners, Wade," Carly calmly declared, choosing to ignore his ongoing concerns about her fitness for the job. "Of course I'd prefer professional fire fighters if they were available, but with the whole southwest going up in smoke, I'm grateful to have any fresh crews."

Carly knew that both of the men were already painfully aware that this was probably the worst fire season in the southwest in twenty-five years; half the departments in California were down to skeleton crews. Carly, herself, had been called out of state on several occasions to back up some section of the Forest Service that was strapped for manpower, and she figured that chances were good Wade had been, too. It was no time to complain about convicts.

"If we've got to use prisoners tonight, give them to me, Bill," Wade volunteered. "Carly's got no business up there to begin with, and if those criminals see a pretty girl, they're liable to—"

"They'll do what they're told," Bill interrupted him firmly. "There's a guard assigned to watch them at all times, in addition to the crew bosses from the Tejon County Fire Department. Besides, Wade, I've already got two other convict crews assigned to your side of the fire. I want to balance them so we have some professional people working both east and west."

After that admonition, Wade fell silent, and Bill quickly sketched out the night's plan. Wade was supposed to hold the line on the east side, where spot fires still smoldered in a dozen narrow canyons peppering the mountainside. Carly, assigned to the west, had a creeping ground fire to contend with, which threatened to flare up at any time. If the Santa Ana winds started up again tonight, as the forecast predicted, the fire would be pushed in her direction.

After they'd reviewed a sketch map of the area, specific communications procedures and scheduled locations of all the crews, Wade and Carly took a brief helicopter ride over the fire. It was still daylight, but the choking smoke gave the illusion of dusk. Carly could see only the heads and necks of the mighty sycamores that looked as though they might be dying by asphyxiation; she was finding it hard to breathe herself.

As the pilot took them around the current perimeter of the fire so they could check out special trouble spots, Wade was free with his advice. As always, it was good, but unnecessary; Carly had been fighting fires almost as long as he had. But she did feel a lot more secure about the task that lay ahead once she'd gotten a clear picture of the ground she'd be covering later in the dark.

It was a rough area of heavy rocks, sharp ridges and dense brush that the flames were lapping up like kindling. Scrub oak, chamise and manzanita cloaked the khaki-colored hillsides, waiting to help fuel the crowning fire. Carly knew that it wasn't likely to be the worst night she'd ever spent fighting a fire, but it wasn't going to be an easy mission, either.

She and Wade returned to fire camp when it was time for both helicopters to ferry the crews up to the designated helistop near the base of the burning hill. After tugging on her fire gear, Carly consulted briefly with Paul Jeffries and the other four Tejon County crew bosses, but she didn't actually see the prisoners until she returned to the fire. She kept a mask of perfect calm upon her face, but secretly she had to admit that the sight of so many criminals unnerved her.

There were dozens of them assembling in ten-man squads. They weren't in chains, or even in prison garb. They were dressed just like the regular fire crews—yellow fire shirts, black goggles and canteens, the latter strung like ammo belts across their backs. They were armed with McLeods, brush hooks and Pulaskis, which were designed to cut brush or dig down to mineral soil, but any fool could see that in the wrong hands, the heavy tools could serve just as well as weapons. Carly couldn't help but notice that the inmates all had the look of starved wolves, even the ones who were overweight. And when one of them spat an obscenity at her, she couldn't suppress a shiver.

A moment later, she shivered again. But this time it was because one of them smiled.

He was a tall man in his middle-thirties, with striking, bushy white hair that contrasted vibrantly with his warm blue eyes. The spontaneous grin produced two deep dimples that belonged on a Boy Scout, not a felon. And a felon he had to be, because Carly knew that mere miscreants did their brief time in the county jails. The state prison at Tejon—correctional institution, they called it these days—housed only serious offenders, even though she'd been told that only those who were judged "safe" were trusted to take on work assignments outside of the prison walls.

Every one of Carly's professional instincts told her that the white-haired man who now offered her such a disarming grin was no better than the leering, buck-toothed con who'd sworn at her an instant earlier. Surely he'd committed some heinous act and was deservedly being punished for it! She didn't intend to be cruel or degrading to any of these inmates, but she didn't think that an exchange of cocktail-party smiles was an appropriate way to establish her authority, either. Even when her woman's instincts—carefully smothered beneath her heavy Nomex and years of training—urged her to return that glorious smile with her own beguiling one.

Division Supervisor Winston won the battle, and she coldly stared the grinning prisoner down. Slowly she watched the appealing dimples relax, the soft, sensual lips tighten in regret. The laughing blue eyes grew sober, then glanced down at the ground.

Carly should have felt victorious, but instead she felt unaccountably sad. Too late, she flashed a cautious, apologetic smile in the snowy-haired felon's direction, but he did not look at her again.

She tried to tell herself she was glad.

AT MIDNIGHT, Gary Reid swung the Pulaski deep into the earth and breathed a heartfelt, peaceful sigh. Despite the acrid smoke, the falling ash and his increasing muscle fatigue, he took great satisfaction in battling the smoldering flames on the south edge of Camelback Ridge. Considering his current options, there was nowhere that he'd rather have been.

It was the first time in nearly a year that he'd been in open country...not to mention outside the prison walls without a guard dogging his footsteps. Although his daytime assignment at Tejon State Correctional Institution was fairly decent—his medical work involved examination, treatment and minor surgery on inmates—it was still a job inside a prison, and when the outside doctors left for the night, Gary was never free to go. Despite his passion for living things and his sense of loss when he saw a fire-charred forest, he'd been thrilled to receive a chance to participate in this dangerous mission with the regular convict crews.

It had been arranged by his cell mate, Clifford, a kind-hearted ex-big-league pitcher and flimflam man who'd served on the convict crews for years and had reached the pinnacle of power for a prisoner. Clifford—a huge black man with a toothy smile that he struggled to suppress when he wanted to look mean—was a squad boss, in charge of a group of ten trained men. One of them had come down with the flu, so Clifford had drafted Gary to fill in.

Clifford's list of reasons why going to fire camp was worth the risk of injury included the exercise, the excitement and the terrific food. There was also the magical reprieve of spending a few days with real people—who were neither guards nor fellow inmates—who by and large judged a man by his performance on the fire line instead of on the morbid details of his conviction. An inmate serving as a fire fighter, Clifford maintained, could almost pretend he was a free man.

Almost. That was the operative word. For the past eleven months Gary had lived in a cage, and no amount of happy-go-lucky optimism or hope for the future was ever going to change that dismal fact. Nor was his flawless performance as a model prisoner ever going to clear the felony conviction from his record. In all likelihood, that ugly mark would prevent him from ever practicing medicine again. And, worse yet, it could keep him from regaining custody of his children, especially since Michelle's mother had taken advantage of his arrest to quickly ensconce the girls in her home.

Still, he refused to give up hope. He wrote to them once a week, and even though he'd never received a reply, he prayed that the older one, Shelley, had not completely forgotten him. His lawyer had gotten word to the blue-eyed four-year-old that her daddy had to go away for a while, but he would not be gone forever like her mother was. He loved her dearly, and he *would* be back. It was just a matter of time.

Gary wasn't sure how much time it took a four-year-old to forget her father; he figured that a lot of it depended on the people around her, and surely nobody in Ruth Everhard's circle of friends would be likely to say loving things about Shelley's convict dad. As for his baby, Patsy—ten months old when he'd been sentenced—Gary knew he'd have to start all over from scratch when he got her back again. But he still remembered every nuance of her puzzled expression when they played peekaboo, every quirk of her laughing eyes when he tickled her feet, every freckle on her little back that he counted while he gave her a bath. Near the end, Michelle hadn't been able to do much of anything for the girls, and whenever Gary had been home he'd been quick to fill in for the housekeeper. He'd done everything in his power to make Michelle happy the last few months of her life.

He'd also done everything he could to save her.

"Hey, Doc!" Clifford's voice suddenly broke through his melancholic reverie. "Watson wants you!"

Gary wouldn't have been surprised to receive a summons from Paul Jeffries, the Tejon County Fire Department crew boss in charge of Clifford's squad. But Watson was one of the prison guards, whose sole duty was to watch the convicts, gun in holster, to make sure that none of them caused any trouble or tried to escape. While it would have been stretching things to call him sadistic, Watson was a weasel of a man who enjoyed lording it over the inmates and drew personal satisfaction from their helplessness. The other guard on duty, a seasoned veteran named Smithson, was a stern man but a fair one, who judged each man based on his own behavior. Gary walked on eggshells with all the guards, and had earned Smithson's trust, so the graying guard gave him a lot of slack. Unfortunately, Watson outranked him.

"Where is Watson?" Gary asked Clifford as his friend hurried toward him, scrambling over roots and heavy piles of decaying leaves. "Do you know what he wants?"

"He's over that ridge with one of the college crew bosses, Doc, and you're supposed to hotfoot it over there right away. Some kid got hurt real bad."

Instantaneously Gary's mood changed. Watson, cretin though he was, knew perfectly well that Gary was an excellent trauma physician, and more than likely the only person on the cliff tonight with more than a rudimentary background in first aid.

Dropping the heavy Pulaski, Gary bolted up the ridge past Clifford, heedless of prickly clusters of chamise that barred his path. The fatigue of long hours battling the blaze fell off him; as a young resident, he'd worked for twice as long on half as much rest. Somebody, somewhere needed him. Everything else vanished from his mind.

Even that pretty brunette at the helistop who'd deliberately snubbed him when he'd smiled just to assure her that none of the convicts was going to do her any harm.

THE INSTANT Carly's radio crackled with word that one of the college crewmen had been injured, she rushed up the smoky fire line to his side. As she scrambled toward him, she could hear him moan, even while he tried desperately to mask his pain. Carly couldn't help but wonder if he would have been so proud if he hadn't been trying to save face before a woman. But she certainly was not about to cast aspersions on his manhood for anything he said, with that gaping hole in his leg. She was sure he was in agony.

Around him stood a group of his buddies, some struggling for nonchalance, others visibly wringing their hands. One redheaded boy crouched beside the kneeling crew boss, patting his young friend on the shoulder with awkward tenderness. His eyes were dark with frustration, fear and concern.

Another fire fighter galloped up the ridge from the south, just as Carly reached the fallen crewman. She didn't recognize him as a Forest Service fire fighter or a Tejon County crew boss, but he carried himself with the authority of a man who was accustomed to making firm decisions in the midst of a crisis.

"I'm Dr. Reid. Captain Watson sent for me," he announced to the boy on the ground, apparently oblivious to all the other people gathered around him. Quickly shucking his heavy fire shirt, gloves and headlamped hard hat as he knelt beside his patient, he asked, "What happened?"

He was a big man, tall and tautly muscled, with snow-white hair and deep blue eyes. Carly recognized him at once; that white hair was a dead giveaway. He was the convict who'd greeted her earlier with such a beguiling grin. With those dimples, it was hard to think of him as a prison inmate... let alone a dangerous felon! Besides, nothing about him seemed to fit the prisoner mold. He didn't look sullen or cowed or angry with life. At the time Carly had first seen him, he'd looked happy to greet her and eager to work. Now he ignored her utterly, intent on the job he had to do.

"He was grubbing the manzanita over there, and the Pulaski slipped and jammed into his leg," the Tejon County crew boss informed the doctor when the boy seemed unable to respond. "I don't know if it's cut an artery, but..."

His unfinished statement hung ominously in the air as the doctor ripped off the rest of the boy's pant leg to make a tourniquet. "Who's got the authority to radio a chopper here?" he barked.

"I do," Carly replied at once. Actually, she'd already used her "handy-talky" radio—H-T, for short—to report news of the injury to Bill, and knew that he was standing by for details. She was tempted to point out to Dr. Reid that she knew how to do her job, but she decided that the young crewman's safety was far more important than her pride.

Brusquely the doctor turned to face her, but she read no trace of recognition there—nor surprise that the senior supervisor on the hill happened to be a woman. In a hushed tone obviously designed to protect the frightened boy, he ordered, "We need a chopper here on the double. Have your people call ahead to the trauma center in Vista Mar. He doesn't have a lot of time." Despite his obvious sense of urgency, his rich bass voice reflected full confidence that she'd carry out his command.

He was right. It never occurred to Carly to question his expertise, let alone to balk at taking orders from a convict. Quickly she called Bill back to relay the information.

In the meantime, Dr. Reid returned his attention to his patient. "What's your name, son?" He used a gentle tone, deliberately casual. No hint of the urgency with which he'd spoken to Carly lingered in his voice.

"Gary Markison, sir."

"Hey! Gary's my name, too," he responded as though they'd just met on the street. "Now, Gary, you happen to be in luck because I'm a trauma specialist, and before that I was a medic in Vietnam. I've seen hundreds of injuries just like yours, so believe me when I tell you you're going to be just fine."

"Really?" the young man asked uncertainly. Carly noticed that his doubt—and relief—was mirrored on the face of his redheaded friend.

"Really." There was no doubt whatsoever in the doctor's tone. "You're going to be in some pain, son, but nothing a strong man can't stand. And it won't last too long because the chopper is on its way and it'll whisk you off to the hospital where they can fix everything up just right."

To Carly's amazement, the injured boy began to breathe more easily, and the deep creases of pain and fear began to ease from his face. Dr. Reid continued to talk to him in a quiet, never-ending stream of reassuring conversation while he took his pulse and checked the tourniquet. Despite the soot on his face, everything in the doctor's bearing spoke of his professionalism, his experience and his expertise. Carly was vastly relieved for the injured student, and suddenly grateful that such a competent physician happened to be on one of her crews.

It took over twenty minutes for the helicopter to arrive, and Carly knew they would have been endless ones for the boy on the ground without the assurances of his cheerful doctor. Dr. Reid barely took his eyes off his patient except for furtive, urgent glances at Carly that seemed to ask why she couldn't hurry up the chopper. She did everything she could, and so did Bill at the other end, and the helicopter actually arrived in record time.

While Carly helped the crew boss load the boy onto a stretcher and six men carried him up the hill, Dr. Reid chatted with his patient about everything that could possibly distract a young man—girls, baseball, the hottest rock bands. By the time their small party reached the helistop, Carly was sweating profusely, but the soot-streaked doctor who knelt on the ground looked completely at ease.

"Well, here's your taxi, Gary," he calmly announced when they loaded him aboard. "You enjoy the game on TV tomorrow night, and remember what I said—if Orel pitches, the Dodgers are going to cream those cocky Astros."

The boy mustered a pained, grateful smile as Dr. Reid squeezed his hand. While Carly radioed one last message to Bill, the group on the hillside breathed a communal sigh of relief as the helicopter's rotors whirred emphatically, whisking the patient away.

One of the college students, the injured boy's redheaded friend, wiped the sweat from his face as he gratefully reached for the doctor's hand. "I can't thank you enough, Doctor. I don't know how you ended up in prison, but... well, what I mean is... you're okay by me."

Dr. Reid found one of his fetching smiles for the boy as he shook the proffered hand. Ignoring the praise and the reference to prison, he said simply, "Don't worry too much about your friend, son. He's in worse shape than I let on to him, but we really did get to him in time. I know the work of the trauma center staff where he's headed—I used to work right across town—and he's going to be in excellent hands."

A wave of fatigued relief swept through the squad as Carly and the crew boss congratulated everybody on their swift assistance and called for a break. While the college squad straggled back down the hill to a clearing near the spot they'd been working, Carly used her H-T to check in with her other four crews. When she finished her calls a few minutes later and turned to head back down the hill herself, she realized with a jolt that she was the only one left at the helistop except for Dr. Reid.

For the last half hour she'd shared an intense experience with him. As anyone would in such a situation, she'd felt uncommonly close to all of those who'd helped with the injured boy, especially to this man, who'd done more than anybody else... and had briefly shared with her the mantle of command.

But now, in retrospect, Carly suddenly recalled that he was a prisoner, a convicted felon serving time for heaven knew what ghastly crime. And doctor or no doctor, she wasn't at all sure that she wanted to be alone with him on the side of a rocky cliff in the middle of the night.

Carly was completely unprepared for the sudden rolling wave of fear that engulfed her. She chewed her lower lip as she glanced around for a guard, wondering if it was too late to call back the crew boss, or even one of the college kids. Although the nighttime fire's low roar was half as loud as it was in the daytime, she knew it would obscure the sound of a woman's screams from the ears of anyone more than ten feet away.

Carly swallowed hard as she tried to decide what course of action to take. Determinedly she studied the distant fire to avoid meeting the white-haired convict's steady gaze, but she whirled around, eyes wide open in alarm, when he suddenly reached out in her direction.

"Sorry if I startled you," his soothing tone instantly reassured her as he tucked his right hand into the pocket of his firepants. Too late, Carly realized that he'd been about to offer to shake her hand as he introduced himself, but—reading her poorly disguised panic—he had thought better of it. "I just wanted to make sure you didn't need anything else before I went back to my squad."

Startled and ashamed by her absurd response to his gesture, Carly held out her own hand in apologetic and belated courtesy. "I'm Carly Winston," she managed to say.

For a moment those deep blue eyes stared at her unhappily, and she knew that her clumsy efforts to cover her apprehension had failed.

"I really appreciate your help," Carly continued, not sure whether or not he was going to take her outstretched hand. "And I know that young crewman was grateful, too."

To her relief, the sadness receded from the doctor's eyes and he slowly reached for her hand with a cautious, dimpled grin. Carly didn't know whether it was that magical smile or the touch of his fingers that gave her an unexpected tremor, but she suspected that this time her visceral reaction wasn't triggered by fear.

Now apparently eager to forget their awkward shared moment, the doctor introduced himself as though they'd just met at a party or an office or the home of a mutual friend. "I'm Gary Reid," he informed her casually. "Hope I didn't step on your toes when I started giving orders."

Carly marveled at the warmth of Gary's hand. It didn't feel like a convict's paw, grimy or tainted with murder or lust. It felt like the hand of a virile, caring man; it made her brief moment of earlier fear seem laughable. And as she stared into those deep blue eyes, mesmerized by the kindheartedness she read there, she found herself doubting that this man could be guilty of any kind of a crime. He was warm and conscientious; he was a gentleman. How had he been convicted of a felony? What crime could he possibly have committed?

"Don't give it a second thought," she assured him. "In a crisis the important thing is that the job gets done."

He nodded, releasing her hand almost reluctantly, as though it were a wounded bird that might not be able to fly without his valiant assistance. "Glad to be of service. My buddy, Clifford, does this sort of work every summer and he tells me that injuries go with the territory up here."

"You're right, unfortunately," Carly had to agree, wondering whether Clifford was a professional fire fighter or another convict. She decided not to ask. The less said about prison on this dark, lonely cliff, the better. "Between the fire, the equipment, the terrain and the darkness, problems are inevitable. And we don't usually have a doctor who makes house calls."

He smiled, but it was a bittersweet smile that didn't quite reach his deep blue eyes. When that darling pair of dimples punctuated his guarded smile again, Carly felt a pang of grief for him. How on earth had this fine physician ended up behind bars?

"I hope I wasn't... overbearing when I started issuing orders, Mrs. Winston," he apologized again, as though he were reluctant to leave but wasn't sure what else to say. "When I'm with a patient in trouble I tend to forget that there's anybody else around."

Now it was Carly's turn to smile. "Believe me, if I were the patient I wouldn't want it any other way." And then, for absolutely no good reason that she could think of, she tacked on, "And it's Miss."

"Miss?" he repeated, as though he were not quite sure what she was referring to.

"Miss, or Ms., but certainly not Mrs.," she clarified. "Though the proper professional term is really 'Supervisor.'" Then, as his face broke into a genuine boyish grin that really did light up his eyes, she heard herself admit, "Actually, I'd just as soon you called me Carly."

"Carly," he repeated, as if to memorize the name. Slowly his eyes drifted over her face, taking in all of her features—the wide smile, the upturned nose, the bright green eyes—and the warmth of his expression made it clear that he liked what he saw. "Not too many women would have the gumption to do your job," he told her in an admiring tone. "My hat's off to you."

It wasn't quite the reaction she'd expected. Most men she met fell into one of two camps: either they were traditionalists who thought she had no business in fire fighting at all; or they were liberated men who truly believed there was nothing extraordinary about her choice of occupation. Apparently Gary Reid was old-fashioned enough to think it was unusual, but contemporary enough to find it a mark of strength rather than weakness.

"Thank you, but actually it's not really a matter of gumption so much as personal taste. I'm trained in ecology and I love these mountains far too much to stand by and watch them go up in flames. And I'm not the kind of person who could survive in a nine-to-five job year-round. I'd never make it in an office, locked up all day without—" she broke off abruptly as a shadow eclipsed Gary's face.

"Yes," he agreed without a trace of his earlier warmth. "It must be hard for you to imagine being locked up."

A wash of regret swept over Carly. How could she have been so thoughtless? But then again, where in her extensive social training as an Air Force "brat" had she ever learned the rules for making small talk with a prisoner on the edge of a cliff in the middle of the night?

But a sudden gust of panic whisked away her regret. Gary Reid's gaze had hardened suddenly, and his boyish smile simply vanished. "It was hard for me to imagine, too," he finished bluntly, "when I was first charged with murder."

Carly struggled to frame a reply to that bold declaration, but as the word "murder" echoed in her mind like a hammer banging on a crooked nail, her mouth went dry and her hands began to shake.

CHAPTER TWO

FOR A MOMENT Gary held Carly's gaze and let her contemplate the terrible words he'd hurled in her direction. He didn't know why he'd done it; after all, she had no way of knowing what a deep cut her off-the-cuff comment had gouged in his soul. But it was the first time he'd felt compelled to explain his incarceration to an attractive young woman; in fact, Carly was the first female he'd even spoken to in months. The first one he'd even *wanted* to talk to since his wife's lingering death.

I'm sorry, he longed to assure her as she struggled to regain her poise. *I didn't mean to scare you. In the end it was ruled involuntary manslaughter, anyway. And I swear to you, lady, you have nothing to fear from me.*

But before he could speak, Carly straightened before him and her fingers ceased to tremble. Her eyes took on a brand of determination Gary had rarely seen in a woman—not even in Michelle—and her knees locked as she tossed her head back with quiet confidence.

"I don't believe it," she boldly declared. "I don't care what the prosecution maintained or how the jury voted. You never killed anybody, Gary Reid. At least, not on purpose. Probably not even by mistake."

In spite of himself, Gary smiled. The tension of the moment—of the last half hour, for that matter—seemed to vanish, and an absurdly sunny mood took hold of him. Some women might have made that proclamation as an act of bravado or self-defense, but his instincts told him that Carly Winston was simply in the habit of speaking the truth. For whatever reason, she'd decided to toss the facts out the window and stake her money on her instinctive appraisal of Gary Reid. It surprised him, honored him, filled him with pride. After all the months of shame he'd endured, even the hint of such high praise was worth fourteen-karat gold.

"What makes you so certain?" he asked her, a teasing note crawling into his deep bass voice, as he regained his verbal footing with this terribly appealing female. "I've been convicted, you know. I'm doing—" he faked an actor's comic exaggeration of the term—"*hard time*. I'm not up on Camelback Ridge tonight because I'm a counselor at a Boy Scout camp."

Carly laughed, a delightful sound that exuded warmth and confidence. "I've never seen a killer with dimples, Gary. I mean, Clint Eastwood you're not."

Gary couldn't help but chuckle right along with Carly. It was incomprehensible to him that a beautiful woman in her position could so quickly take his situation in her stride. Then again, this brief moment in the moonlight was just an interlude in her very exciting job. It wasn't the first contact with the outside world she'd had in months.

"I guess that leaves out acting as a second career," he admitted, ridiculously pleased that this brave, beautiful woman didn't think he was a killer.

"Not to mention trying to make it as a hit man for the mob."

Again she laughed, and Gary freely laughed with her as he picked up his fire shirt from the ground and dusted off some ash that was falling heavily on his bare right arm. Even this far from the fire—a good two hundred yards—the heat was intense, and he had no desire to put his protective covering back on one minute sooner than was absolutely necessary.

Meeting her eyes with more sobriety, he admitted, "Actually, I've been trying to come up with an alternate career. I've got to find a job before I can get out on parole and I'm not likely to have a thriving practice by December."

Her laughter dimmed, but her smile continued to warm him. "Surely you don't intend to give up practicing medicine just because of a little bad luck. You're entirely too good a doctor."

This time, Gary's laughter was bittersweet. Legally there was still a chance that the state Board of Medical Quality Assurance would some day reinstate his license, but his diligent research on the topic had convinced him that it wasn't too likely. But he didn't want to drag any depressing legal facts into this carefree conversation, so he decided to tease her instead. Amiably he asked, "I take it you're an expert on medicine?"

Unabashed, Carly shook her head. "No, but I've been a patient lots of times and I...got to observe a lot of Air Force doctors up close when my mother was...ill...when I was young. I know medical compassion when I see it, and I think it's too valuable a commodity to be lost."

Gary slipped both hands in his fire pants' pockets and studied Carly quietly, knowing intuitively that her mother was dead. Despite the strength of character he read in her eyes, she couldn't hide the wistfulness of childhood loneliness from somebody who'd been there himself. But despite his strong belief that Carly's youthful parental loss must have mirrored his own, it seemed presumptuous, or at least premature, to express such private thoughts out loud. Instead, he simply thanked her for the generous praise.

Carly smiled. Impulsively she touched his arm as she assured him, "I was serious." Her fingers landed half on the sleeve of his prison-issue T-shirt, half on his bare biceps. The skin-to-skin contact was warm and healing, arousing memories of softness, memories of home. It was, Gary realized with a jolt, the first time a woman had touched him in over a year.

"I know," he managed to reply to her statement. "And to be perfectly frank with you, that kind of praise means a lot to me. It's been a long time since anybody's referred to me as a good doctor." He could have added that it had been a long time since he'd felt good about much of anything, but he didn't want to burden a total stranger with his troubles. Especially one whose very presence seemed the essence of all things good and bright.

But suddenly her eyes met his with something that had nothing to do with medicine, nothing to do with the fire. He'd told her nothing about his life and his hardships, and had deliberately sidestepped a painful discussion of the bizarre scenario of events that had caused him to end up serving time. Yet he sensed that Carly Winston truly believed that he'd never deliberately wound another human, even one he'd hated with all the passionate fury he'd felt for Tom Everhard. Without one single word of entreaty or invitation, she'd crossed that mystical line that separated prisoners from the rest of the world; she'd ignored the fact that Gary was a convict and simply accepted him as a human being. The warmth of her trusting gaze filled his whole chest, and he felt, for the tiniest breath of a second, as though he were a free man.

There were a dozen different conversational steps Carly could have taken at that juncture, a dozen safe topics for small talk—or they didn't have to talk at all. This was her bailiwick; he knew she could have ordered him back to his squad and taken off for another one. But she'd declared a break for all the crews, and—as incredible as it seemed to Gary—she now settled down casually against a nearby rock as though she'd decided to spend her precious break time with *him*.

Following her lead, Gary slowly dropped his fire shirt on the ground and used it as a mat while he leaned against a twisted oak. Cautiously he studied Carly, afraid to say anything that might offend a division supervisor or a sensitive female...afraid to do anything that might break the spell.

Carly didn't skirt around the obvious gap between her professional situation and his own. Forthrightly, but in a gentle tone, she now asked him, "How have you learned to survive in prison, Gary? It must have been a terrible adjustment for you."

Just like that she broke down all the barriers, laid out the rules for the two of them. They weren't a male convict and a free female with technical authority over him; they were just two people fighting a fire in the middle of the wilderness, a man and a woman on a rugged cliff in the wee small hours of the morning.

From this vantage point, the crackling flames of the fire on the next hill were glorious, a dramatic painting of orange and yellow light. It was hard for Gary to think of the fire as the enemy at times like this, not when it was so beautiful to look at and had brought him so close to...well, to this enchanting female. She seemed so strong, so feminine, so open, when it would surely have been safer to remain aloof.

He could only honor her honesty with candor of his own. "I haven't adjusted at all, Carly," he confessed, "at least not in my mind. In order to do that, I'd have to start thinking like an inmate; I'd have to grow tough and hard like the rest of them. Instead, I decided to treat my time in prison like boot camp, where I did whatever I could to stay out of trouble and still hold on to a few tattered shreds of my human dignity at the same time."

Carly's gaze softened. "It must be very hard."

He shrugged, but he did not deny it. "I've devoted myself to becoming a model prisoner, the exception to all the rules. I'm serving a two-year sentence, but I've got enough 'good time' saved up to be eligible for parole in a hundred and thirty-six days." He gave her a rueful grin. "But who's counting?"

Carly smiled back. "Is there any reason to think you won't make it?"

He lifted his hands in a helpless gesture. "A thousand reasons. But if my luck holds, the parole board will have no call to turn me down. It should be obvious from my record that I've bent over backward to demonstrate my willingness to 'reform,' and the nature of my 'crime' doesn't make me a danger to society. So it's really a question of keeping out of trouble until then."

"With the guards?" she asked.

He laughed mirthlessly. "Just Watson and one or two others, actually. Most of the officers are really decent fellows. Watson's a bitter man, though, and he hates just about everybody. I do my best to stay out of his way." He stretched out his legs in the dust and got comfortable against the tree when Carly pulled up her knees to her chin as though she meant to stay awhile. "Actually, I'm more worried about the other prisoners," he surprised himself by confessing out loud, though he was quick to assure Carly that she didn't need to worry about any of the convict crews on her particular hill. Peterson, the bucktoothed inmate who'd sworn at Carly earlier that night, had a foul mouth but Gary knew he wouldn't hurt her, and all the other prisoners were fairly well behaved. They were, after all, the "best" of Tejon's convicts. The truly unsavory characters were always kept behind bars.

"There are two or three inmates who are always out for blood," Gary explained. "They don't like the way I cotton up to the guards and they think I'm uppity because I don't carry a shank—that's a knife carved from a spoon—or join any of the prison gangs. I've only got two things going for me to keep me safe in there. Clifford—he's huge, and has most of those guys buffaloed into thinking he's a mean one—and my medical skills."

Carly's emerald eyes showed more concern for him than naked fear. "I can guess what Clifford does for you, but how does being a doctor help?"

"Well, the warden tends to listen to me, so sometimes I can get medical care for the men when nobody else takes their infirmities seriously. Especially the beatings from the guards."

"The *guards* beat the inmates?" she asked in horror.

Immediately Gary decided he'd made a mistake telling Carly the grim truth about prison life, and he resolved to change the subject as quickly as possible. But first he assured her, "It's not too bad at Tejon. The two guards who were really vicious were called on the carpet when the new warden took over. One was fired outright—the one who worked Clifford over the first day I arrived—and the other quit a month later." He hadn't intended to mention that terrible beating, but it still haunted him. Clifford wasn't a demonstrative man, but his loyalty to Gary was unimpeachable largely because he was convinced that if he'd had anybody but Gary for a cell mate on that occasion, he would have died.

"Didn't anybody report the beating?" Carly asked with touching naïveté.

"Of course," he answered patiently. "But wardens aren't known for taking the word of a convict over that of their own men. The only reason this new one listens to me is that we both went to Stanford, and in his eyes that separates me from the other inmates."

Actually, such a distinction was more of a curse than a blessing in the tiny prison world where anonymity was often a man's best form of protection. Determined to move on to a lighter topic of conversation, Gary now asked more cheerfully, "So how did you get involved in fire fighting, Carly? You mentioned growing up in the Air Force, so I'd guess that you don't come from a long line of firemen."

Carly's smile confirmed that Gary had just hit upon her favorite topic of conversation. "Actually, being in the Forest Service isn't too different from military life, Gary," she proudly informed him. "A lot of our people served at some time in their lives. It feels perfectly normal for me to be involved in a chain of command that requires me to throw my schedule to the wind at the drop of a hat."

Her comparison of fire fighting to the military didn't surprise Gary, because Clifford had described fire camp as a mobile Army base. "Do off-duty Forest Service personnel live in some kind of group quarters?" he asked curiously.

"Only while we're fighting a fire," Carly explained. "The rest of the time we live in apartments and houses like everybody else. Actually, I don't live too far from here. Have you ever heard of a tiny town called Sespe?"

Gary shook his head.

"It's just south of the Los Padres range, which is about as close to the forest as I can get. Besides, I like the people there. We set up a fire camp at the Sespe High School football field about nine years ago, during a terrible fire. We were there a whole week, and the local folks did everything they could to make us feel welcome. They made us brownies and doughnuts and wrote glowing letters to the weekly rag. I guess that sort of thing is pretty typical of small towns, but to me Sespe feels like the close-knit community of an Air Force base. Everybody knows everybody's business, but everybody takes care of their neighbors in a pinch."

Although Gary remained silent, he couldn't help but mentally compare little Sespe with the prison community at Tejon. Everybody knew everybody else's business there, all right, but they used the information to spy on each other. Camaraderie was almost nonexistent behind bars, which was one of the many reasons Gary considered it a minor miracle that he'd been placed, at random, in Clifford's cell. A year ago he would have said that he had absolutely nothing in common with a nearly illiterate criminal. Now he could state unequivocally that Clifford was the best friend he'd ever had in his life.

"I got to know one of the local doctors because he was helping us with first aid," Carly continued jovially, "and when I found out that he had a small apartment for rent, it just seemed like a natural place for me to go. Now Willard Jameson is just like family."

"How...uh...old is this Dr. Jameson?" Gary asked, hoping she'd tell him that Jameson was a bald, ugly geezer. *And what difference would that make?* he asked himself sharply. *She said she was single; she didn't say she was uninvolved.*

The absurdity of his reaction—the very notion of thinking of Carly or any other decent woman as a potential special person in his life—would have struck Gary as hilarious if his true situation hadn't been so pathetic. Even if he were stupid enough to take a vibrant interest in Carly Winston, she'd never bother to look at him twice. A year ago he'd turned down female advances on a regular basis, but that was before he'd become a convicted felon.

Yet Carly seemed gratified by Gary's inadvertent revelation of his envy. She grinned as she admitted, "Gary, he's sixty-three and looking forward to partial retirement as soon as his son finishes up residency and comes home to join him. We don't have too many doctors in Sespe, as you might imagine, and Willard Jameson is everybody's first choice. He's basically been turning away patients for the last few years because he just can't handle any more by himself. His son is going to be walking into a perfect setup, though he doesn't act like he's particularly grateful."

"I'm not surprised," Gary answered without thinking.

"Why do you say that?"

To him it was obvious. "No man worth his salt really wants to have his future handed to him on a silver platter, Carly. Oh, it might be nice to start off with a ready-made career. But where's the payoff? When do you get to look back and say, 'I came from ground zero and *now* look where I am?'"

Respect deepened the rich green hue of Carly's lovely eyes as she answered, "It sounds as though you're speaking from experience."

He shrugged. "I can't say that I actually ever got where I was going career-wise because I ended up in prison just about the time I reached the pot of gold at the end of the rainbow. But I had the opportunity to let a rich man pay my way through school—at least the last few years—and set me up in the practice of my choosing. I told him I'd keep my pride intact, thank you kindly, and in spite of everything that's happened since then, I've never regretted my decision."

Carly studied him quietly. "Would it be inappropriate for me to ask who this unwelcome benefactor was?"

"My father-in-law," he said bitterly, then corrected himself by saying "ex-father-in-law" when he saw Carly's eyes blink as though it might have troubled her to think of him as married.

Gingerly she asked, "Were you divorced before you went to prison, Gary?" apparently realizing what a toll prison could take on marital love.

Gary shook his head, finding it hard to admit that Michelle was dead. "I'm not divorced, Carly. My wife..." He sighed deeply and started over again. "Michelle would have stood by me, no matter what. But she was...no longer alive...when I was convicted."

A strange mixture of relief and sympathy colored Carly's expression. Selfishly, it warmed him; for Michelle's sake, it made him mad.

But her voice quavered with sincerity when she said, "I'm so sorry, Gary."

For a moment he couldn't look at her. He studied the fire, wild and angry in the distance, as wild and angry as he'd felt when he'd first learned that the world's most perfect wife was going to die before her thirtieth birthday. It was much later that the numbing grief had set in. Even now, at times it seemed to suffocate him.

But there was no way Gary could bring himself to explain all that to a stranger. He swallowed hard and tried to remember all the reasons he was thrilled to be spending these precious few minutes in casual conversation with Carly. But "I'm sorry, too," was all he could manage to say.

After a moment's painful pause, she rescued him by reigniting the conversation. "You were going to tell me about Michelle's father," she gently prodded.

Gary met her eyes with unveiled gratitude, eager to dwell on anything other than the way he'd lost Michelle. "Tom

Everhard thought I was scum because my family had no particular social standing," he confessed to Carly, "but once he realized that nothing short of death was going to pry his only child away from me, he decided to make me over in his own image. I refused. Not just to let him pay for medical school. I mean, I refused to let him buy me. He tried in a dozen ways." Carly didn't ask about Tom's methods, and Gary didn't bother to explain. "The whole thing caused Michelle a lot of grief, but she never asked me to toady up to him for her sake. She loved me just the way I was, and no matter what her father said, she always believed in me."

Sympathetically, Carly offered, "He must have had a lot to say when you ended up in prison."

Gary shook his head. "He would have, but by then he was dead." He realized that his tone was harsh and vindictive, but he couldn't help the great anger he still felt for the man who'd done him so much harm in life. Even his death had caused Gary nothing but grief. Now he looked Carly in the eye and quietly confessed, "I was convicted of killing him."

This time she didn't flinch, and her calm carriage mirrored his own belief in his innocence. Her mute faith in him made Gary want to stand up and cheer.

Gently she answered, "If you want to tell me about it, I'll be happy to listen, but if you'd rather talk about something else, I understand."

Her eyes met his with such great acceptance that Gary suddenly wanted to offer her the world—a ridiculously chivalrous notion that he was quick to squash. The only smart thing to do was to back away from any more intimate confessions. Besides, it was bad enough that Tom Everhard had spoiled so much of his life with Michelle. He wasn't about to let the bastard steal the only time he'd ever have with Carly.

"We were actually talking about setting goals, weren't we? About going the distance to succeed in your own career."

Carly nodded as though there had been no conversational detour. "You were going to tell me how you managed to do it all by yourself."

Gary couldn't stifle a quiet smile of gratitude. *Carly Winston, you're really something!* he longed to tell her. *I've never met a better listener in my life.* Out loud he said simply, "Well, to tell you the truth, I don't think I ever would have ended up a doctor if I hadn't joined the Army. I enlisted at seventeen, partly to take advantage of the GI bill. I was absolutely certain I could drag myself up by my own bootstraps. On top of that, I was old-fashioned enough to believe that I had a duty to Uncle Sam." He said the words partly in jest, then realized that in Carly's family such patriotism was probably taken for granted. In his neck of the woods, it had been considered a bit passé, if not downright reckless. "My dad worked hard all of his life—he owned a gas station—but he died very young of a heart attack. My mom died just before I graduated from high school, so if I hadn't enlisted I would have gone to work anyway.

"Army life really wasn't that bad while we were stateside," he admitted. "I was trained as a medic more or less by accident, and at first I was a little disappointed. I was afraid I wouldn't see too much action." He shook his head in disbelief at the memory of his own youthful foolhardiness, and Carly honored him with her sweet chuckle. "Well, to make a long story short, nobody asked me to do any killing, but I was surrounded by death and dying all the time. I got obsessed with my duty—keeping men alive—and when I got home, I decided that somehow I'd drag myself through medical school so I could learn everything there was to know about saving lives. By my first year as an intern, I was beginning to think I'd lost my mind. Most of the time I was so exhausted that I thought *my* life was in jeopardy. But the first night I ended up in the emergency room with an accident victim who looked like she didn't stand a prayer, I knew why I'd sweated through all those years. She had a hysterical husband and two teenage children sobbing in the lobby, and I vowed I'd find a way to save her—or die trying."

"And?" Carly asked, as though his answer really mattered to her.

A smile broadened Gary's face—a glowing smile of satisfaction and professional pride that even a year of prison couldn't erase. "Somehow I performed a miracle. I felt as though she'd died and I'd brought her back to life." Triumphantly his eyes met Carly's. "To this day, I can still remember the way I felt. It was three o'clock in the morning and I'd been on my feet for nineteen hours. But I was delirious! I'd never been so happy in my life."

As he poured out his tale, Carly leaned forward, as though to catch every word. Vaguely he realized that her legs now sprawled perilously close to his own, though she didn't seem to notice. But he knew she couldn't miss the change in his expression as he remembered the look on Michelle's face when he'd come home that crucial night. Joyfully she'd celebrated with him, just as he'd expected her to. It wasn't until the next day that she mentioned that she'd been up all night herself walking the floor with a teething infant.

"Shelley—our firstborn—was just a baby, then," Gary reminisced, no longer fully aware of his audience. "We had trouble with her formula, trouble with her ears. I was gone all the time, helping other people get well, and I never realized how badly my family needed me at home."

Suddenly it all came back to him: Michelle dying, his precious little girls in tears, his father-in-law demanding that his granddaughters come live with him, livid with rage when Gary flatly refused. They were *his* children; they were all he had. He would do anything to keep them by his side. Just as he would have done anything to save Michelle.

But there was no cure for bone cancer.

"Michelle never complained about anything," he heard himself muttering, almost to himself. "Never let me know when something bothered her. If I'd just paid more attention in the beginning, maybe..." He stopped abruptly, his eyes on Carly as he suddenly remembered that he barely knew this woman—and in all likelihood, after tonight, he'd never talk to her again. How could he tell her that half of the guilt the jury read in his eyes had to do with all those nights at the hospital while he'd left Michelle alone? How could he begin to express the rage and frustration he'd endured when he'd realized that after all those years of medical training, he still hadn't known enough to save his own wife?

Vaguely he realized that his voice had trailed off, that he'd ceased to focus on the beautiful woman before him. He glanced up, startled, expecting her to look peeved, but her eyes were kind and generous as she read the unhidden pain on his soot-blackened face.

"I lost my mother when I was nine," she confessed, in a quiet, soothing tone. "I can't say that I know just how you feel, Gary, but I know that sometimes it just takes a long time."

Once again she reached out to touch his arm, her fingers tenderly offering the comfort of one caring human being to another. To Gary's amazement, the moment's pain instantly melted away. In its place sprang a buoyant feeling of comfort and fresh hope.

And the first flutter of desire.

Slowly he smiled, delighting in the answering grin he saw on Carly's lovely face, a smile full of warmth and understanding. And maybe—unless he was crazy to even imagine it—a misty hint of something more.

For a moment their mute communication was utterly perfect. Incredibly, he felt good all over.

And then, abruptly, Watson's grating voice erupted from the stand of manzanita off to Gary's left.

"Reid!" the rotund guard bellowed, heaving with exertion. "Where the hell have you been? That injured man's whole damn crew came down the hill ten minutes ago!"

Gary battled the bile in his throat that always choked him at moments like this. Of all the trials of prison life, none was harder than enduring humiliation at the hands of this simian being. And having to submit to Watson's power in front of Carly made it ten times worse! For the last few minutes, she'd actually helped him to forget his situation. They'd been sharing conversation like normal people who'd just met but intuitively knew they had a lot in common. It was almost as though they were on their first date.

No, it's far more special than a date, he realized in wonder. *It's as though we've known each other all our lives.* He wasn't sure what Carly was feeling as she hopped to her feet and faced beer-belly Watson. But her composure was flawlessly professional as she did the one thing he never would have expected from a stranger.

She covered for him. She took his side against a guard.

"I dismissed the men for a break a few minutes ago, Captain Watson, and since then this crewman hasn't been out of my sight," she declared, making it clear that she, at least, hadn't forgotten that she was a division supervisor overseeing a convict crew. She didn't come right out and say that she'd ordered Gary to stay with her, but she managed to give that impression. "We're grateful for his help with the injured boy."

Gary knew she'd saved him an official reprimand—the sort that could end up in his file—but it was a toss-up whether or not his gratitude outweighed his injured pride. No man of Gary's stripe wanted to be bailed out of his troubles by a woman. Especially one he genuinely wished he could impress.

"If that's all, Supervisor," he declared quite formally, "I'll return to my squad."

"That will be all, Crewman," Carly excused him in the same official tone, but her eyes met his with an unspoken intimacy that promised that everything he'd shared with her would remain in confidence. "Thank you for bringing this physician to our attention, Captain," she said crisply to the guard.

Watson mumbled something about sending girls to do a man's job as he trailed Gary out of the clearing, but Gary didn't bother to reply. Nor did he comment when Watson continued to rail about having to hike up and down the fire line combing the burning chaparral for prisoners who larked about instead of doing the job they were getting paid for.

Gary didn't bother to mention that the convicts' firefighting pay was about a dollar a day. Nor did he mention that—on Watson's command—he'd rushed to the injured crewman on the double. His mind was too full of the memory of laughing green eyes and brave, forthright answers... and Carly's graceful form, which even a Nomex fire shirt couldn't hide.

Once, when they were crossing a rocky patch of ground, Watson stumbled and fell heavily against Gary, who righted the other man without a word. But in his mind he compared the feel of the heavy guard's flabby fingers to the gentle touch of Carly's hand where she'd gripped his biceps just minutes ago. He could still feel the warmth of her skin against his own....

CARLY WAS too busy coping with spot fires after her break to dwell on the unexpectedly intimate moments she'd shared with Gary Reid. When she did think of him—when she found herself scanning the working line of prisoners for a glimpse of white hair or cherubic dimples—she caught herself with a harsh word and attacked the fire with greater force.

He's been convicted of killing a man, Carly reminded herself sternly. How she longed to hear his side of that tale! But when she'd given Gary a chance to set the record straight, he'd neatly sidestepped her question, hardly what she would have expected from an innocent man. And yet... she believed he was innocent, solely because he had told her that he was.

Common sense warned Carly to put a safe distance between herself and the beguiling prisoner, but she knew it would be easier said than done. When he'd smiled at her she had felt like a teenager on her way to her first prom. But Carly was a long way from her teens, and she knew trouble when it came and bit her on the leg. She could practically see the tooth marks already!

It's just an overabundance of sympathy, she assured herself. *It's such an unfair situation, and it's so obvious that he's a decent man.* She repeated the lie over and over again, but it didn't help get Gary off her mind.

Nor did it help that the first words out of Wade Haley's mouth when they met after the lunch break had to do with the injured crewman. Carly had barely had time to say hello before he'd asked in his most unctuous tone, "So how are your summer crews doing? I heard there was an accident earlier tonight."

If it had been anybody but Wade who'd asked her the question, Carly would have confessed how worried she'd been about the teenager—and how relieved that a doctor had been there to do emergency first aid. As it was, she snapped defensively, "Accidents are hardly uncommon in our line of work, Wade. It could have happened to anyone. Besides, we happened to have an excellent physician at hand, so the crewman was never in great danger."

"A physician? You mean they've added a full-time doctor to our staff?"

"Not exactly," she admitted.

Wade laughed; he knew perfectly well what resources were available to the fire crews. "Is he a college kid or a con?"

Carly's lips tightened, for some reason more offended than usual by his arrogant jesting. "He is a highly qualified trauma specialist who just happens to be serving time at Tejon because of some legal misunderstanding. I doubt that his conviction has anything to do with his medical skills, Wade. I saw him in action, and his professionalism was most impressive."

"You mean his bedside manner?" Wade teased. "I don't know how much he impressed the injured man, but he obviously made an impression on *you*."

Carly glared at her cohort, more irked than usual by his demeaning jokes. But before she could summon up a proper answer, he teased, "Why, Carly, you're blushing! Surely I didn't hit a sensitive nerve?"

"I am not blushing, Wade," Carly retorted, suddenly afraid that her cheeks might actually be growing flushed. "If my face is red, it's just because I got too close to the flames."

It was true in a strictly metaphoric sense, Carly assured herself as she said goodbye to Wade and went back to work on her assigned terrain. Reluctantly she acknowledged that something about Gary Reid's story had touched her deeply, something she couldn't seem to ignore...any more than she could deny that her tolerance for Wade's teasing had been much lower than usual. For some reason, she wanted to defend Gary Reid's medical skill and protest his innocence, but she couldn't think of any way to do it without giving Wade the ammunition he needed to find yet another new way to embarrass her.

Sometimes Wade reminded Carly of her college roommate's big brother, who'd mercilessly razzed both girls about absolutely everything. Carly, raised an only child, had assumed that he hated his little sister until the night he spotted her fiancé cuddling up with another woman and socked him in the jaw. For days he'd seemed almost more upset than Carly's roommate; over and over again she had heard him say, "I should have known; I should have found a way to protect her from that jerk."

Carly's father had echoed the same sentiment, almost word for word, when her own fiancé had strayed and broken her heart. Colonel Winston had devoted a two-week leave to drying his daughter's tears, and he'd never once said, "I told you so," though he'd warned her about Rodney Haywood right from the start. Rodney was a weak man, the sort who leaned on anybody who was handy. But after a lifetime of being bounced about from pillar to post and often feeling in the way, Carly had adored feeling truly needed. It had come as a blow when she'd finally realized that Rodney hadn't needed *her* in particular, and he'd found somebody else to hold his hand when her career had taken her away so often.

"You deserve so much more in a husband, Carly," her father had told her when she'd called off the engagement. "You need a man who's as strong as you are, who can give you love as well as freedom." Later, when she was half recovered, he'd winked as he'd suggested, "Next time, why don't you let me pick him out?"

For some reason, Carly's memory of her father's words triggered a sudden vision of Gary's dimples, and she vanquished the image at once.

Three hours later, utterly drained and covered with soot, Carly crouched inside one of the choppers as it hovered above the helipad at the fire camp. When it slowly descended through the smoke and falling ash, she watched the previously delivered crewmen clear the landing area, wearily dragging themselves toward the rows of trailered showers to wash off the night's grime.

The white hair of one man shone like a beacon in the pale light of sunrise as he lowered his head to dart toward the landing chopper, reaching out one hand to Carly as though he were about to help a lady out of a high-seated truck cab. He took two steps in her direction, then froze and stared at his outstretched arm. The absurdity of his instinctive courteous gesture seemed to embarrass Gary; abruptly he thrust his hand deep in his pocket and turned away. Without a word to her, he quickly followed his big black squad boss back toward the camp.

As Carly watched him go, her stomach suddenly lurched with an elevator-drop sensation that might have been fear or joy. She tried to see Gary Reid through her father's eyes, but it was a blurred double image, a dichotomy she could never resolve. Carl Winston would like the fact that Gary was a doctor, a caring individual, an instinctively courteous man. But he'd never even notice these traits once Carly admitted how she'd met him. There was no way on earth that her straight-arrow father would ever approve of a romance between his daughter and a felon.

There was no way Carly could approve of it, either.

CHAPTER THREE

"WE'VE GOT A wedge shape moving up Lion's Tooth Peak," Bill Lundgren informed his staff, when they convened in the operations trailer at 4:00 p.m. on the second day of the fire, "and it's been crowning all day. We hoped it would die down by this evening, but the Santa Anas have moved in, with a vengeance. It's going to be a long night."

By the look of Bill's bloodshot eyes, he hadn't had much more rest than Carly had. She couldn't blame all of her sleeplessness on Gary Reid, though she had to admit that thoughts of the man were lingering in her mind. She'd tried to snatch a few hours of daytime sleep, but the fire camp had been about as peaceful as a construction site. The logistics people were building what was, in essence, a miniature city up on Camelback Ridge. In addition to the cooking trailers and the long rows of showers and sinks, there were separate office trailers for each major component of the firefighting effort: logistics, finance, fire plans—where fire-suppression strategy was constantly evaluated and redesigned—and operations, from which Bill executed the fire plan and directed the actual attack on the fire. And, of course, there was also a residential neighborhood of the fire camp—a collection of cots divided roughly into a convicts' section, a college kids' section, and the professional fire-fighting crews' section, where Carly slept. Or tried to, at least, amidst all the hubbub.

But exhaustion was par for the course for a professional Forest Service employee in the summertime, and Carly didn't waste much time bemoaning her fate. Instead, she turned to the business at hand and asked her boss, "Have they held the line on the west side where it was last night?"

Bill shook his head unhappily. "It got away from us around noon. Tonight your crews are going to have to start out on the far-west side of Camelback, Carly. Make sure you don't get too close. With that wind beating the flames, anything can happen."

Carly knew what he meant. In fire fighting, there were always three factors to be considered: weather, fuel and topography. At the moment, she had all three going against her. The bone-dry air had been thrashing like a demon for most of the day, the underbrush was heavy with twigs, leaves, grass and debris, and the land itself on the west side of Camelback—crisscrossed with tiny gulches and narrow canyons—was impossible to hike over safely and incredibly easy for a fire to leap.

It was imperative that they clear a wide firebreak path up-slope that night, but around eleven Carly got a call on the radio from Paul Jeffries informing her that the line to be cut, marked earlier in the day when visibility was so much better, was no longer discernible to his crewmen. Carly knew there were dozens of reasons why the red flags could have disappeared: high winds could have blown them away, falling branches might have obscured them, spot fires may have burned them up, or small animals could have carried them off into the brush. Now somebody would have to plow through the dense growth in the darkness and remark the original line or create a new one. That somebody was Carly; it was what she got paid for.

By the time she hiked up to the lead crew's position, Paul had selected two crewmen to accompany her—one squad boss and his choice of an assistant. The squad boss Paul introduced was named Clifford—it was the big black man with whom she'd seen Gary the previous night—and the second crewman, beside him, was Gary himself.

Carly was irritated by the tiny tremor of anticipation that swept through her the instant she saw him. She had a job to do; it was inconceivable that her response to a man she'd just met could be intense enough to interfere with the execution of her duties. She tried to remember just what Gary had said to her the night before, and how many of her disquieting feelings she might have revealed. But her mind went completely blank as she met the penetrating gaze of those deep blue eyes. She knew that Gary wasn't looking at the supervisor for Division A. The dimpled smile that brightened his soot-blackened face was a personal greeting just for Carly.

She found the strength to limit her greeting to a quick nod of recognition, hoping he'd understand the need for a show of cool discretion in front of the other crewmen. But it was impossible to tell what he was thinking; his expression looked sober in the gloom.

"You'll each need to take a brush hook," Carly ordered briskly, starting into the up-slope thicket with her shovel at her side. "The chamise is terribly thick in through here."

"No matter how thick it is, we'll chop a path for you, Supervisor," Clifford promised her. "I'm an old hand at this. I know just what to do."

His words meant to reassure her, but as his teeth gleamed at her in the darkness, she remembered Wade's warning about the convicts; she remembered that Gary had been convicted of killing his father-in-law. The unexpected ghost of worry haunted Carly. What if she was wrong about her ability to handle these men?

I'm not wrong, her heart insisted blindly. *I'm Carl Winston's daughter; I can handle anything fate sends my way. Besides, every instinct I possess tells me that I could trust Gary Reid with my life.* And Squad Boss Clifford, after all, was a man whom Gary proudly called his friend.

At first, their trek uphill was difficult but uneventful. The men hacked at the underbrush with cheerful determination, exchanging friendly insults and rarely speaking directly to Carly unless she spoke to them. Gary was courteous but distant whenever she made a comment that was specifically directed at him, and his eyes seemed to focus on some aspect of the scenery whenever he could just as easily have met her gaze. She couldn't think of any subtle way to let him know that such strict formality was unnecessary now that they were practically alone and the third party with them was his good friend. But under the circumstances, she decided, it was better to err on the side of excessive propriety than to risk any misinterpretation of her motives by an overt show of friendliness.

After half an hour of battling the heat, the needle-sharp goat's head stickers and the obstreperous stands of manzanita that seemed determined to block their progress, Carly called a halt to reconnoiter. Rarely had she found reflagging such rough going. With such dense ground cover, she concluded, no wonder the forest was going up in flames!

Gary's face was beaded with sweat as he worked close beside her, breathing hard, while she pondered their situation. By now it was obvious that they weren't likely to find the original flags, but they were in such dense brush that it would be difficult for the crews trailing them to build a new line by morning. On the other hand, if they didn't clear a firebreak by dawn, the flames would overrun this ridge once the midday heat joined forces with the wind, which was predicted to increase in velocity considerably by tomorrow.

Carly knew that her fatigue was starting to interfere with her ability to make decisions. Every muscle in her body ached, and she desperately craved some sleep. But the last thing she could do was risk sitting down to take a brief rest. Few things were more dangerous for a drowsy fire fighter on the line than giving in to fatigue.

"Okay. We're just going to have to cut a trail through this mess until we spot a clearing," she decided, announcing her plan out loud. "Let's just keep going till we come out on the other side."

Carly took a deep breath as she thrust her shovel into the dirt to move a low-growing piece of chamise. A moment later, she felt Gary's arm around her shoulder. It was a platonic gesture of camaraderie, or perhaps medical concern, but it filled her with a buoyancy that wasn't typical of the way she usually felt while working a fire.

"Why don't you take a break while we carve out a path, Carly?" he suggested in a low, soothing tone. "You're just about to drop."

The same words from Wade would have infuriated Carly, but from Gary, they were a source of inspiration which gave her the strength to go on.

"I always look this way after a night or two without sleep," she assured him, finding a grateful smile as she met his eyes in the semidarkness. "I really don't feel as bad as I look."

"I'm glad to hear it," he responded with a grin.

"Flatterer," Carly teased.

They shared a moment's chuckle, each too tired to indulge in a full-bodied hearty laugh. But the work seemed a little easier after that, and Carly found her spirits immeasurably brighter. For the next few minutes she and Gary worked side by side, with Clifford just a few feet ahead of them, and Carly grew increasingly confident that they'd soon find an easier path.

And then, without warning, Paul's worried voice on the H-T suddenly jarred her out of her placidity.

"Division A?"

"Division A, Paul. What's up?"

"Carly, we've got a sudden twenty m.p.h. wind heading your way and the fire's starting to cook up like crazy. Suggest you return down-slope at once, or find protective cover."

It wasn't his words so much as the slightly frenzied tone in his voice that frightened Carly; it was out of character for laid-back Paul to sound so alarmed. A fingernail of fear seemed to scratch her spine as she recalled that the tragic demise of her friend John Campbell had occurred under very similar circumstances. One minute he was flagging line, then the wind had changed abruptly; now he was dead. Carly struggled to exorcise the image of his charred body from her mind.

Quickly she glanced back at the rough trail they'd hewn through the manzanita, and she knew they'd never be able to retrace their steps in a rush. "We copy, Paul," she radioed back at once. "We'll have to find a safe spot up here."

It was easier said than done. Not only wasn't there enough clear ground to easily return down-slope, there wasn't enough bare soil anywhere in sight to carve a ring of safety around three people.

For one brief second Carly's eyes met Gary's, then Clifford's, as they silently shared their realization of their imminent danger. She didn't need to spell it out for them.

Neither man wasted any time arguing over who ought to take charge—both instantly placed their fate in Carly's hands. The responsibility was awesome, but Carly knew that her extensive experience and training could very well make the difference between life and death for all three of them. Any time lost in a power play with a man of Wade's chauvinistic mind-set could easily prove fatal.

"We passed a little knoll off to the east about thirty yards back that looked pretty bare," Carly informed the men, her voice steady and calm. "I think it's our best shot."

Both men scrambled down the hill after Carly at breakneck speed, attacking the brush around the small clearing the instant they reached the knoll. Diligently Carly shoveled out the top layer of dirt until she reached safe mineral soil which wouldn't burn in a ground fire. Gary used his brush hook to carve off great lumps of chamise and sage while Clifford alternately hacked at the chaparral and tossed the cut brush as far out of the clearing as possible.

For the next ten minutes, none of them said a word. They were too immersed in battle. The fire was the enemy in this to-the-finish war, and they all knew that the only way any of them would survive it was if they worked as a unit, and worked until they dropped.

It was so hot that Carly found it hard to believe that the fire was still a good fifty yards away. Sweating profusely, she longed to strip off her saunalike fire shirt, but she didn't dare.

Paul called in to report the fire's movements every few minutes, and Carly knew that they were running out of time. She couldn't even stop to answer him. The bare truth was that if the wind didn't change in the next few minutes, all the fervor in the world wouldn't be enough to save them. They might as well stop digging and pray.

When Carly's arms ached so badly she didn't know how she could lift the shovel even one more time, Gary silently grasped it and handed her his brush hook so she could rest one group of muscles and exhaust another set. The world closed in on her, and she couldn't see past her hands as they wielded the heavy curved tool; she couldn't hear anything but the two men's labored breathing.

She tried not to think about all the things she might never get to do, or the forever farewell she wouldn't get to give her father. Irrationally, she felt grief that Gary would die without seeing his children, then rejoiced that at least he'd die a free man. Once his eyes met hers in the murky light, and she knew his thoughts were just as grim.

In that moment, it didn't matter that she was a supervisor and he was a felon; it didn't matter what dreams had been shattered in his life. As the roar of the flames bore down on them, they were partners battling fate, two strong oxen pulling the same yoke. Fear and desperation had forged a link between them that not even survival was likely to break.

And then, abruptly, Paul's voice sang out on the radio, "Carly, the wind's turned! Can you hear me? The fire's lying back down!"

Carly wasn't sure she caught all his words, but she couldn't miss the joyful relief in his voice. She heard Clifford give a triumphant whistle as he slapped her on the back. Then Gary threw one arm around Carly and the other around his friend as he whooped in celebration. Carly did the same.

"We made it! We made it, Paul!" Clifford hollered into the H-T. "The wind turned in time! We're going to be all right!"

It took Carly a moment to realize that Clifford was kneeling on the ground as he gripped the radio; she was the only one still crushed in Gary's arms. There wasn't any doubt in her mind that he'd first seized her in a glorious thank-God-we're-really-safe hug. But now, with Clifford absent from the tiny circle of celebration, she knew that Gary didn't have any good reason to keep on holding her so closely. And if the look in his eyes was anything to go by, Gary knew it, too.

She could have pulled away then; it was the logical thing to do. But Carly's feelings were in a whirl of relief, fatigue and something stronger...something she couldn't walk away from but was not about to name.

For one instinctive moment, her arms tightened around those strong shoulders as she leaned against Gary's chest. While he cradled her tightly, his warm breath fanned her temple, and she had the feeling that he might kiss her hair.

And then, just as suddenly as he'd grabbed her, Gary let her go. In fact, he all but dropped her on the ground.

For just a moment his eyes met hers with unveiled fear that he'd broken some stringent code in the wake of exuberant relief. But underneath the fear was another emotion, better hidden, that had something to do with the life-threatening experience they'd just survived together... but somehow went beyond that natural bond.

Carly had formed that bond with more than one stranger on the fire line in the tense hours of the night, yet she'd never felt quite so reluctant to see the celebrating cease. That hug had been too short, too swift, too wonderful, and for no logical reason whatsoever, she ached to press herself into Gary's arms again.

Instead, she took the H-T from Clifford's hands and radioed to Paul in a calm voice that gave no hint of her turbulent emotions. "We're okay and heading back down. Thanks for keeping us posted."

Just like that it was over. For a fire fighter, it was a typical hour.

But the night's tension had taken its toll, and by the time Carly returned to Paul's crew with Gary and Clifford, she didn't have a single shred of patience for the hulking guard who descended on their weary trio.

"You men have been out of my sight for hours!" Watson bellowed, as though they'd deliberately gone AWOL just to spite him. "You watch your step with me, you bastards. You know the rules!"

The intrusion was so blunt, so rude, that it elicited a gasp of dismay from Carly. "Gary, does he always speak to you that way?" she quickly whispered.

But Gary didn't answer. As a tide of anger swept across his handsome face, he steeled himself and clenched his teeth as if to trap his fury inside his mouth. Then he turned around briskly, nodding once to Carly before he and a grumbling Clifford marched away.

Carly knew why Gary had to endure such harsh treatment, but she had no such constraints. Quickly she stalked over to the obese guard and declared with moxie, "Captain Watson, those two men nearly died on that hill tonight. They deserve a commendation, not a reprimand! I know you have a job to do, but our first priority up here tonight is finding a way to control this fire. It's my understanding that you're only supposed to interfere if there's some kind of a problem with your men."

"I'll interfere any damn time I feel like it, girlie," he snarled. "And if you get in my way again, I'll have you booked for aiding and abetting a criminal and interfering with an officer in the performance of his duties!"

She felt, more than heard, Gary's sharp intake of breath behind her, and she knew she had to act quickly or Watson would goad him into doing something he'd regret.

"Don't be absurd, Captain. You know that nobody on Camelback Ridge has any intention of breaking either of those laws. But it might interest you to know that there's another one on the books which makes it a misdemeanor to hinder a fire fighter on the line. If you hassle my crewmen again without a good reason, you'll be guilty of violating Penal Code Section 148.2 and believe me, I won't hesitate to report you to your superiors and to mine."

Watson's mouth hung open, his jaw slack, as he realized that she meant every word. Knowing when to call it quits, Carly smugly whirled away from him, then thanked Gary and Clifford for their good work in her most professional tone.

"Any time, ma'am," Clifford promised her.

And Gary said, "If there's anything else we can do for you, Supervisor, you just let us know." The promise wasn't an idle one; she heard a tone of barely banked fury beneath the simple vow.

For just a moment Carly met his eyes in the eerie backdrop light of the fire, and she read there a new kind of anger with the constraints of his prison life. It was directed at the officious guard, but this time it had nothing to do with Gary's pride, his parole, or even with his children. She'd seen the look in the eyes of dozens of officers and enlisted men on Air Force bases around the world: proud, vigorous men who could tolerate rough treatment of any kind without flinching, but went berserk the first instant that one of their women was threatened. She saw it now in Gary's eyes. He'd been able to ignore Watson's abuse until the guard had bad-mouthed *her*.

As it turned out, Carly had won the power play with Watson on her own, so Gary hadn't had to risk his tenuous parole position to rush to her defense. But she couldn't stifle the tiny flip-flop in her heart when she realized that if any man ever truly threatened her, Gary would toss away his "good time" in an instant, to save her honor or her life.

She only hoped he'd be so valiant with her heart.

"GOOD MORNING," a bright, feminine voice greeted Gary as he stood in line for breakfast the next day. Returning her greeting, he quickly turned to flash a smile at Carly as she sauntered up beside him. Her fatigue was still evident, but, nonetheless, her green eyes sparkled with an inextinguishable zest for life. She wore no makeup, but her lips were soft and pink, anyway, the smooth natural texture of her skin inviting. He had to stifle an urge to lean down and kiss her hello.

Whoa, Reid, he ordered himself crisply, checking the unexpected impulse. *Does not compute. This is a pristine lady. The last thing she needs is to be tarnished by a con.*

Mentally he shook himself, remembering how perilously close he'd come to getting into trouble in the midst of his survival euphoria last night. Making a pass at his division supervisor this morning—or doing anything at all that she might misconstrue as one—was at the top of his list of "thou shalt nots" if he expected to be granted an early parole. And the likelihood of that early parole was the only star on his horizon. He shined it daily as if it were a precious jewel.

Gary shuffled along behind the haphazard line of fire fighters waiting for breakfast, hoping that Carly would fall in silently behind him or pull rank and go on ahead. But she did neither. Companionably she strolled along beside him, her hands casually tucked into the pockets of her jeans, her small but exquisitely shaped breasts fully outlined by her clean blue T-shirt.

"I hope I didn't get you in trouble last night," she whispered in a conspiratorial undertone.

Although Gary knew she was sympathetic to his plight, and had talked back to Watson on his behalf, the dour truth was that sooner or later, Watson would make him pay for her chutzpah. Briefly he toyed with the idea of suggesting that Carly spare him any future favors—the boomerang potential was just too great—but he couldn't bring himself to ask for her help. The whole situation made him feel furiously impotent, which was the last thing he wanted to feel with her.

On a physical level, he knew that his first glimmerings of desire for this woman could easily be fanned into flame. That risk was one of many reasons he knew he should keep his distance from her, but fate had a way of throwing them together. At least, he assumed it was fate. She couldn't possibly be seeking him out, could she?

"No trouble," he lied bravely. "Don't worry about Watson. He's not exactly known for his largesse, but his bark is worse than his bite."

Carly laughed. "In the movies, when they show scenes of rich lawyers interviewing their clients in prison, none of the convicts ever use terms like 'largesse.' I'm telling you, Gary, you're really miscast."

Again, she managed to make him smile about his bleak situation; again, she warmed him with her insistence on treating him as an ordinary man. Taking her lead, Gary asked conversationally, "So what role do you play, Carly? In real life, I mean. Away from the fire."

Carly looked surprised. "Gary, this *is* my real life. I'm a resource technician for the Forest Service and I have some other duties. In fact, right now I'm officially working on a project that involves restructuring a campground about fifty miles north of here, though I don't expect to get much done until fire season is over. I haven't put in more than two days on it back-to-back since fire season started in the spring." She did not appear particularly troubled by the fact. "From May to November, I often drive straight from one fire to another. I work all the time, overtime, double time—"

"Sounds like residency in an urban hospital."

They shared a smile. Then Carly said, "Except that I rarely go back to the same place—I practically live out of my truck, except when I check in at home to do my laundry and feed my cat. It's kind of like being in the Air Force, you know? When the troops are called, I have to go."

"Even if you have other plans?"

She nodded emphatically. "I've got two hours to report, once I get a call. That's one reason I don't have much of a social life during fire season."

As Gary took a step toward the serving area, matching his long stride to Carly's shorter one, he thrust away his apprehensions and allowed himself to enjoy the moment. So what if she was only being kind? So what, if it was pure luck that she'd ended up behind him in line this morning? The air was crisp and clear, with only the vague haze of smoke so early in the day, and even the smoke smelled like a wondrous summer camp fire.

"What's the other reason?" he asked, eager now to draw her out. Carly's thigh accidentally brushed against his as she walked beside him, but she showed no awareness of the fact that the brief contact forced him to take a deep breath and count to ten.

"I can't say that I often find a man who understands my devotion to my work," she confessed with a rueful grin. "Unfortunately, the few who do are usually professional fire fighters, which means they don't have any more free time than I do. Besides, they tend to be pretty chauvinistic, and neanderthal isn't my cup of tea."

Gary laughed, then gestured with his shoulder at Wade Haley and Bill Lundgren, who sat together at the far end of the collection of picnic tables trucked in for the duration. "You mean those two fine fellows don't appreciate your chosen career?"

"Well, Bill does, but he thinks of me as a daughter—or at least a protégée. Now Wade is another story, altogether."

"Oh?" Gary muttered, surprised at the twang of jealousy triggered by her words.

"Well, he's a real hotshot fire fighter; don't get me wrong. And after all we've been through together, I'd have to call him a friend. But he's also a pain in the neck a good deal of the time. He's always trying to protect me from something. At least that's what he says he's trying to do. Personally, I think his machismo is threatened by the very notion that a woman can do his job as well as he can." She turned to meet Gary's gaze squarely, as though his reaction to her words really mattered to her. "I imagine some doctors have the same concern."

"Not I," Gary replied with a grin, then tacked on, "but even if I did, I don't think I'd be stupid enough to confess it to a woman like you!"

"And just what kind of a woman do you think I am?" Carly demanded in mock umbrage, planting one fist on her hip. The gesture made her look remarkably saucy, and it pulled her T-shirt tightly across her very shapely breasts.

Struggling not to look at them—struggling to thrust from his mind the imagined sensation of running his fingers over those smooth, inviting curves—Gary asked, "Do you really want me to answer that?" He meant it as a joke, but the moment the words were out of his mouth he realized that Carly's question was a loaded one, and he could only entangle himself by attempting any sort of a reply.

Apparently Carly's thoughts mirrored his own, because abruptly she grew silent; for a long moment, her lovely green eyes studied his blue ones. Despite the clank of serving trays and the low rumble of conversation around them, a tent of privacy seemed to encase their tiny corner of the universe as they tried to speak without words. It seemed as though they were a man and a woman alone in the great southwest, surrounded by all the beauty and hope of a brand new day.

Gary clenched his fists as he strove to keep his hands by his sides. He wanted to kiss this strong, gentle lady. He wanted to take her in his arms. There were a thousand reasons why he knew he shouldn't do it, but at the moment, he couldn't seem to think of a single one. He also couldn't veil his need from the perceptive woman who stood before him.

But tension ridged the lines of her neck as she dropped her gaze and turned away abruptly, the gesture an unmistakable rejection of any further unspoken intimacy.

I guess the real question is what sort of man I am, isn't it, Carly? he wanted to ask, but he knew he couldn't do it without bitterness coloring his tone.

Oh, he didn't blame Carly for his situation. He was actually relieved that she wasn't planning to toy with him while they lived in fire camp, considering his restraints. Yet he couldn't help but rail at this foretaste of what it might be like for the rest of his life every time he met a decent woman. Would they all shun him when they found out about his past?

While he endeavored to conceal his conflicting feelings, Carly mercifully picked up the conversational ball. Unfortunately, her choice of topics only heightened his discomfort.

"You know, Gary, you never did tell me just how you ended up in prison," was her next breezy comment. "How on earth did you manage to get yourself convicted on a charge of murder?" Despite her unspoken rejection of him as a potential lover just moments earlier, her casual tone made it clear that she still considered him unjustly accused.

Gary appreciated her faith in him, but he didn't want her pity. Besides, he'd told the story of Tom Everhard's death to so many officials who didn't believe him—not to mention the jury that had voted to convict—that he was loath to repeat the details all over again. And even if he did eventually decide to share the whole gory tale with Carly Winston, he didn't want to go into it while they were surrounded by hungry fire fighters at the crack of dawn.

Dryly he informed her, "Actually, by the time they finished hashing out all the details, they had to be satisfied with 'involuntary manslaughter.' The D.A. realized he couldn't make a second-degree murder charge stick."

"I'm surprised that the manslaughter charge did," Carly retorted, her trusting emerald eyes meeting his once again. "Anybody who really looked at you could see that you'd never deliberately hurt another person."

It was just the sort of thing Michelle would have said; she'd had that kind of blind faith in him. Even though the man he'd "killed" was Michelle's own father, Gary knew that his beautiful wife would have stood by him. She always had. But then again, if Michelle had been alive at the trial, he wouldn't have been in a state of shock, and he would have found a better way to defend himself. "Apparently I didn't strike the jury quite the way I strike you, Carly," he mused aloud.

A sudden pink tide washed over Carly's face that had nothing to do with the law, nothing to do with Gary's conviction, nothing to do with the instant camaraderie that can spring up between two people who share a mutual crisis. What Gary read in her eyes was an age-old calling, a reflection of the snap of need he'd felt when she'd accidentally brushed his thigh.

But this time it was even harder to stifle the sudden stirring in his loins because he knew that it was more than the reawakened hunger of a man who had slept alone too long. Along with the flame of desire came a sudden ache deep in Gary's heart.

Again his fingers balled into a fist as he fought the urge to touch Carly's round, perky face, the urge to seize her hand. It was so sudden, so intense, that he had to plant both feet firmly on the ground just to stay upright.

Guiltily he looked at Carly, and to his amazement, her sparkling eyes were still trained on his. She looked as stunned as he did—embarrassed, hopeful, afraid—as though she, too, saw a reflection of his own vision.

A candle in the window, an image of home.

Dear God, I thought it was just me, Gary moaned inwardly. *But if she's feeling it too, then this battle is going to be twice as hard.*

"Carly, it's not easy for me to...talk about the trial," he belatedly confessed, his throat constricting as he tried to steer their conversation away from emotional quicksand. "Besides, it would take a long time to explain everything that..." *That I wish I could share with you.*

The absurdity of the thought all but staggered him. He didn't know this woman; he never would. She'd offered him a moment's kindness, maybe even a glimpse of physical desire. But it would be stupid—maybe even catastrophic—for Gary to misinterpret this breathless moment of understanding. *Think of the girls, Reid,* he commanded himself tersely. *Just count the days to parole.*

It was Carly who found her tongue first. "I'm sorry, Gary. I didn't mean to pry," she whispered just before they reached the serving trays. When the convict-cook asked her what she wanted, she made her culinary requests quickly, without relish, despite the lavish selection of bacon and ham and homemade biscuits, pancakes and two kinds of eggs. Gary tried desperately to rejoice in the food and ignore the woman, but he couldn't keep his eyes off her shapely backside as she said goodbye in the most cursory fashion before she darted off to join the other fire fighters, leaving Gary to join his own kind—the other men who were serving time.

"You're playing with fire, Doc," Clifford muttered, as Gary plopped down beside him dispiritedly. "And I'm not talking about this giant blaze."

Gary hunched down over his tray and longed for darkness to cover his face from his perceptive friend. At the moment, the early morning sun illuminated his discomfort all too clearly. Still, he decided to feign ignorance. Maybe if he ignored his turbulent feelings, he reasoned irrationally, they might just go away.

"If I said I didn't know what you were talking about," he pleaded, "would you let it be?"

Clifford shrugged his broad shoulders and replied, "No skin off my nose. You want to make a fool of yourself, be my guest."

Gary swallowed hard. "It's not that bad yet, is it, Clifford?"

Clifford sighed sympathetically. "Well, since that pretty li'l boss lady is friendly to everybody, you might be safe so far. But I've seen the way you look at her, Doc, and it's mighty damn clear that you've got it bad already. Don't think I can't read the signs.''

Gary told himself that Clifford was exaggerating—he was a long way from being smitten with Carly Winston. So what if he'd felt a twinge of desire? Was that so bizarre for a man in his situation? It was a moment's weakness, he assured himself. Nothing more than that.

Still, it was damn hard to ignore Carly's pluck and her beauty. So casual, so understated. He wondered what she looked like in a dress. He wondered what she looked like in a bikini or a pink-lace teddy like the one he'd bought Michelle for her birthday, shortly after Patsy's birth.

"Get a grip on yourself, Doc," Clifford ordered him, looking downright stern. "I've been down this road more than once. You can lie to yourself all you want, but it's only going to make things harder in the long run."

Gary didn't ask his friend to explain; he knew what Clifford meant. The whole sorry story had spilled out in bits and pieces over the long, dark months they'd spent together. At the age of eighteen, Clifford had married his high-school sweetheart, right after he was sent to Arizona to pitch for a B team called the Eagles. Gary had seen pictures of his friend's bride—a beautiful girl with a smooth Afro and big brown eyes. She'd adored Clifford, and was mesmerized by the possibility of being married to a world-famous pitcher. She'd never tired of quoting a local sports reporter who—after seeing Clifford pitch his first B-league game—claimed that Clifford had a fastball that would make his name a household word one day.

Nobody would ever know if Clifford might have been good enough to achieve that dream. Within two years of the start of his minor-league career, he started having trouble with his pitching arm. Five years and three operations later, he was an unemployed high-school dropout who was functionally illiterate and had no experience and no employable skills. By then, his young wife was thoroughly disenchanted with the reality of raising babies on welfare. In desperation, Clifford had let himself get sucked into nonviolent crime, playing a minor role in an extensive real-estate-investment scam. He got caught when he broke down and warned an elderly widow not to give up her life savings. His wife left him as soon as he went to jail.

For years after that, Clifford had simply felt sorry for himself, dwelling on his lost opportunities, getting involved in one flimflam scheme after another whenever he was released from prison. He never got a transitional parole job, because there was no one willing to take a chance on him. Once, about ten years ago, he'd fallen in love with a dashing woman who'd been the mastermind behind one of his more artful swindles. When he was caught, he kept mum about her part in the crime so she was not convicted. She came to see him faithfully for months... until the police found new evidence to convict her, too. He'd swallowed his pride to ask his lawyer to write her a letter at the women's prison, to which she'd replied that he was a chump—for whom she'd only feigned affection to keep him from implicating her. Now that she was behind bars, she had no further use for him.

There was another woman who had once claimed she loved Clifford—a good woman, he still maintained—but the awkward visitations had taken their toll. After nearly six months of Saturdays spent with watchful guards, leering cons and no quiet moments of joy to sustain her love for him, she'd tearfully told Clifford that she just couldn't take it anymore. She'd pray for him, but she wouldn't be coming back.

After that, Clifford had been unable to envision any future beyond the walls of prison.

Now, he counseled Gary firmly, "Trust me, Doc. Carly Winston is a lady, and no lady looks twice at an ex-con. And you're not even an 'ex' yet. You're still in prison! You mess with that girl and you'll blow your parole, sure as shootin'. And once I'm out, buddy, you don't want to hang around inside."

For just a moment, Gary's eyes met Clifford's. Then he shivered and looked away. He'd told Carly the truth about the way he'd coped with prison life, but maybe he hadn't given enough credit to his cell mate. Clifford was the one ray of light that warmed his life behind bars.

Gary had never lost his revulsion for Tejon, but once he'd realized that he'd accidentally found one person he could really trust and confide in, he'd started to believe that he might survive the ordeal. He knew that prison would be a thousand times worse if Clifford got out and left him behind—and Clifford was up for parole a few weeks before Gary. He also knew that every month he stayed in prison was cataclysmic—not only to his safety and his peace of mind, but to his first-and-foremost mission: regaining custody of his girls.

"You really think you're going to make parole this time?" he asked Clifford in a low tone, knowing that Clifford would have to find a job on the outside and someone to vouch for him if he hoped to be released before his term expired. "They always seem to turn you down on some pretext or another."

"Yeah, but I've been a little goody two-shoes since you've been my cell mate, Doc. You're made me so respectable I disgust myself." His lopsided smile diffused the negative words, and Gary, as always, found himself laughing with his big friend.

"I hope some of that carries over on the outside, Clifford. You sure as hell don't want to end up back in prison."

Clifford shrugged amiably. "Don't make too much difference to me either way. There's nothing waiting for me out there."

Unfortunately, Gary couldn't refute that sad assertion. He hoped that after the hours and hours he'd spent teaching Clifford to read, his friend might have enough skills now to hold a productive job once he got out of prison. But nobody could hand Clifford the self-esteem and will to succeed which had been Gary's birthright from his poor but determined parents. Without it, he suspected that he'd be planning a life of drifting, too.

Even though he knew his life as a physician was probably gone forever, Gary was determined to rebuild the pieces of his life one way or another. It wouldn't be the first time fate had knocked him down and he'd picked himself up again. And he didn't figure it would be the last.

"Maybe I'm trying to make friends with Carly so I won't have that problem," Gary suggested in a light, teasing tone. He marveled that now, a year after Michelle's death, he could speak of loving some other woman, even in jest. "I kind of like the idea of having a beauty like her waiting for me on the day I'm released." Gary's laughter echoed Clifford's, but it was bittersweet. Actually, the idea of Carly Winston waiting for him when he got out of prison was a wondrous fantasy that filled him with warmth and aroused him with masculine need. But no dream on his horizon was less likely to be fulfilled, and only a fool would waste a moment dwelling on such an absurdity.

Gary reminded himself that he had more important things to worry about. At this point in his life, no pain was greater than the realization that by now his baby, Patsy, had probably forgotten him. And if he didn't get out of prison soon, even little Shelley might well give him up for dead.

BY THE TIME Carly found herself cold trailing at midnight, she was beginning to feel a personal rage against the Camelback Ridge fire. For two days and nights her crews had been fighting this flaming enemy and nobody yet dared to call it "contained." Although neither she nor anybody else on the operations staff had made any glaring errors, Carly always felt that she'd somehow let down the forest when it took so long to snuff out a blaze.

At the four o'clock meeting, Bill had informed them that a new fire had broken out—arson was suspected—about six miles north of Old Grizzly Peak. If it headed south and the Camelback blaze moved north with much velocity, the two could join in a major conflagration. Not only would the destruction be incredible, but there was even a chance of the fire-fighting line getting caught between the two walls of flame. With the east winds working against them, anything could happen.

Carly's five minutes at breakfast with Gary had been the brightest spot in the whole grim day. At least it had been a bright spot until she'd inadvertently revealed that he'd sparked within her an unwelcome flicker of desire. He'd been a gentleman about it—actually he'd seemed a bit embarrassed by her mute confession—but he'd made no attempt to seek her out since then, nor even to catch her eye in passing.

How could he seek you out, you fool? Carly chastised herself. *With Watson on duty he might as well be bound and gagged.* Of course, her own restrictions were almost as binding. Once the fire ended, she would no longer be Gary's supervisor, but he was always going to be a felon, no matter what he did or didn't do. And though she truly believed in his innocence, his reluctance to share the details of his conviction troubled her—even though she knew she had no right to quiz him about it. He owed her no explanations.

What's the matter with you, Carly? she berated herself for the hundredth time since she'd first laid eyes on him. *The guy is a prisoner! Can you imagine introducing him to Willard, if you ever take him home? Can you imagine explaining him to your Dad?*

The last thought was sobering enough to keep Carly distinctly subdued the next time she passed a white-haired head—when she hiked down-slope around 3:00 a.m. the next morning. It had been a difficult shift, partly due to the gusty winds and partly due to the fact that she'd gotten too near the flames and now sported bracelets of reddened flesh where her gloves didn't quite meet her fire-shirt sleeves. She'd slopped on lots of salve, but it wasn't helping much. She tried not to look at Gary, even when he glanced her way, but that didn't help much, either. She even tried to pretend that her stomach didn't do a neat three-hundred-and-sixty-degree turn when his muscular form abruptly stopped, ax in midair, to study her face... and then her hands.

She didn't know whether it was Dr. Reid or her friend Gary who was alarmed at the sight of that red skin. But he didn't waste more than a moment worrying about the task at hand—widening a trail that was already well cleared—before he threw down his ax and scrambled over to her side. He didn't pull off his fireshirt as he had to examine the injured college crewman on the night they'd met, but he did tug off his gloves before he flipped on his flashlight and aimed it at her wrists.

With calm assurance Gary lifted one of Carly's arms, then the other, into the beam of light, taking infinite care not to touch her blistered skin. But it wasn't the doctor's touch she felt, nor the doctor's sturdy chest she longed to melt against as a strange form of weakness filled her body. *He's a convict. Just one of my crewmen for the night,* she reminded herself fiercely. *More than that he can never be.*

"What kind of salve did you put on?" Gary asked, oblivious to her thoughts, as his breath warmed the shell of her ear.

Carly mumbled the brand name, trembling at the magic of his casual touch. If he felt any similar tremors, he concealed them well. His blue eyes radiated concern, but she couldn't tell whether it was vibrant concern for Carly Winston or generic compassion for any patient in his care.

"That's good, but there are some that are better," he informed her in a professional tone, listing three other choices with medical precision. "How bad is the pain?"

Carly shook her head. "Not too bad. Nothing I haven't weathered a dozen times before."

He massaged her forearms gently, as though he longed to soothe the wounded flesh a few inches farther down. "Burns are serious, Carly. You can't afford to take any chances. You surely can't risk doing this to your skin all the time." Suddenly his eyes narrowed as he studied her face. "Your lashes are singed and so are your eyebrows," he pointed out more sternly. "You've got to be more careful."

"Yes, Dr. Reid," she replied with a shaky grin. "I'll do my best to follow your prescription."

Based on their past interaction, Carly expected Gary to make a joke of his own, then release her. But now his eyes met hers gravely, as though to indicate his interest was much more than simple medical concern. For a moment, she was absolutely certain he was going to reach out to touch her face, and by now Carly realized that she was aching for him to do just that. *Willing* him to reach out and touch her, to make the first move, to break all the rules so she could say *It was his idea; I had no choice.*

Instead, he dropped her hands, flicked off his flashlight and picked up his ax. As he stepped away and went back to hacking at the brush, Carly battled a sense of crushing disappointment that was simply too acute to ignore.

How could I possibly yearn for this man's touch? the voice of reason railed at her. *To feel anything for Gary Reid but human compassion is simply absurd.*

Yet inside her soul Carly felt intensely rising warmth for this man of tenderness and strength—a smoldering ground fire of passion that she could not put out with a swipe of her ax or McLeod. But somehow, Carly knew, she had to find a way to douse the flames.

If it wasn't too late already.

CHAPTER FOUR

AFTER ANOTHER long night and a few daylight hours that passed for sleep, Gary tugged on his prison-issue boots and ambled over to the dining area in hopes of scaring up a snack. Apparently he wasn't alone in his culinary interest. A handful of other inmates were gathered at one of the tables, sipping orange juice and playing cards. Carly, Wade and Bill Lundgren were chowing down on chocolate chip cookies at the far end of the clearing, and one of the college kids zipped in to grab a bag of peanuts before he joined a group of his schoolmates who were involved in a noisy game of Three Flies Up.

Gary looked over the gathering and decided to overrule his instinctive desire to go chat with Carly; the rules of the game required him to mingle with his fellow inmates. Any fraternization between Carly and himself would have to be strictly at her instigation. Besides, he reminded himself brusquely, he didn't want to risk getting friendly with her anyway. His double-time heartbeat when he'd checked her burns the previous night had had nothing to do with the feminine essence of this casually sensuous woman. He would have rushed to the side of any burn victim, wouldn't he?

He tried valiantly not to watch her, but when she glanced up at him with unmistakable pleasure, Gary couldn't turn away. With a slow, pixie grin she raised both hands above her head. At first, he thought she was making a bad joke about being arrested, but when she lightly tapped her wrists together and then gave him a cheery "thumbs up" gesture, he realized that she was telling him that her burns weren't giving her much pain.

It was a medical comment, patient to doctor, but intimate nonetheless, and the answering, dimpled smile he gave her revealed as much delight with the way she conveyed the information as with the news itself. He marveled that in such a short time he'd developed a sort of secret code with Carly Winston, who must surely see him as no more than another convict on her fire line.

In her eyes, Gary reminded himself, his only distinctive feature was his medical degree. But when the nervous flutter of her eyelids belied that modest assessment, Gary wasn't sure whether he ought to feel happy or sad.

As Carly licked her lips and focused again on Wade Haley—unconsciously giving Gary one last glance—he concluded that he hadn't imagined her vibrant interest in him. He'd been in prison a long time, and married for years before that, but he hadn't lost all of his instincts where women were concerned. They'd just been lying dormant. And every male instinct Gary Reid possessed told him that if he'd just walked into a cocktail party or a hospital cafeteria, within the next few minutes Carly would have found a way to saunter over to his side. *Or I could have worked my way around the crowd to her,* he mused, fighting the frustrating reality that prevented him from doing so. Apart from Clifford, he had nothing in common with the prisoners playing cards except for the fact of their mutual incarceration, and everything in common with Carly and the other two educated men. Yet if he stayed in the dining area to socialize, there was only one group he was free to join.

His thoughts were crystalized as Carly turned slightly to the left—either to hear Wade better or to turn her back to Gary—at the same time that Clifford called out, "Hey, Doc! Should we deal you in?"

Gary found a smile of greeting for his friend, but he shrugged noncommittally. He'd had more than his fill of cards during the long months in prison. During this brief respite in fresh air, it seemed like a waste of precious time. "I don't know," he mused, his gaze following Clifford's toward the college kids who were cheering wildly as they scrambled to catch the dog-eared softball. "Is there anything else going on?"

Clifford, normally the most cheerful of fellows, suddenly looked morose as he eyed the impromptu ball game. Gary knew how much he missed baseball. He loved to talk about it, loved to watch it on TV, loved to toss the old ratty ball he kept in his cell back and forth from his left hand to his right when he was nervous or just longing for the past. To have a real live game going on underneath his nose and not be allowed to play was more than his friend could bear, Gary knew. Yet he couldn't argue with Clifford's logic as he said, "The kids don't like to mix with us at fire camp, Doc. They act like we've got some contagious disease. I don't think they'd welcome us breaking up their tea party."

Gary's glance shifted back to the impromptu ball game for a moment, then he found it necessary to embrace Carly's face with his longing gaze. She was still listening to Wade Haley, but now she looked more irritated than entranced. Gary took comfort from the memory of her description of Wade as—what was her word?—neanderthal. A fine term indeed.

"Who's on-duty right now?" he asked Clifford thoughtfully. It was a vague question that would have been greeted by blank stares from half the crewmen in fire camp—the professionals and the college kids. But from the inmates' point of view, only one chain of command affected their immediate happiness. The duty schedule that interested them had to do with the guards.

"Constantine and Jackson," Gary's cell mate reported cheerfully. "Day shift all week."

Gary smiled. Both of them were reasonable corrections officers. They wouldn't put the nix on a ball game if the men played fair. All he had to do was get the college kids excited about the idea; if he used his trump card, that might not be so hard to do. "See that redheaded kid over there by that scrub oak?" he said to Clifford as his idea began to take shape.

Clifford nodded.

"He thanked me for saving his friend. He didn't exactly say, 'If there's ever anything I can do for you,' but I think he'd be happy to do me a favor."

This time Clifford grinned, and Gary grinned back as he made up his mind. A game would certainly cheer up his cell mate, and Gary wouldn't mind playing himself. He wasn't about to throw away a few hours of outdoor freedom playing poker, especially when it was just remotely possible that Carly might be in the mood to play softball herself. Anything that would break down the barriers between them would be an improvement. For the moment, he tried not to think about the root of that kind of thinking, or where it might lead.

Instead, he trotted over to the redhead, gave him his best dimpled smile, and asked if he'd mind if the convicts joined the game. The boy was eager to accommodate Gary, especially when Gary suggested that Carly's Division A challenge Wade Haley's Division B...and mentioned that Division A had a ringer.

It took a few minutes to get everything organized. Bill Lundgren decided not to play but thought the game would be good for morale—as long as one of the day guards followed the erstwhile athletes to the nearby clearing chosen for a diamond. Constantine, the elected guard, decided that a few immense flat rocks would serve as bases, and he reminded the prisoners that the game would be zapped in a second if anybody got out of line.

"Division B formally accepts your challenge," Wade Haley informed the men with a smug grin when he came over to take his place as "captain" of his team. He was greeted with a chorus of good-natured hisses and boos when he continued, "Prepare to get stomped!"

"Forget it, Wade!" the redheaded boy called out. "We've got you licked six ways from Sunday!"

"You heard him, Wade!" a feminine voice, full of baseball fever, seconded the first. "You don't stand a prayer!"

Almost as one body, the men turned to stare at Carly as she trotted out from under the trees, heading straight for the infield. As always, Gary had trouble keeping his eyes off her, and he hated knowing that every man there probably hungered for her as much as he did. In a casually provocative sort of way, she was a beautiful woman; more important, she was fair and kind. Most of the convicts had been behind bars a long time, and even the ones who were granted occasional conjugal visits with their wives had plenty of time to store up desire for an attractive female. Although Carly was nearly a decade older than most of the college boys, she was lithe enough to attract their interest, too.

Maybe this happens whenever she fights a fire, he thought sheepishly. *Some damn fool convict falls for her every time.*

He thrust the notion from his mind, as Wade cheerfully mocked Carly. "What's this, little girl? You gonna be Division A's mascot?"

"Mascot?" Carly retorted smartly. "Smokey The Bear is our mascot, Wade. I'm playing second base!"

Another communal whoop swept through the crowd, this one of approbation. Even Division B applauded Carly's gumption. Foulmouthed Peterson, unfortunately, was already playing second for Division A, and he found it necessary to give Carly a rather carnal leer as she approached his position. "Couldn't keep your hands off me, huh, princess?" he taunted her. "I knew it was just a matter of time."

Gary, who was only a few yards away playing shortstop, felt his hackles rise as he stepped instinctively closer, ready to intervene the instant Carly needed backup. Apparently Wade Haley felt equally protective; he took a step toward second, eyes narrowing as he studied the bucktoothed felon.

Carly, however, didn't need any man's help. She took the crude remark in her stride.

"Sorry to disappoint you, Crewman, but I grew up playing infield with the rest of the Air Force brats. My dad taught me how to hit, throw and catch like a boy, and my aim is deadly; I just don't have the power for long-range fielding."

"I've got the power," bragged Peterson, witlessly falling into her trap.

"I'm sure you do," Carly answered, her confident tone stopping just short of flirtation. "That's why I'm counting on you to collect anything that slips by me in center field." She turned away from him briskly as he trotted out to his new position, calling out to Wade, "Let's play ball!"

As far as Gary was concerned, the next two hours were positively glorious. It was great to feel the hard thump of a well-fielded ball in his hand, great to feel the mighty *thwack!* of a solid grounder or tree-smacking home run. The two teams were pretty evenly matched. After Clifford had dazzled everybody with his incredible screwball, he took pity on Division B and occasionally threw pitches they could hit, and it turned out that one of Wade's college crewmen played varsity baseball at school.

The only surprise of the afternoon was Carly, who really did know how to play ball. While nobody would have called her the strongest member of the team, she wasn't the weakest, either. She fielded as many balls as Gary did, and was usually good for a single at bat. A dozen times they dived for the same ball, learning to take the other's cue while one or the other called for it. Sometimes they high-fived on a victory; sometimes they shared the brief pang of playful defeat. And while they waited for their turns at bat, they usually ended up fairly close together, even though Clifford's lineup didn't require it. All the barriers seemed to fall down as they shouted encouragement to their teammates and jumped for glee.

For one blissful afternoon, Gary forgot all about Tejon State Correctional Institution. He even forgot about the fire. The men around him were just pals from the neighborhood, and Constantine was only in uniform because he was the ump. Gary's body felt strong and agile and his eyes were rewarded by the sight of a brave, plucky female who seemed to find numerous excuses to cast cheerful glances in his direction. And on top of everything, it was a beautiful, beautiful day.

For the first time in a year, he felt downright happy. Truly overjoyed to be alive. Once Carly caught him grinning for no reason whatsoever, and the smile she tossed his way told him that she understood his private celebration... or that maybe she felt the same way.

And then, sometime in the middle of the seventh inning, Wade smashed a hard grounder just to Gary's side of second base, and he dived for it just as Carly did. For once their communication failed, probably because both were so eager to stomp on the arrogant fellow who'd kept up his bragging all afternoon, no matter what his team's performance had been. Gary was never quite sure how it happened, but he came down wrong on his left foot while Carly was awkwardly poised on her right, and the ball struck the ground between them just before they collided and went down.

It wasn't a hard fall, and Gary knew that neither one of them was hurt, so his thoughts were not of safety as he found himself sprawled out in the dirt more or less on top of Carly. The dust swirled up around them like a curtain drawn at night, and Gary was struck by the sudden sensation that they were all alone behind the protection of the nearby tumbleweed. He had an eerie feeling that life had suddenly slipped into slow motion, and he realized, as if from a distance, that he should have been making great haste to stand up, or at least to roll off Carly. But he couldn't bring himself to move an inch.

He told himself that the wind had been knocked out of him, and he needed a moment to catch his breath. After all, he seemed to be having a lot of trouble breathing. But as his arms tightened around the woman who made no effort to straighten up beneath him, he had the definite sensation that she was struggling to breathe normally, too.

Those vibrant green eyes confessed that her respiratory trouble had nothing to do with the fall. Carly's cheeks were flushed and the skin of her waist, suddenly exposed where her T-shirt rode up from her jeans, seemed hot and pliant beneath his hands. Try though he might, he couldn't seem to stop his fingers from splaying across her spine. He met her gaze with apologetic longing, but the desire he read in her eyes told him that he'd done nothing for Carly to regret.

For the briefest of moments, there was nobody but the two of them on the face of the earth. Gary couldn't hear the rest of the ball players, couldn't hear the guard. He didn't care if Wade Haley scrambled around all four bases and made a home run. All he cared about was the look on Carly's face, the unmitigated longing for him to take her in his arms.

"Gary?" she whispered, with an ache that masked the sound. As he instinctively pulled her closer, her lips parted and her head lifted toward his. For help? For comfort? For the kiss he desperately wanted to give her?

Desperately struggling for control, Gary told himself he was only trying to help her to her feet; that was why he couldn't release her. Besides, she was gripping him tightly, as if for support. But he wasn't making any progress in pulling her up; she seemed to be pulling him back down. For one crazy, dizzy moment, he had the feeling that she was leaning against his chest. Hot fire sprang into his loins as her fingertips pressed against the small of his back.

He was still struggling to get both of them back on their feet when Wade Haley's voice came crashing through the cheering baseball hubbub like a father who had caught his teenage daughter in a parked car on a Friday night.

"Carly! Are you okay?" the division supervisor demanded, his face hot and red as he galloped toward them.

At the penetrating sound of the other man's voice, Carly's eyelids fluttered with the startled look of a blue jay about to take flight. Gary could feel her trembling, as he willed himself to release her—after all, he wasn't making much headway helping her stand upright—but the muscles in his fingers wouldn't seem to let go.

"Carly!" Wade hollered again, nearly at second by now. Then his tone grew bellicose and strident as he commanded, "Crewman Reid! You release that woman this instant!"

The shutters went down over Carly's shining emerald eyes just like the final curtain of a comedy on a dark and rainy night. Abruptly she sprang to her feet, awkwardly leaning on Gary as she tried to steady herself. He was stung by the red tide that arced across his face while Wade berated the guard for not intervening sooner. Mercifully, Constantine calmly pointed out that Reid was a model prisoner and was only helping the girl to her feet; Wade was the one who'd gone off the deep end.

While Carly dusted off her jeans and her pride, she whispered, "I'm sorry, Gary. That's just the way Wade is. He's overprotective because you're a convict, but *I* know you'd never lay a hand on me."

Abruptly Gary dropped his hands from her midriff, as though she'd slapped him in the face. Her tone could not have been more gentle or sincere; it was reality, not Carly's words or even Wade Haley's, that hit him so hard. The sad truth was that he'd never dare touch Carly in the heat of passion, with or without her consent. The risks were too great—to her feelings, to his freedom, to his two precious girls.

And yet, as the game resumed, Gary realized that it was going to take every ounce of his willpower to keep a safe distance from this exhilarating woman. When she smiled at him, he wanted her so much he could hardly think straight. Worse yet, he now had proof that Carly craved him just as much. If he didn't make the first move the next time they found themselves without an audience, he was sure she'd find a way to issue a subtle but straightforward invitation.

And somehow he'd have to find the strength to turn her down.

THE MINUTE the baseball game was over, Carly confronted Wade. "I need to talk to you alone," she declared in a tone that brooked no opposition.

"Sure, Carly," he agreed amiably. "As soon as I—"

"Now."

This time he studied her dark expression and stuck both hands in his pockets like a chastened schoolboy. He followed Carly toward the dining area, where they were out of earshot of the other men. Carly didn't know where Gary had gone; she'd judiciously kept her eyes off him ever since their seventh-inning collision. She'd figure out what to do with him later. First, she had to deal with Wade.

"Wade, this has to stop," she told him bluntly. "I've done my best to ignore your smart remarks, your smothering overprotection, your antediluvian thinking where women are concerned. But this afternoon you embarrassed me in front of my crewmen—in front of people who simply must take me seriously if we're to get the job done. And that's why we're here, Wade. Not to indulge in good sport at a colleague's expense. The one thing you and I have always agreed on is that the enemy is the fire." Carly considered it a victory of sorts that Wade let her finish before he interrupted, but that was the extent of her triumph.

"If you think I hollered at that con during the game to embarrass you, Carly, then you really don't know me at all. I *like* you, Carly," he admitted, as though the words jammed in his throat. "I don't want you up here fighting fires because I don't want to see you or any other woman get hurt. I don't want you trying to handle convicts because I don't think you can control such a seedy group of men. I said as much the minute Bill assigned those con crews to you, and what happened today only proves that I was right."

"Wade!" Carly burst out in frustration. "Absolutely *nothing* happened!" She owed him no explanations of what had happened in her heart. "We just crashed and went down! End of story."

He shook his head. "Only because the guard and I were there. If you'd been alone on some hilltop with that bunch of mangy dogs, you'd—"

"Gary Reid is not a mangy dog!" Carly said hotly, before she could stop herself. "Can't you see he's not like the others? He's just a decent guy who got a bad rap!"

Too late, Carly realized that she'd given Wade all the ammunition he needed to make his point. "If you believe that, Carly, then I've got a bridge to sell you in Brooklyn! You're not safe with any of those prisoners, even if you're on your guard! And if you've already fallen for a line one of them has been feeding you—"

"Nobody's been feeding me a line, Wade," she interrupted him.

"No? Then who told you this con was innocent? Somebody in the Forest Service? Somebody you've known for years? Somebody you can trust?"

Carly couldn't meet his eyes. What could she say? Gary had told her he'd committed no crime; her heart had told her the same. But to confess as much to Wade would be admitting that he'd been right all along, that she wasn't tough enough to handle herself with such hard and cunning men. He'd say it was proof that she was out of her league.

Stiffening, Carly said, "Wade, the point here isn't whether I'm right or wrong about Gary Reid. The point is that I'm entitled to make my own judgments. You're not my father, my big brother or even my superior on this job, and your behavior is hindering my effectiveness as a division supervisor." Reluctantly she concluded, "If you interfere like that again, I'll have to discuss it with Bill. I know you mean well, but I can't do my job in an atmosphere of sexual discrimination."

Wade didn't look intimidated by her warning, but his mouth tightened in disgust. "If you're worried about sexual harassment up here, Carly Winston, you're looking in the wrong direction. For your sake, I just hope to God I'm nearby the next time one of those guys gets out of line."

After Wade stalked off, Carly took a deep breath and tried to tell herself that he was a chauvinist whose opinion meant less than nothing to her. But the sad truth was, she respected Wade as a colleague, although he was often a royal pain, and his reaction to Gary Reid was probably what she could expect from most of her other fire-fighting friends. Even when she tried to imagine herself having the same conversation with Willard or her dad, she knew that the result would have been the same. They might have been more courteous, or offered more faith in her judgment, but anyone who loved her would shudder if they knew what had really been going on in her head when Gary had landed on top of her this afternoon.

She wanted him.

From the first moment they'd met, she'd wanted to bask in his dimpled smile; from the first time they'd talked, she'd wanted to listen to his life story and share the joys and sorrows of her own. And with each passing moment they fought the common enemy and learned to share their hopes and fears without the burden of public words, Carly found herself more eager to weave herself into Gary's life.

She knew he never would have touched her when they were working on the line; even in the casual atmosphere of the camp, their bodies would never have come so close together if fate hadn't intervened in the form of the baseball game. But the simple truth was that it had felt so natural to Carly to feel his torso pressed against hers—so right—that the only reason she'd bothered to move away from him, at all, was that they were in public. If he ever reached for her when they were alone, during her off-duty hours, she knew she'd never find the strength to turn away.

In the same breath, she realized that Gary would never deliberately seek her out in that fashion. If she'd met him anywhere else, she was absolutely certain that he'd have asked her for a date by now; if he'd been a professional fire fighter she'd met on duty, he would have asked for her phone number and address and promised to track her down as soon as they both had a free moment between fires. And in the meantime, he'd be meeting her for meals and breaks whenever he didn't have other obligations with his crews.

But Gary could do none of these things, even if he was absolutely sure that Carly would welcome his advances. And he couldn't take the risk that she might be offended by any overture he made, not when any false move he made could end up in his file and cripple his early parole.

Carly told herself that she'd made no decision, that she'd find the willpower to put Gary right out of her head. But when it came time to call a lunch break on the night shift, she was equidistant between Paul Jeffries's crew and and one made up of college kids, and she found herself brown-bagging it with Paul.

At least, she started off greeting Paul. But then, with determination born of need and courage, she took her lunch and strolled around in search of a good boulder that was only about twenty feet from Gary. She waited until she caught his eye, then settled down where there was room for two. Bravely she gave him her best "I came here just to see you" smile, in case he had any concern about pushing himself where he wasn't wanted.

Carly knew that about the only decision a convict was allowed once he'd volunteered for fire-fighting duty was which rock he'd use as a chair during his midnight break. But after all the subtle ways Gary had indicated his interest in Carly, she hadn't the slightest doubt that given his choices at the moment, he'd pick a lunch bag off the pile and head her way.

He didn't. With a nod of greeting that he might have given to a total stranger, he sauntered past her—and past Clifford, who'd found an old stump nearby—and strolled as far away from Carly's boulder as a man could go and still stay in sight of the rest of the crew. He sat on the ground by himself and focused all his attention on his ham-and-cheese sandwich, while Carly reeled with a sense of rejection she hadn't experienced since her wallflower days in high school.

She hoped the slow blush on her cheeks wasn't visible in the dim firelight; she hoped that the crewmen nearby interpreted her deadly silence as tension or fatigue. Desperately she tried to figure out how she'd managed to be so stupid. How could she have misread the man so utterly? He was a convict, shut off from women of every kind, but he'd still chosen solitude over the warm company she'd offered! He couldn't have made himself more clear.

Carly mentally recapped the events of the past few days, but she couldn't pinpoint just where she'd gone wrong. All the data had indicated that something very special had been growing between the two of them. She'd been certain that the ball was in her court, that Gary had been hamstrung by circumstances beyond his control and was waiting for her to make the next move.

She'd never even considered the possibility that Gary didn't want to play the game.

CHAPTER FIVE

IT WASN'T UNTIL late the next afternoon that Gary came face-to-face with Carly again. During the restless midmorning hours that had passed for sleep, he'd tried to tell himself that he'd misread her subtle invitation, not to mention the deep hurt his deliberate rejection had caused her. But such rationalization did nothing to ease the knot of tension in his stomach. He knew he'd done the right thing for his own future, and he was also sure he'd done the right thing for Carly. But he hadn't expected to see so much pain in her eyes when he'd mutely made it clear that any special relationship between them was out of the question. He'd never imagined that he already meant as much to her as she meant to him.

They both rolled into the dining area about the same time, eager to devour the the day's afternoon snack. But Carly had barely picked up a piece of corn bread when she spotted Gary coming, and she briskly said "hello" without a shade of warmth before she turned away. Quickly she started off on the path toward the deserted helipad.

For maybe thirty seconds he told himself he was glad; he reminded himself that it had to be this way. And then he realized that he was jogging after Carly, determined to catch up with her before she disappeared.

"Carly?" he called out, reaching her before she'd gone more than twenty yards. When she stopped and turned to face him stiffly, he slowed to a stop and asked humbly, "May we talk?"

Beneath the singed lashes, her green eyes were dark and unreadable. Bright spots of color splotched both cheeks, but he couldn't be sure whether her skin was red because she was angry, or because she'd come too close to the fire. Suddenly he couldn't remember anything he wanted to say to her; he couldn't imagine why he'd gone charging after her at all.

"What is it, Crewman?" she asked coolly. "Am I needed at Operations?"

It was a faultless answer—courteous, professional and utterly remote. Suddenly it occurred to Gary that he might have made a big mistake. If he really had hurt her feelings, then she might find a way to use her authority to punish him. And if he'd read her wrong and she wasn't interested in him after all, he was going to look like a fool.

"I...wanted to speak to you on a personal matter, Supervisor," he said quietly, echoing her formal tone. "If this isn't a good time, it can wait."

For just an instant a gray cloud of pain flitted across her lovely face. She bit her lip before she relented. "What is it, Gary?" she asked softly, but without hope. "Is something wrong?"

He couldn't stifle a sigh of relief at the way she said his name. The wistful tone that colored the word had nothing to do with power or revenge. In public, she always held on to her professional facade. But face-to-face, alone with Gary, she just couldn't hide what she felt for him.

Mutely he took a step forward, met and held her gaze. As gently as he could, he said, "I'm really sorry, Carly."

She didn't ask what he meant. Despite the awkwardness between them, they still understood each other without many words.

"Don't be," she replied, her voice trembling only slightly. "You've got enough to worry about. It's not the first time I've taken a shine to a man who didn't return my feelings." She found a valiant smile. "I doubt it'll be the last."

Helplessly he shook his head. "I thought we understood each other better than that, Carly. If I were free..." He left the rest of his thought unspoken; he knew he couldn't hide the hunger for her written on his face.

Carly's eyes asked a million questions as she visibly rejoiced in his fresh admission of desire. "You told me your wife was dead, Gary. Unless you've got some other female tucked away somewhere that you forgot to mention—"

"I've got *two* little females tucked away somewhere, Carly. And I did mention them to you right off the bat."

Renewed frustration tightened Carly's lips. "Gary, *I'm* not the one keeping you from your children! Don't you think I'd help you get back to them sooner if I could?"

"How?" he asked, more sharply than he'd intended. "By throwing your weight around with the guards? By letting your partner accuse me of some heinous crime? By getting me into a prison-yard brawl with some scum like Peterson because he says things to you I just can't abide?"

Carly took a sharp step back as though he'd struck her in the face. "I had a right to reprimand Watson! He was interfering with my duties and he was grossly out of line. As for Wade and Peterson, you can't blame me for that! Besides, I talked to Wade after the game and—"

"I'm not *blaming* you for anything, Carly. I'm just trying to be up-front with the facts. Even if I were willing to watch your world topple by letting you get involved with a convict, *I* just can't take the chance."

Carly swallowed hard as she came to grips with his meaning. "Gary, I'd never take a risk with your safety!" she protested. "I never would have said a word to Watson if—"

"It's not my *safety* I'm concerned about. At least, not with Watson. He gets his kicks out of humiliating us. But I can stomach that—" he nearly choked on the words "—because I know that every reason he comes up with to report me to the warden can slow down my parole. Don't you realize that if he'd been umping that game instead of Constantine, I'd be back at Tejon right now?" He gave her a moment to digest that grim fact before he charged on.

"Every month that goes by for me in prison is one more month without seeing my little girls. Do you have any idea what that means to me?" Suddenly his tone grew hard as the injustice of the whole situation flooded him. "Dammit, Carly, they're so young! Patsy wasn't even talking when I left! As it is, I'll be lucky if even *Shelley* remembers me, at all."

For several moments, Carly said nothing, but aching compassion suffused her lovely face. Slowly she took a step closer to him, and—without waiting for an invitation—gently took his hand. He knew he should have pulled away, should have run from the inner swell of joy and desire triggered by that simple gesture.

Instead, his fingers curled around her hand.

"Oh, Gary," she whispered, her emerald eyes meeting his with aching tenderness. "How on earth did this happen to you?"

Gary looked away, the old shame—the constant shame—flowing over him anew. "The jury didn't think it just 'happened' to me, Carly. They're sure that I brought it on myself."

Slowly, tentatively, Carly edged closer, kneading his tingling fingers, struggling to cross the natural barriers of his inner prison walls. He knew he should release her; he knew he should drop her hand and step away. He should never have let things go even this far, and he knew that he'd have to act quickly to keep things from going any further.

Vaguely, in the distance, he could hear the sounds of the resting camp. A cook called out a question; a crewman laughed out loud. The cheerful cries of some college kids tossing around a Frisbee brightened the mood of midday. Gary reminded himself that he and Carly were surrounded by people, but at the moment, he realized with keen longing, the people were all pretty far away.

And then he heard Carly whisper, "I'm not the jury, Gary. I'm not your judge. I'm just somebody who wants to be your... friend."

When her voice broke on the last word, he couldn't help but ask, "Is that all?"

She didn't answer right away. Her tongue darted out to moisten her smooth pink lips, and her free hand tugged nervously on a stray curl of black hair. Then her fingers slipped more intimately between his own.

"It looks like that's up to you, Gary," she quietly confessed.

He longed to tell her she was out of her mind, but he ached for her so badly he thought he'd go crazy if he couldn't kiss her soon. Somehow he managed to hold his ground while he reiterated his dark position.

"Carly, I'm in chains. These last few days are the nearest I've come to feeling free in months, and right now you're the boss, so it seems to you that we can work around the rules. But this fire will be over in a day or two, and then I'll be right back in my cell." He couldn't keep the agony of that prospect from haunting his grim tone. "There's just nowhere for us to go from here."

"Gary, you'll be out on parole in just a few months," Carly reminded him with determined optimism. "I'm not going to elope with an oil baron or an earl in the meantime, you know, and I'm not looking for a one-night stand. If we just—"

"We?" he burst out, knowing he had to make things crystal clear right now—or it would surely be too late. "There is no 'we,' lady. There's just Gary Reid, ex-M.D., all by himself, stripped of every damn thing in the world that he holds dear. For the rest of my life I'm going to have a felony on my record, Carly. I'll probably never practice medicine again. I may never even be able to reclaim my own kids! No decent woman in her right mind would ever have anything to do with me." When Carly's eyes flashed hotly on the last line, he tacked on more urgently, "Carly, I don't want to see you tarnished by what I've become! Can't you see that? I don't want you covered with prison dirt!"

Abruptly she disengaged herself from his hand. "It sounds like you don't want me, *period*."

"You know that's not true!" he heard himself roar. "I don't want to end up lying in my cell aching for you night after night, even if you might be crazy enough to wait for me! It's impossible, Carly. Can't you see that? It's too hard for me—and too damn risky—and I *know* it would be a mistake for *you*."

For a moment only, the sound of a chattering sparrow punctured the silence of their little glen while Carly's gaze pierced him. Then, abruptly, she looked away. He watched her cover both eyes with her hands, then rub her temples. She heaved a great sigh before she spoke to him again.

This time her voice was firm but gentle. "You'll have to decide what's right and wrong for yourself, Gary, but you can't make my decisions for me."

Helplessly he closed his eyes, willing every ounce of strength to fight against her nearness. He just might have made it if she hadn't cheated.

"Don't you think I've thought about all of this? Don't you think I realize what a gamble I'd be taking to get involved with a convict, no matter how honorable he seems to be?" she whispered huskily just before she laid one tender hand against his unshaven face. "Don't you think that I've racked my brain trying to find a way to keep from falling for a man in your situation?"

"Don't fall for me, Carly," he ordered her in a low, despondent tone. He tried to step back, to push her hand away from his face, but to his dismay he found himself leaning closer. "Good God, it's bad enough that my own life is in tatters. Don't let me bring you down with me."

"To me, it's not a matter of bringing each other up or down, Gary." Her thumb swept low, over his jaw, across his chin...teasing the corner of his lower lip. "It's a matter of walking hand-in-hand. I can't explain why I think there could be something very special between us, but there are times when I'm so damn sure of it that—"

"Don't!" The word was no more than a desperate croak as he caught her teasing thumb between his hands. "It would never work, never in ten thousand years." Even as he said it, even as he struggled fiercely to push her away, he felt the iron wall he'd worked so hard to erect between them collapse.

For one staggering, electrifying moment, Gary wrapped his arms around Carly and pulled her against him, hard. His lips found hers with an anguished, searching hunger that cried out for the tenderness she'd offered him. Her mouth was honey-sweet and warm, but strong and self-assured, not pleading. He relished the moment when Carly's hands slipped up and over his broad shoulders; then back down to burn his chest. Her trembling fingertips slipped inside the neck of his T-shirt to tug ever so lightly on the coarse hair that shielded the hollow at the base of his throat.

A groan rose from somewhere deep within him, as his tongue slipped between her teeth, hungrily exploring the sweet, secret recesses of her eager mouth. Her black curls were thick and lush between his fingers; he cradled the nape of her neck in the palm of one hand, while the other slipped down to the small of her back to press her urgently against him.

He was already swelling with hunger, aching and hard, when the sound of a landing chopper broke them apart with a guilty start. Carly's eyes looked huge with surprise and need, as though she couldn't believe he'd had the audacity to kiss her like that...let alone that she'd given herself to him completely, without a moment's hesitation.

There were a thousand things he could have said to her, and maybe just as many she could have said to him. But suddenly the helipad came alive as footsteps rushed toward the chopper, and somebody started calling, "Carly? Carly!!!" The voice seemed to be nearby.

Still a bit breathless, she met his eyes with longing-laced confusion. "I'm sorry, Gary," she whispered, "but I think I have to go." A moment later he was watching her dart away with the quick, graceful motions of a white-tailed deer. It wasn't too hard to convince himself that he'd imagined that incredible moment when her soft, willing lips had sought his own. How could such an incredibly delectable woman actually have chosen him?

It was a miracle. It was a nightmare. It was something that he could not allow ever to happen again.

EVERY NERVE OF Carly's body was still aflame with desire, when she went on-duty that night. All of her reservations had vanished; she'd handed over her heart to Gary Reid.

But she still didn't know just where she stood with her reluctant lover. *Dear God, how I want you!* his kiss had proclaimed. But only after he'd spent ten minutes vowing, *No, no, no.* Their parting had been so abrupt that she wasn't at all sure what to expect from Gary the next time she saw him.

From the moment she had crawled out of the helicopter on Camelback Ridge at seven, the fire had managed to erase all thoughts of Gary from her mind. It was crowning like crazy in the wind, turning directions at the drop of a hat. One squad had to scramble over the edge of a small precipice to get out of the way, and an hour later word came to Carly on her H-T that when the fire had abruptly changed course, one of the prison guards had run for cover and fallen off a cliff. The fire had moved on without actually touching him, but he was still lying, perhaps unconscious, on an unstable ledge.

Instantly Carly radioed Paul Jeffries, the Tejon County man in charge of Gary's crew. But when Clifford answered her summons, she just couldn't manage to stay formal with the man after what they'd been through.

"One of the guards is injured," she told him instantly, relaying the exact location as she scrambled there herself. "I need Gary right away."

I need Gary, she'd told the world by way of the H-T. She hadn't said, "I need the doctor," or "Send the Medi-Vac team," or "We'll need first aid." She'd called Gary because he was a doctor, but suddenly Carly realized that she would have wanted him beside her if he'd been a gardener, a truck driver or a clerk. In any crisis, she would "need" Gary—to help her think, to stand beside her, to hold her hand.

At the moment she wanted Gary to help her decide how to move the injured man.

She felt no sense of vengeance when she learned that the guard on the ledge was Watson, just genuine regret for his pain. From her vantage point it was obvious that his injuries were so severe, he could be paralyzed for life...or have no more life at all.

She decided not to risk any of her crewmen until she checked out the actual situation of the unstable terrain. Cautiously she started down the cliff alone. It took her almost ten minutes to reach the injured guard, and by that time his pulse was weak and erratic. He moaned softly when she spoke to him but could not articulate any words. She clambered over to the beefy leg that hung precariously over the cliff and gently braced it with her own body, clinging to the roots of a massive sycamore to help steady herself. Again she reached for her radio and signaled for help.

"Operations supervisor, Division A."

"Operations," came the quick reply.

"We have an injured guard requiring evacuation. Request paramedic team as soon as possible and transport to trauma center. Stand by for location."

As she strained for the sound of Gary's arrival, the voice crackled again, "Division A, can you transport to helistop 4?"

"Negative," she decided quickly, terrified to leave Watson lying there any longer than necessary, but certain that Gary would insist on special support for his neck and spine. "Require backboard and stokes."

"Copy. We'll get back to you."

The next voice she heard was Gary's, tight with strain.

"Carly, are you all right?" He was far above her on the slope, sliding down almost recklessly in his haste.

"I'm fine, Gary," she called back. "It's Watson. From the way he's lying here, I think his spine may be critically injured. I'm not sure how to move him."

For a moment there was no reply. Even the sliding stopped. Carly wasn't sure whether it was the guard's identity or the state of his injury that had brought Gary up short, but for a moment he held stock-still, clinging to a tree, while the sound of the fire grew louder and louder. Carly had the eerie feeling that she was still all alone.

"Gary?" she called again.

"I'm here," he assured her belatedly, his tone almost harsh with command. "I'm on my way down. Whatever you do, don't move him until I get there."

She held perfectly still in the darkness, keeping her flashlight on as a beacon while she listened to him shuffle through the dead leaves and chaparral. Her heart thumped erratically as she rechecked Watson's pulse. She could hear him breathing in short, uneven rasps of pain. Uncertain whether or not he was fully conscious, she continued speaking to him in a low, soothing tone.

"I've radioed for a chopper to take you to the hospital, Captain Watson," she assured him, "and Dr. Reid is on his way."

A moment later Gary reached Carly and the guard. Before he touched Watson, he briefly squeezed her arm in mute assurance. In that instant, she knew that she could turn things over to Gary; no matter what had caused that brief silence, that strange lapse up on the cliff, he was Dr. Reid again, ready to practice medicine.

While the radio crackled again, with specifics regarding the pickup location of the injured man, Watson's eyelids fluttered open weakly and he spoke for the first time. "Please, Reid." The words came out in a painful gasp that startled Carly. "Don't try to get even now. I'm begging you."

Carly thought she knew what he meant. If Gary had ever had any reason to harm a man, this guard deserved his wrath. And with all he knew about medicine, it wouldn't take much to guarantee that Watson's injuries would haunt him for the rest of his days. But Carly never doubted Gary for an instant, not even when Watson gasped incoherently: *"No, Reid. Don't snap my neck. Not like the guy you croaked."*

It was Carly's first clue as to the specific nature of Gary's alleged crime, and she wondered if Watson was referring to something that had happened on the operating table—or, at least, in the line of medical duty. She longed to hear Gary's explanation, but she knew that she didn't dare ask him again; she'd pressed him too much already. Someday, when Gary had learned to trust her, he'd tell her the whole story. She'd simply have to wait until he was ready.

Gary's face looked black and harsh in the dark firelight as he assimilated Watson's accusing words, but his tone was even when he spoke. "Hush, Captain," he ordered softly. "Don't remind me of how I got to prison when I'm trying to be the best damn doctor I know how to be."

A painful grimace crossed Watson's face, but Gary touched his hand ever so lightly. "We're going to brace your back and then load you into this basket-affair to make sure that nothing goes wrong," he assured his terrified patient, as though they were the best of friends. "Just try to relax. They'll give you something for the pain the minute the chopper sets down in Vista Mar."

Slowly, the mist of reluctant trust passed over Watson's face, and he closed his eyes and let Gary do what needed to be done. In the meantime, Carly radioed the rest of the necessary information, including Gary's request to ask the other guard, Smithson, if he could accompany his patient in the chopper.

"How bad is it, Gary?" she whispered, too low for Watson to hear. "You didn't fly out with the college boy who cut his leg."

Gary shook his head. "I should have, but Watson never would have trusted me loose in a hospital alone. Smithson will give me the okay."

He was right. It took a few moments for somebody to track Smithson down, but by the time the night-flying helicopter found a nearby spot, he'd radioed back his approval for Dr. Reid to accompany the patient.

It took five other men to help Gary tuck Watson tightly into the stokes and carry him up the hill to the pinpoint of land where the helicopter was waiting. Carly heaved an enormous sigh of relief when they ever-so-gently strapped him on board. And then, in a great flurry of dust and smoke, the helicopter lifted from the ground and disappeared in the darkness.

With Gary Reid inside it.

FROM THE MOMENT the helicopter disgorged its human cargo, Gary was a different person. For the first time in eleven months he was not a prisoner, a felon, a cretin trapped behind bars. He was a doctor in a civilian hospital, trained to save lives. He felt like a man, again.

Nobody told the emergency room staff that he was a convict. Not even Watson, who had mercifully passed out before Gary could bark out a report on his condition in medical shorthand that had instantly marked him as a physician. After the intern on-duty had taken over, one of the nurses had come back to thank Gary for his help. The only awkward moment had been when she'd asked, "How did you happen to be up on the mountain, Doctor? Do you fight fires on your days off?"

"It's a long story," Gary had told her. "I'm just glad I could help out."

Gary was eager to get out of the blood-soaked hubbub of the emergency room. He wasn't sterile, for one thing—he was filthy with smoke and dirt—and in the E.R., he knew from long experience, anybody who couldn't help was definitely in the way. Technically, Watson was his guard, but Watson would be in surgery for hours. It occurred to Gary that he really had no idea just what was expected of him, at the moment, yet what he decided to do until somebody came for him might well affect the length of his prison stay. Prudence suggested that he wait in the lobby, alerting somebody in an official capacity that he was a convict waiting to be herded back to his cell. But everything in his doctor's bones curled up in revulsion at the notion of letting hospital personnel know he was a convict. How many years had he ached for the respect of his peers, longed for the right to sign his name with the tag, M.D.? How could he just go up to a nurse, or even a volunteer, and say, "By the way, I'm a doctor—but I'm also a felon, and they'll be sending somebody to wrap me in chains later tonight?"

Feeling like a chastened schoolboy, he plodded toward the pretty young girl manning the main lobby desk. Carefully he prepared a line that would cover his situation without revealing his ugly status. "My name is Dr. Gary Reid," he told her truthfully, "and someone from the county sheriff's office should be arriving to meet with me later. Would you please direct him to the cafeteria when he arrives?" It wasn't the usual place for authorities to meet with hospital staff, but the girl nodded cheerfully and Gary made a mental note of her name, in case he needed a witness to corroborate his intentions later on.

After that he was ignored. *How long will I have to wait?* he wondered. The only times he'd ever had to wait for a ride at a hospital were those instances when Michelle had come to collect him from their home, less than two miles from St. Paul's. They had lived in a modest neighborhood on the east side of town, in contrast to her parents, whose home was in the ritzy beachfront area of Vista Mar, about ten minutes from where he now stood. The address was permanently etched in his brain; it was where he sent his weekly letters to his children.

Forcibly Gary turned his thoughts back to Camelback Ridge, which he'd vacated in such a hurry. Smithson, doing double duty guarding two crews now that Watson was gone, surely would have better things to do for the next few hours than worry about his most trusted prisoner, and the Forest Service people might not think of it at all. Gary smiled ruefully as he remembered that since Carly was the division supervisor, it was probably her job to send somebody out to retrieve him. Would she do that right away, with the fire still blazing on that ridge? Would she try to give him a few serendipitous hours of pseudofreedom? Or would she realize that if he sat around in this hospital for hours with nothing to do, he'd find himself aching for the touch of her fingertips on his lips and skin once more?

Oh, Carly, what am I going to do about you? Gary asked himself, as memories of that single, explosive kiss swamped his senses. *I want you so damn much! But I can't let you get involved with me.*

He marched out of the lobby in an intensely restless mood. He vowed not to think about Carly or his children; the next few minutes were too precious to waste in self-pity. How thrilling it was to be all by himself, free from the constraints of prison! There was nobody with whom he had to clear his next move; nobody to bark if he broke the rules. He took the longest possible route to the cafeteria, celebrating the sight of so many noncriminal strangers: proud old men, middle-aged women who smiled like his mother, long-haired teenage boys and unbearably appealing babies. He wandered into the gift shop and looked at romantic cards that he wished he could have sent to Carly; he saw cute little teddy bears that he would have loved to give his girls.

By the time he reached the cafeteria, Gary was hungry. Glad that he had a handful of change in his pockets, he bought a stale bologna sandwich and pressed himself into an inconspicuous corner of the room. Between his soot-stained fire pants and T-shirt and his eerie situation, the last thing he wanted to do was encounter somebody he knew—which was entirely too likely in a hospital in the very city where he used to practice medicine, even though, fortunately, he'd done his residency elsewhere.

He was mentally recalling his years at St. Paul's when he spotted a tiny little girl about two feet away from him, clinging to a tall man's hand.

"When do we get to see the baby, Daddy?" she asked eagerly, her blue eyes sparkling as she jumped up and down. She was three, maybe four, and her long blond hair swirled angelically around her face just the way Shelley's used to. "Is Mommy going to be all right?" she wanted to know.

The father, a good-looking young man seemingly in his late-twenties, picked up his daughter and gave her a noisy kiss as he settled down at the tiny table next to Gary's. As she giggled, he assured her, "Mommy's going to be just fine, sweetheart. And I'm going to sit right here with you until the doctor says we can see your baby brother or sister."

Gary deliberately turned away from the poignant sight; the memories were just too painful. With a terse grimace he plodded back to the vending machine and spent his last few coins on a bottle of apple juice, heading for a seat as far away from the darling child as possible.

But there were so few people in the cafeteria at this hour of the night that her father let her skip from table to table, and five minutes later she found Gary again. Her eyes sparkled despite the lateness of the hour, and she giggled as she pointed at his smoky T-shirt.

"How'd you get so dirty?" she demanded to be told.

Gary swallowed hard. It was the first time in a year that he'd heard the sweet voice of a child speaking directly to him. "I was fighting a fire," he managed to answer.

Her eyes grew big. "In the hospital?"

"No, in the forest with Smokey The Bear. Far away from here."

She nodded proudly, as though she'd known it all along. Then her little face grew terribly earnest as she asked, "Are you here because your mommy is going to have a baby?"

Gary struggled with all the painful memories—his life's work, his children, his precious late wife. And then, for no good reason, he thought of Carly, and realized with surprise that when he'd been kissing her, he hadn't once thought of Michelle.

He shook his head, desperately wishing that this precious child would go away. What would her father do if he realized she was speaking to a felon? "I... I already have a baby," he told her, deciding not to bother with explanations about the difference between a "mommy" and a "wife." "And I have a little girl about your age."

The child clapped her hands as though he'd just given her a present. "Oh, boy! Where is she? Can I play with her while I wait for my mommy?"

As Gary battled a surge of paternal feelings, he suddenly realized that both of his little girls lived less than ten minutes away from where he sat, and there was no way on earth that a county sheriff would come looking for him within the next hour.

What I'd do for a moment with my babies! his heart cried out. *If I could just hold them in my arms for an instant, or even stand in their bedroom doorway long enough to watch the peaceful rise and fall of their tiny chests while they sleep.....*

He knew he couldn't get away with it. He'd have to break into the house to get by Ruth Everhard, and she'd instantly call the police. But when the little blond charmer at his knee smiled at Gary, his heart hurt so much that he almost thought it would be worth the risk.

When she climbed up on his lap a moment later, he was sure of it.

BY THE TIME Carly met Wade at the half point of her shift, she was certain that their luck had finally turned. The winds had died down considerably, and Wade was feeling very optimistic. "I think we've almost got this fire licked, by golly!" he exuded, oblivious to the fact that she was still mad at him. "It's real quiet on the east side of Camelback, and looking good on your side, too. If the wind doesn't spring back up again, we might have it contained by 2400 hours."

Carly had only a moment to celebrate the good news—and wonder if it meant that the prisoners would be shipped back to the prison before she had a chance to see Gary—when a message came in on the radio. Since both she and Wade were carrying their H-Ts, either one of them could have answered, but as usual, Wade beat her to the punch.

"Division B, but Division A is also standing by."

It was Bill, and he wanted to speak to Carly.

"We've got a problem up here with the Tejon County Sheriff's people, Carly. We called in Sergeant Smithson's request for them to pick up that convict doctor at the hospital tonight, but they can't seem to find him. Did you see Crewman Reid get on the helicopter with your own eyes or was that a plan that fell through?"

Carly froze. Even though Wade stood right beside her—his eyes on her face like a hawk with claws outstretched to seize its prey—she could not mask her fear.

She wanted to protect Gary. She wanted to say that it was all a mistake. But she had no options; not even a lie would help him. All she could do was tell Bill the truth.

"I saw him get into the chopper, Bill," she admitted slowly. "He was very concerned about the injured guard."

"He hated that guard, Carly," Wade reminded her the moment she finished the call. "All the convicts in my crews called it poetic justice that Reid was the one who was supposed to help Watson after he got hurt."

Carly might have thought the same thing if she hadn't seen the way Gary handled Watson. Besides, she knew Gary; not as well as she would have liked to know him, but she was pretty sure that in most situations she could guess what he might do.

Would he run away if he got the chance? Not without the girls. Could he kidnap them from wherever they were, or convince whoever had custody to help him? Suddenly

Carly realized that she didn't even know the most basic facts about this man who'd stolen her heart in a handful of quiet moments on this mountain. She'd let him kiss her—she'd let him claim her body and her heart—and he'd never even told her his version of what the courts claimed that he'd done.

But none of that mattered now. A terrible sense of emptiness overcame Carly...a sense of irrevocable loss. If Gary had escaped, he wouldn't return to fire camp in the morning; if the wind stayed down, she wouldn't see him again even if he'd done nothing wrong. And if Gary wasn't coming back to Camelback Ridge, how could she figure out what was going on between them? He'd told her to forget him, but there was no way she could just pluck him out of her heart!

It's for the best, Carly, and you know it, she reminded herself tersely. *He was right, when he said that loving him would be a big mistake.* But Carly felt no relief at this logical conclusion. Her stomach tightened in a rare brand of grief.

Although her instincts promised her that Gary was just a victim of some bureaucratic snafu, she realized, with aching regret, that if he *had* run away, he'd never qualify for early parole...if they caught him and sent him back to Tejon.

She knew that Gary was a cautious man; a pragmatic one. He wouldn't run away without a plan, without some place to go. Of course the police would know his family and all his friends; they'd know just where to search. He'd only be safe with someone he trusted that they'd never suspect. Somebody like...

Oh, my God, Carly moaned as she was blindsided by a new thought. *Somebody just like me.*

In a blinding moment, she realized that Gary had more than enough information to find out exactly where she lived, and he knew that it would kill her to turn him in. If he really had escaped, would he come to her? And if he did, what on earth would she do? Red flared on her cheeks as she considered her options, battled with her warring feelings of fear and exhilaration. She wasn't sure which option sounded more terrible—finding a convicted felon on her doorstep when she got home, or facing the fact that she might never see Gary Reid again.

CHAPTER SIX

BY MORNING the Camelback Ridge fire was officially contained. Carly should have been overjoyed and relieved, and, of course, the fire-fighter part of her was. It was the woman inside her who didn't want it to end. She just couldn't bear to give up all hope of finding out what had happened to Gary. No word had yet come regarding his whereabouts, even though Carly had taken the risk of asking Bill about it three separate times, just in case that tidbit of news had passed her by.

It was not until she spotted the convict crews filing into three huge trucks with Tejon State Correctional Institution emblazoned on the side, that she realized there was something she simply had to do.

Carly camouflaged her urgency with a flurry of "Good work, men" and "Thanks for all your help" farewells for the group as a whole, while her eyes sought out Clifford, who was leaning silently against a massive oak near the last truck. She didn't have time for tact or propriety. She just marched right over to his side.

"You know Gary's missing," she declared, trying to keep her voice low. "Do you think he bolted?"

Clifford's eyes grew cold. "I think that if you have to ask that question, you don't deserve the answer. You don't deserve the Doc, either."

Carly swallowed her embarrassment and curiosity about how much Clifford might know. Instead she said, "If there's another explanation, why don't you give it to me? I might be able to help him."

Warily Clifford shook his head. "All you can do is get him in trouble, Supervisor. I mean no offense. But it takes a certain kind of woman to stay with a man who's doing hard time... a certain kind of love that doesn't spring up in three days in the bushes." His big lips flattened, as though the pain of some ancient wound suddenly pierced his heart, again. Yet his tone softened when he assured her, "You're a good lady, Supervisor. Don't get me wrong. And I know you can tell that the Doc's a special guy who's got no business being in prison." He sighed hopelessly. "But if you want to do right by him, just forget him now. You made him feel like a man again, and that's a lot more than he ever hoped for when he signed up to come to Camelback Ridge."

Color rose to Carly's cheeks, and this time she knew it had nothing to do with the fire. Still, she wasn't about to let a convict tell her how to run her life, even if he was Gary's friend.

"If he didn't make a run for it, Clifford, where is he?" she pressed. "How did he just disappear?"

For a long moment Clifford didn't answer. When he finally did, his words were not particularly reassuring. "Sometimes men just disappear in prison, Supervisor. I've been in the slammer a long time, and I've seen it all. Sometimes it's bad. Sometimes it's permanent. In the Doc's case, my guess is that somebody botched things up at the County Sheriff's office. It happens all the time."

"So you think he'll be sent back to Tejon eventually?"

Slowly, Clifford nodded.

Carly tried to tell herself that she'd found out all she wanted to know; she tried to say goodbye and walk away from Clifford. But she couldn't seem to do it. Not without leaving some sort of a message for Gary.

"Would you tell him... tell him I'm listed in the book? Tell him... I'd really like to hear from him."

"I'll tell him." The burly black man shrugged, as though the subject were now closed. As though his edict weren't breaking Carly's heart. As he marched off toward the last truck, he tossed back over his shoulder, "But I wouldn't stay up nights waiting for the phone to ring if I were you."

Carly knew it would be tough advice to follow.

RESTRAINING HIS ALMOST overwhelming need to go see his children was one of the hardest things Gary had ever done, but somehow, he escaped the darling blond child who was breaking his heart and roamed the hospital halls until morning. Once Watson was out of surgery, he'd stopped by his room once every hour or so to ask the nurses how he was doing. Gary was standing by his bed when the guard woke up at noon.

Watson opened his eyes slowly, peering at Gary through a haze of malice and pain. At first, he didn't speak; it took him a minute to get a grip on his surroundings.

"You didn't kill me," he finally said.

Gary shook his head.

"Did you make sure I'd never walk again?"

"I did my best for you, Watson," he said tiredly. "The doctors aren't sure about your future yet, but from what I've heard, I think you'll be fine. Just give yourself a little time."

Before Watson could answer, a nurse fluttered in and began asking questions, which her patient answered with as much embarrassment as rancor. He seemed to forget Gary's presence, and Gary decided it was time to leave the room...and the hospital, too. Although he was in no hurry to return to Tejon, he was afraid to spend too long "unsupervised" for fear that somebody would think he'd escaped. He was trying to decide how best to word his situation to a nurse or administrator downstairs when one of the doctors he'd met in the emergency room the night before entered the room.

"Still here, Doctor?" he asked Gary with an empathetic grin. "Not quite sure you can trust us with your patient?"

Gary tried to smile. "Oh, I'm sure he's in good hands. I'm just—" he tried to tell the doctor why he was there, but couldn't quite bring himself to say the words "—I'm just waiting for my ride to show up."

The doctor gave him an odd look, but didn't press for more details. But after he'd answered Gary's medical questions about Watson's conditions—which looked quite promising, all things considered—he asked a question of his own.

"When you got on that chopper in the mountains last night, Doctor Reid, was there a prisoner on board? There was a sheriff waiting for me when I got out of surgery, asking if I'd seen one. Apparently he was one of Watson's charges."

Gary's face flamed; he couldn't hide his humiliation. The last thing he wanted to do was admit his true situation to this fellow medical man, who had treated him as a peer. But—with a siege of sudden despair—he realized that now he was going to need this man's help.

"I'm...the prisoner," he admitted in a near whisper, trying to ignore the shocked look on the doctor's face. "I really am a doctor, but I'm a prisoner, too. I told a young woman at the main desk where to find me when the authorities came, but I guess...I guess she forgot, or misunderstood me."

"I see," the other man said awkwardly, though it was clear that he didn't see at all. In fact, Gary had the odd sensation that he had taken a step back—even though he hadn't moved—to put some distance between himself and the seedy felon his "fellow doctor" had suddenly become.

"I was here all night," Gary told him, hating the pleading sound of his own voice. "I'm sure the night nurse would remember me. My parole could be delayed indefinitely if the guards report me as...missing."

He was starting to sweat. The doctor was looking at him curiously, digesting the information, apparently trying to decide what, if anything, he should do about it. At last, the other man said, "Let me check my patient, then I'll make a few calls."

His calls, Gary discovered later, were to the floor's night nurse, the girl who'd been on the front desk and the County Sheriff. From what Gary could gather, none of the hospital staff had realized that the "doctor who brought the injured guard in" was also the prisoner, so they'd informed the first officer who'd arrived that Watson's charge was nowhere to be found. By the time another officer showed up in mid-afternoon and Gary explained the whole situation to him again, he was fatigued beyond words, not to mention furious, when the powers-that-be decided that he had to spend the night in the county lockup until his "missing" and "found" paperwork could be properly processed in the morning.

But in the morning, the guards on-duty had no idea what Gary was talking about when he asked about his return to Tejon; and when he asked to speak to the officer who brought him in, they told him that the man was home with the flu.

SEVEN DAYS AFTER he delivered Watson to the emergency room at Vista Mar, Gary lay on his back in the day room at the county lockup, too full of anger to speak. Was it not bad enough that he'd been forced to spend three weeks in this hellhole when he'd first been arrested? It was ten times worse than the prison at Tejon. County was so overcrowded that less than a third of the men fit in the handful of cells designed to hold them, so the "less dangerous" types were given one of the wall-to-wall bunks, which consumed what had been designed as a recreation area. Gary had been assigned to a lower bunk. The guy above him, who found it necessary to drop something on Gary almost every time he climbed up or down, was currently charged with selling heroin to a pair of sixteen-year-olds, but he'd been quick to tell Gary he'd once done time for murder.

Gary had explained to everybody who would listen that he had a perfectly good cell waiting for him back at Tejon, but the guards here at lockup didn't have the authority to move him, and whoever did have the authority, somewhere up the mysterious prison hierarchy, either didn't know about the snafu or just didn't care. Although he was prepared to tell his story over and over again, if necessary—complete with the names of the hospital personnel who could back it up—the official position was "Let's wait until the officer involved gets back and files a complete report." Nobody, as far as Gary knew, had tried to track the man down. He might have been back on-duty or dead by now, or maybe he'd filed the report before he'd come down with the flu. Clearly, it didn't matter to anyone but Gary.

In desperation he'd used his one phone call to contact his lawyer, but John Henton was on vacation with his family in Bermuda—Bermuda, for Christ's sake!—and his secretary couldn't do a thing for Gary until he returned. Gary could have called another attorney, but thought better of it. In the time it would take to convince some slowpoke to take his case, John would surely return to town.

In the meantime, all Gary could do was stay on his toes, keep out of trouble, and do his damnedest to remain alive. The constant fear and harassment had one benefit, he told himself; at least, it kept his mind off Carly. How blind she'd been to think she could ever carry on a relationship with an imprisoned man! How could she have imagined that he'd ever let her dirty herself by coming to see him in a place like this? She couldn't even imagine the torture he'd told her he'd endure, counting the minutes until he saw her again... reliving every memory of the brief time they'd shared.

Desperately he pushed away the memory of that one perfect kiss, the one moment when his resistance had collapsed. He regretted—would always regret—that he'd never been able to tell Carly goodbye. Just once, she had a right to know how much she meant to him. Gary didn't want her to remember him often, but when she did, he wanted her to feel good about their brief involvement. Sooner or later, she'd regret having yielded so completely to a convicted felon. He wished he could soften the blow by letting her know that—for whatever it was worth—his own heart had tumbled just as recklessly.

But that was a futile dream, to be stacked in the corner of his mind where all his other regrets now lived. Right next to the sorrow at how he'd overruled his passionate need to go see his girls and wasted all those hours in the hospital, only to be hauled back to the county lockup as though he really *had* run away!

He didn't have long to dwell on his pain before the inmate who inhabited his extra bunk returned, deliberately mashing Gary's right hand as he clambered up to his own bunk. The hand hurt, but not as much as Gary's pride. He wondered, for just a moment, what it would be like if the drug dealer actually broke his hand someday. He felt a moment's alarm as he realized that he might never be able to operate again.

Then despondency replaced the alarm when he remembered that, hand or no hand, he'd probably never be able to practice medicine again anyway.

CARLY HAD ONLY half a day between the Camelback Ridge fire and her next assignment down in the southern part of the state. She napped for three hours, did a quick load of laundry in Willard's garage, and spent maybe five minutes cuddling fluffy Homer while she leafed through her mail.

There was a new stack waiting for her when she returned but nothing from Gary. She wasn't surprised; just keenly disappointed. But she'd learned young to take life's lumps like a "good soldier," and it was pretty clear that in the long run Gary Reid was only going to be another bruise.

She'd accepted that reality in her mind, but her heart was still another matter. Willing herself to forget Gary had done Carly precious little good; she still felt hot when she remembered his rare caresses. And worse yet were all the unanswered questions. Had he made it back to Tejon? If not, why hadn't he? And what set of circumstances had resulted in his erroneous incarceration in the first place? Had Clifford given him her message and had he decided not to call? Or was he waiting to see if Carly had meant what she'd said and was willing to buck the system to be with him?

She was still trying to talk herself into forgetting him when a knock on the door—three long raps and one short one—signaled the arrival of Willard Jameson, her loquacious landlord.

Willard was about her father's age, but the two men were as different as night and day. Willard was blond; her father had dark hair. Willard was round-featured, though not at all overweight, and Colonel Winston had square planes on his face and shoulders. Carly's father was generally wary about new ideas or changes, but Willard was always cheerful, buoyant, eager for whatever the future might bring. There had been a time, right after his wife, Thelma, had died, when he'd grown quiet, almost morose. Carly, along with all of his other friends, had been concerned about him. But about the time his only son, Willie, had started medical school and promised to go into practice with his father when he finished residency—a lifelong dream of Willard's—his sunny disposition had returned almost overnight.

He'd once also cherished the dream that Carly, whom he loved dearly, would someday marry his son. But fortunately, he was now reconciled to the fact that she and Willie had no particular interest in each other. They'd gone out once to make Willard happy, and had cheerfully agreed that they had almost nothing in common.

Today, Willard was a bundle of energy, bouncing on one foot, then the other, as he prepared for his daily run. "Carly! Glad you're back. Homer and I were getting tired of batching it."

"Oh, I hope he hasn't been a nuisance," Carly replied, knowing that many landlords in Willard's position would not have allowed her to keep a pet. "I always leave him plenty of food and water, and he comes and goes through that hole in the floor."

It was a unique arrangement that suited everybody involved. Willard had built the apartment himself and had never gotten around to polishing off one of the closets. As a result a small cat-sized hole remained, which gave Homer free access and kept burglars out, a wonderful compromise for Carly.

"Oh, he's no trouble," Willard insisted, scratching the purring cat beneath the chin. "We keep each other company when the nights grow long. He just misses you; that's all."

I wonder if anybody else does, Carly ached to say. *I wonder if Gary ever thinks of me.*

Willard, never one to let a conversation lag, quickly popped another question to his young friend. "So, what's new in the fire business? Anything exciting out there in the chaparral?"

Carly forced a smile. "Well, you know how it goes. Every fire is exciting, but I'm bushed. I'm planning to sleep all weekend."

Willard nodded, then peered at Carly a bit more closely. "I think that's a good idea. You look positively exhausted."

Carly didn't argue. In addition to her physical fatigue, she feared that her emotional weariness might also be visible. She felt overwhelmed with frustration. Common sense told her to forget that she'd ever been put in charge of a convict crew, but the ache within her told her she never would.

"What is it, Carly?" Willard now asked perceptively. "Bad news?"

No news is more like it, she longed to reply. Instead she replied, "Of course not. I've just had a difficult week and I haven't quite let it go yet."

Willard touched Carly's chin, as he met her eyes. In a doctor's no-nonsense tone, he said, "Tell me what the trouble is, Carly. Maybe I can help. And even if I can't—" he gave her an encouraging smile "—I can certainly listen."

Carly was undecided. It would help enormously to share her confusion with somebody who cared about her, but she wasn't sure just how much she wanted to reveal. Discreetly she admitted, "I was placed in charge of a convict crew, Willard. Not at yesterday's fire, but the one before. It was an eye-opening experience."

She expected Willard to fuss over her, to say "Is that safe, young lady?" or something along those lines. Instead, her friend seized on one word, realizing that there was more involved than fear. "Eye-opening, Carly? How so?"

Carly took a sip of her coffee, then sat down on a nearby kitchen chair facing Willard. "At first, I thought they were all scum. I guess I was a little bit scared. And some of them were pretty awful, though all of these men were convicted for fairly nonviolent crimes. Or, at least, crimes of passion that involved a specific set of circumstances not likely to be repeated again. I mean, there weren't any rapists or psychopathic serial killers or anything like that." She took another sip, wrapping her fingers around the cup. "But I worked with these men—two of them nearly died with me when we got trapped by the fire—and it's hard to think of them as mere criminals. Nonhumans. I mean, they got hungry and cold. They got blisters from the flames. They were as brave as anybody else on the line. And now they're back in prison again."

She met Willard's eyes, hoping the doctor would see her point . . . but not see too much more.

Quietly he took her hand. "I think I understand what you're feeling, Carly. I felt the same way the first time I visited a prison."

"You've visited a prison?" Carly asked, equally stunned by the news and relieved that she had a friend who might be able to tell her what to expect if she ever tried to visit Gary. "How? When? Was it some kind of a tour, or did you know one of the criminals?"

Willard's lips pursed together with a grimace, which was rare for him. "I knew one of the men, but he was never a criminal." His tone was harsh. "He was my kid brother."

Carly gagged on her coffee and spit up a good mouthful. Willard patted her on the back as she apologized—for both faux pas—then asked in dismay, "Why was your brother in jail, Willard? If it's okay to ask." Carly had met Willard's brother one Christmas, and remembered him well. Floyd Jameson was a quiet man of medium height and light blond hair, friendly, unassuming, gentle and warm. It was inconceivable to think of him in prison. As inconceivable as the notion of Gary Reid committing murder.

Willard stood up brusquely, anger lining his cheeks with red. "Floyd was very active in our church when he was young," he told Carly, "and then the war broke out. I mean World War II. It wasn't like Vietnam, you know, where lots of good people took both sides. The whole country was united then, and if you were a patriotic American, you supported the war." He exhaled loudly. "But our church—along with a lot of other churches— opposed all kinds of war, no matter what the reason. The pastor taught our boys to practice pacifism, no matter what the price. Floyd followed his beliefs. He asked for conscientious-objector status, but since our church wasn't widely known, he was turned down." His eyes filled with unashamed tears. "He spent a year in jail. A terrible, hellish year! It would have been a lot longer if Thelma's uncle hadn't gotten him a Citizens' Conservation Corps job, so he could get out."

Carly felt sick; as sick as she felt whenever she thought about a man of Gary's refinement serving time. Although she came from a military family, she could respect Floyd's point of view. The issue wasn't war or peace; it was standing up for one's personal values. "I'm so sorry, Willard," she told her friend. "I never knew."

"Well, it's hardly common knowledge. Floyd's put it all behind him now. He knows that he was true to his own beliefs, so he can hold his head up high." Abruptly Willard swallowed hard. Then he said, "I guess none of your prisoners were in that position. C.O.'s, I mean."

Carly lifted her hands helplessly. "Not that I know of. But some of them—" she studied her friend and decided to come clean "—well, one of them, at any rate, is as innocent of wrongdoing as your brother. He doesn't belong in there and it's destroying him." Tears suddenly washed her tired eyes as she confessed, "And it's just tearing me apart."

"Oh, Carly," Willard murmured. One look at his eyes told Carly that he already had the whole picture. He slipped one avuncular arm around her, but just as he gently tugged her toward him, the telephone began to ring. Too upset to talk, Carly let the answering machine take care of the call, but she couldn't help but listen to the message.

"Supervisor?" a deep voice drawled. "This here's Clifford from Tejon. The Doc's friend, you remember? He's not back yet, and—"

In an instant Carly flipped the dial that stopped the recording. "Clifford, this is Carly. I'm here. What's wrong?"

"Gary's not back yet, Supervisor Winston," Clifford told her at once, nearly shouting to be heard above the background of television and men's rough voices at his end of the line. "I can't reach his lawyer, and I can't get the warden to do anything. When they couldn't find Gary the first night, the warden decided he'd run off and washed his hands of him."

For a minute there was a terrible ruckus that sounded like a fight, and Carly knew that Clifford wouldn't have time to tell her very much. "Tell me what you want me to do, Clifford," she said without hesitation. "How can I help Gary?"

"Find him. Then get somebody to figure out how to get him back here."

Carly blanched. "Clifford, how do you expect me to find Gary? If he's gone, he might not come to me. And if he's lost in the system—"

"Then they've stuck him in some other jail. And wherever he is, it's got to be worse than this one. He'll be buzzard meat without me, Supervisor. Do you understand?"

Before she could reply, somebody else grabbed the phone and hissed an obscenity at Carly. Before the line went dead, she heard what sounded like fist against bone.

IT TOOK CARLY—or, to be more precise, a friend of Willard's—a day and a half to find Gary. Willard's friend just happened to be a County Sheriff, and he generously arranged for Carly to visit Gary in jail.

Normally, Carly spent no time worrying about her wardrobe, but before she drove up to the jail she spent over an hour trying to decide what to wear. It was the first time she'd ever seen Gary when she wasn't covered with soot, and she wanted to look pretty for him. But chances were good that anything she wore would be dressier than his regulation prison garb, and she didn't want the contrast to offend him. After a great deal of thought, she decided to wear a designer pair of lightweight denims with a matching cotton top adorned with colorful kettlecloth flowers. Halfway to the jail, she decided that it was both too casual and too bright, but she knew she'd be just as miserable wearing anything else, so she didn't go back home.

On the outside, the county jail looked like any one of the dozen beige government buildings that surrounded it—rundown, but not quite seedy. Inside was a different story. The main entrance was poorly lit, and the long hallway to the visiting room was downright dark and dingy. A heavy, grizzled guard ushered Carly into a long, skinny room that housed a line of windows reinforced by wire and adorned by brown telephone receivers, but no phone. The guard motioned Carly to the third phone, and she settled uneasily into the metal chair beside it.

She licked her lips as she waited. She glanced around the room. To her left was an elderly man who was apparently talking to his son, a heavily tattooed boy on the other side of the wall. Anger marked their exchange. To her right was a pregnant girl of maybe seventeen, wearing enough makeup for six or seven women. She sobbed constantly, only nodding in response to whatever words she might have heard on her "private" phone. The woman guard who had so vigorously searched Carly had warned her that all conversations at County would be monitored. There was no doubt in her mind that she could expect no privacy with Gary.

She did not, in fact, have the slightest idea *what* to expect in this godforsaken place that made her feel dirty from the inside out. The only thing Carly was sure of was that she'd feel better once Gary's beloved face came into view.

She was wrong.

He looked terrible. The last time she'd seen him he'd been soot-streaked, of course, but that had only proved that he was one of the gang. Now he was dressed in shabby jeans that were a size or two too big and a graying T-shirt with a rip in one sleeve. He hadn't shaved in some time—maybe since she'd last seen him—and the result made him look more like some underworld goon than the hero of *Miami Vice*.

Carly would have been able to bear all of it, no matter how grim, if Gary had simply given her some sign that he was glad to see her. A smile, even with his eyes, would have made it all worthwhile. But he looked like a man who'd forgotten how to smile. Or maybe had never learned how.

He made no haste to reach his side of the wall between them, no haste to settle into his metal chair and pick up the phone. His glare made her shiver, and a tiny voice inside her said, *If he looked like this on the witness stand, no wonder the jury voted to convict him.* For a moment she found her own faith in Gary wavering. How hard it was to put her faith in a story she'd never even heard! The bottom line was, he didn't look like anybody Carly had ever seen before. Or wanted to see again.

At last, in a voice as cold as steel, he said, "Hello."

"Hello," Carly answered, finding it hard to even blurt out that much. But when he made no reply, she clutched the receiver more tightly and tried to start the conversation. "I got a call from Clifford. He was worried about you when you didn't come back to your cell. Are you okay?"

Again he paused, as though weighing every word. Because of her? Carly wondered. Or maybe because he knew that a guard was listening to their exchange?

"I'm uninjured," was his cautious reply.

Physician talk? Or did that mean somebody had tried to hurt him and had failed?

"Willard—my landlord—has a friend who's a sheriff. He managed to track you down. Apparently they had trouble finding you at the hospital because they said they were looking for a prisoner and didn't ask for you—a doctor—by name. The officer who finally put all the pieces together wrote a report, but he forgot to fill in one part, so the next guy up the line decided to kick it back to him before he filed it. But the officer was sick the next few days, and by the time he came back to work, the report had gotten shoved to one side and... well, forgotten, I guess."

Gary said nothing. His eyes were dark.

"Your paperwork has just been sitting on the corner of somebody's desk all this time, Gary," Carly finished, her voice strained and low. "Willard's friend assured me that the situation would have been straightened out sooner or later. He also said that you should be back at Tejon in time for dinner." When he didn't reply, Carly added, "Assuming that's what you want."

"It doesn't have a damn thing to do with what *I* want," Gary snapped. "I'm not even a person to these guys." For the first time, his beautiful blue eyes showed a flash of feeling, and Carly tried to take heart. Even though it was anger, at least it was honest emotion, not the veiled iciness he'd greeted her with before.

"Clifford says it's better there."

His jaw jutted out with stress. "What Clifford means is that *Clifford's* there."

"It's also... easier to talk to visitors, the sheriff says." Her eyes pleaded mutely for him to ask her to come visit him at Tejon. "I guess they have big picnic tables. No glass to keep us apart and—"

"Dammit, Carly!" he suddenly burst out. "The Tejon visiting room is a garbage heap, not a summer-camp barbecue!"

Before Carly could respond, Gary closed his eyes; he took the receiver away from his ear and banged it once against his chest. Hurt, confused, too frustrated with the entire scenario to think clearly, Carly put her receiver down, too. Desperately she battled the tears that welled up within her.

After a moment of terrible silence—punctuated only by the public sorrows of every other criminal in the room—Gary opened his eyes again. This time he looked straight at Carly, really looked at her, with an expression of tenderness and profound frustration that she had seen before... on Camelback Ridge.

He looked like Gary. He looked like the man she adored.

Following his lead, Carly gave up trying to be proud or sensible. She let the tears spill over; she let her love for him fill her eyes. When he reached toward her, just once, to lay one hand on the glass, Carly mirrored his action on the other side. She watched his thumb move back and forth, as though to stroke her wrist. For a blinding moment, she remembered the last time they'd been alone together—when his touch had been so potent, so tender. A flash of ripe, sensual need splashed over her. Then, abruptly, Gary pulled back his hand and picked up the phone.

With less haste, Carly did likewise.

"I appreciate your trying to straighten out this mess," he said quickly, as though he couldn't get the words out of his mouth fast enough. The change in conversational tempo was almost frightening. "And I want you to know that...I'm glad we met, and I'm glad we've had this chance to say goodbye."

Ice hardened in the pit of Carly's stomach. "I didn't come to say goodbye, Gary," she confessed. "They promised me fifteen minutes, and—"

"This is no place to carry on a conversation," he cut her off. "If I'm being transferred back to Tejon, I need to get ready to go."

Carly knew there was probably nothing he needed to do before the transfer that could possibly take more than thirty seconds. His brush-off could not have been more blunt. Stunned, she heard herself babbling, "I'll come see you again, Gary. I'll come see you on Saturday at Tejon."

Again, he stared at her; his lips tightened and the knuckles of his right hand turned white as they gripped the phone.

When he didn't speak, Carly couldn't help but prod him; she couldn't leave without knowing where she stood. If he really didn't want to continue their relationship, she just couldn't force herself on him again.

"Gary," she said bluntly, "this is no time to be proud. I'm willing to go the extra mile—to put up with any roadblocks the prison system throws in our way—as long as I'm sure that you...return my feelings. Now I'm not asking for red roses and sweet nothings, but I need some assurance that I'm not all alone here, Gary. Now tell me straight: do you want me to come see you at Tejon? Do you want me to write to you there? Do you want to see me, again?"

It seemed to Carly that a lifetime passed while she waited for Gary to answer. She watched tiny white lines of anguish frame his full lips; she watched him scratch his half-bearded chin. She even counted the seconds while he raised one hand to the screened window again, as though to touch her face, before he drew back sharply when his fingertips encountered the icy glass.

At last he lifted the receiver back to his face, and clearly enunciated his answer so there could be no doubt: "No."

Only the anguish in his beautiful blue eyes assured her that it was the hardest word he'd ever had to say.

CHAPTER SEVEN

"You sure you're okay, Doc?" Clifford asked him at least three times, when Gary returned to their cell at Tejon just hours after Carly left him at County. "You look sick."

"I'm not sick. I'm a doctor. I ought to know."

"Nobody worked you over?"

Gary shook his head. "Nobody tried. I just told them I was your pal." He tried to summon up a smile to bolster his lame joke, but nothing happened. He was in too black a mood to act happy.

Clifford grew silent then, but Gary began to pace like a caged wolf, slowly at first, but making sharp turns with increasing intensity. Clifford tolerated the action for about ten minutes before he said, "You're gonna rip, Doc. Spill it now. Get cool."

Gary slammed one fist into the bunk, his fury rising by the minute. He was tormented by the memory of his woman—no, he mustn't ever think of her that way—a good woman, a pure woman, subjected to the leers of the other inmates and the suspicious scrutiny of the guards. They'd actually frisked her! Laid hands on her to make sure she hadn't smuggled anything in! Just seeing Carly in that seedy place had been enough to make his blood boil. It was almost as bad as knowing that *she* had seen *him* in the same setting. A convict among other cons. He felt as though he'd had a skull and crossbones tattooed across his chest.

"You shouldn't have called her, Clifford! She never should have come."

Clifford looked a little bit guilty. "I waited a whole damn week, Doc. I tried to reach your lawyer. I didn't know what else to do."

"I've got other friends on the outside," Gary reminded him. "You could have contacted one of them."

"I don't know any of them," Clifford pointed out. "Besides, how many of your fancy doctor friends would dirty themselves for one second with a con like me?"

It was a grim thought, Gary realized, because it was appallingly true. None of his doctor friends was in the habit of fraternizing with criminals. It occurred to him, with shock, that his status was now exactly the same as Clifford's. How much warmth could he expect from his old pals when he got out? He tried to count the men who'd come to visit him in prison, and there were damn few. Of course, he'd told them all to stay away; the shame of it was more than he could bear. But they could have written to him; only the address would be dirty. No matter where a friend was living, the message would still be the same....

"You should have seen her face, Clifford. Looking at me as though—" he shuddered "—I were some heaven-sent miracle. God, it killed me to send her away! I thought she was going to break down."

What hurt the most was that Gary knew she'd never forget the way he'd treated her. But how could he have done anything else? He couldn't take her in his arms with glass between them; he couldn't tell her how he ached for her with a guard listening on the phone. And he certainly couldn't encourage her to carry on with their ill-starred relationship, not when he knew that each trip to the prison would continue to tarnish Carly from the inside out.

"Don't beat yourself up over it, Doc," Clifford advised. "Nobody sold her a bill of goods. She knew who you were going in. Before we left fire camp, she asked me to tell you to call her. I told her you wouldn't, so whatever happened at County shouldn't have surprised her."

But it *had* surprised her, Gary knew. It had crushed her very soul. And the only way Gary could imagine easing her pain now was to vanish from her life so that she might get on with healing, as soon as possible.

Unfortunately, that plan didn't do a thing to alleviate his own misery. What did they say? *Physician, heal thyself.* But for his hunger for Carly Winston, Gary knew there was no cure.

FOR THE FIRST month after Carly saw Gary in jail, she welcomed the incessant demand for her services in a rash of arsonists' fires. She was almost too weary to feel the aching emptiness inside her. And when she had a moment to think—when memories of Gary inevitably flooded her mind and her body—she told herself that she understood why he'd sent her away. But that didn't help her one iota. She simply couldn't forget his beautiful blue eyes and dimpled smile.

It had taken a long time to forget Rodney's wavy blond hair and rakish grin, too, but time had healed that wound. Yet Carly knew she'd never forget the lesson she'd learned from her affair with Rodney. She'd met him when he was going through a "rough patch." His girlfriend had walked out on him right after he'd lost his small computer business. He was flamboyant, exciting and... well, whiny, at times. Carly had tried to bolster his ego in the romance department with exaggerated praise for his so-so skill as a lover, and she'd pored through the want ads looking for possible positions for him, though he never felt any of them was quite suitable. In turn, he told her that she was the woman he'd been looking for all of his life, and he didn't know how he had ever lived a day without her. He showered her with romantic cards and flowers, often purchased with money she had lent him. Never in her life had she felt more needed by another human being, and she had interpreted his clinginess as love.

Carly had believed in Rodney's ability to put his life back together... with just a little more patience, a little more time. She had also believed in his love for her, despite his increasing complaints about all the nights she spent in fire camp, until the evening she was called away on what turned out to be a false alarm. Thrilled to have the night off, she'd rushed home to the apartment they'd shared—although she alone paid the rent. The scene she witnessed—Rodney in a tangle of sheets, on top of a hatefully beautiful blonde—would never be fully erased from her mind. Nor would the scene that followed: the other woman confessing that she'd been seeing Rodney for weeks and had never heard of Carly... Rodney, half dressed, begging Carly for forgiveness, insisting that he couldn't live without her... before he got angry and decided that his unfaithfulness was "all her fault" because her fire-fighting career meant more to her than he did. If she'd ever been home at night, Rodney had maintained, he never would have looked twice at another woman.

The parallels between Rodney's situation and Gary's current condition—mourning his late wife and railing at the injustice that had cost him his children and his career—were painfully clear to Carly. She believed with all her heart that Gary was an innocent victim of circumstance, but then again, she'd once thought the same was true for Rodney. Battling the pain any way she could, Carly told herself that she ought to be glad she would never need to make any more awkward decisions where Gary was concerned. She'd asked him outright where she figured in his life, and his answer couldn't have been more straightforward.

And then, out of the blue, the letter came.

She'd been gone for three days. Arriving home at midnight, she'd grabbed the mail, tucked it under one arm, and opened a can of food for Homer so he'd stop yowling and rubbing against her leg. It was Carly's habit to flip through the mail to see what was there, then take a shower before she read the letters in bed.

Tonight, however, she didn't make it to the shower. She never even finished checking the rest of the mail. The third envelope in the pile, sandwiched between a bill from Sears and a flyer for a discount carpet-cleaning, was a plain white envelope with no return address. The chickenscratched addressee was "Supervisor Carly Winston," and the postmark was Tejon. She only knew two people who lived in Tejon, which meant that the letter was either from Clifford, and concerning Gary...or—dear God, please let it be—a letter from Gary himself.

Carly took a deep breath, then tore open the envelope.

Dear, sweet Carly:
A month has passed since I told you to give up on me, for your own sake, and part of me hopes to God that you have. But another part, the selfish part, hopes that forgetting the brief time we shared is as impossible for you as it's turned out to be for me.

You know what we're up against. With luck I'll be out in five or six months, but I'll always be an ex-con. God alone knows how I'm going to make a living, let alone how I'm going to get my babies back. I know I have no right to ask you to be part of the picture, and the last thing I want is for you to give it a shot out of guilt or pity for the poor convicted man. I mean that, Carly. Don't try to fake it. I'll see right through you, and it'll only make it worse.

I guess you can tell that I'm no good at letters. What I'm trying to say is that I care for you, Carly. Too much for my own good.

You know where I am.

It was signed with a single *G*, and the proper prison mailing address was listed at the bottom of the last page.

Carly skimmed the letter once, then read it again more slowly. The third time through, she tried to imagine what Gary really meant by each and every word. Then she went ahead with her shower and read the rest of her mail. An hour later she read the letter from Gary again. Then she broke down and cried.

ALMOST A WEEK passed before Gary got a letter back. It read:

Dear Gary,
I wish I could tell you that your letter came too late. After the hell you've put me through it would serve you right if I told you to jump in the lake. Instead, I'm going to tell you straight out that I'm willing to put up with anything the prison system has to fling at us—and any garbage still waiting when you're on the outside—as long as I don't have to fight *you*. I don't care how embarrassing it is for either of us to be monitored and forced to mingle with people who make us squirm. If that shame is stronger than what

we feel for each other, then we don't have enough feeling between us to make it work.

Think about it. Be honest with me. I'm dying to see you, but I won't show up on visiting day without an engraved invitation.

Carly

Gary read the letter twice, then closed his eyes as the enormity of his relief flowed over him. He'd told himself that he'd never really doubted what her reply would be, but now he realized that one of the reasons he'd sent Carly away was his fear that sooner or later she'd realize he wasn't worth the trouble. In a way, he was pleased by her anger. It meant she wasn't going to coddle him. She refused to let his prisoner status interfere with honest communication between them.

After some thought as to the best way to respond to her terse note, he dug out some heavy parchment letterhead left over from his life on the outside. In big block letters he wrote:

WHEREAS: VISITING HOURS AT TEJON CORRECTIONAL INSTITUTION ARE HELD EACH SATURDAY FROM TEN TO THREE;
WHEREAS: INMATE GARY REID IS BREATHTAKINGLY EAGER FOR THE SIGHT OF ONE CARLY WINSTON;
WHEREAS: SAID INMATE IS HOPEFUL THAT SAID VISITOR TREMBLES IN EQUAL ANTICIPATION.
THEREFORE: THIS DOCUMENT SHOULD BE CONSTRUED BY ALL AND SUNDRY AS ONE ENGRAVED INVITATION TO SATURDAY VISITATION AT TEJON CORRECTIONAL INSTI-

TUTION FOR THE SOLE PERSONAL USE OF ONE CARLY WINSTON, WHOSE ATTENDANCE IS MOST HUMBLY REQUESTED.

He signed his name, "Gary Allan Reid, M.D.," with a flourish, then delivered the letter to a guard before he could change his mind. For the rest of the week he felt buoyed by all the delirium of falling in love, though he wasn't ready to give that sterling name to his chaotic feelings. On Saturday he paid a fellow in the prison laundry extra for clean jeans and a shirt. The third time he combed his hair, Clifford laughed out loud. But Gary vowed that nothing would trouble him today. He would find a way to make this a good visit for Carly, no matter what happened. He was prepared for any scenario.

Except for one in which Carly simply didn't show up.

THE FOLLOWING THURSDAY, a note of explanation came.

> ...I received your wonderful invitation last week and hope you'll let me take a rain check. Please understand that nothing but a fire would keep me away from you. I was called out of state on Friday and didn't get back until yesterday. We're all working double shifts and covering for each other all over the Southwest. This is the worst fire season in sixteen years....

The rest of the letter was friendly but not passionate, and it did little to relieve the remembered agony of his Carly-less visitation day. Didn't she know what visitation day meant in prison? It wasn't like a date you could just reschedule for another night of the week! After all the weeks he'd tried to forget her, agonized over what to do, he'd finally made the decision! Michelle would have forgone the fire to come to him, Gary knew. Nothing would have been more important than healing the breach between them, comforting her man in prison. Apparently Carly had different priorities.

Gary reminded himself that he'd met Carly at a fire and had seen her dedication on the line; it was partly her professionalism during that harrowing experience which had drawn him to her. But as he recalled those magical few days, he remembered that she'd asked him once or twice just how he'd ended up in prison, and he'd rather clumsily deflected her questions. Oh, she'd insisted on more than one occasion that she believed he was innocent of any wrongdoing, but surely she still had questions in her mind! Why didn't she ever mention the subject in her letters? Was she trying to show her faith in him, or was she afraid to learn the truth? Now that she'd had plenty of time to think through the situation—and plenty of time to forget their one stormy kiss—was she reconsidering her position?

Gary ran over all the lines of logic in his mind, during the long hours of the following week, but no rationale changed the facts: he desperately wanted to spend some time with Carly, and she'd had the opportunity to come see him but had deliberately chosen to go somewhere else.

Still, he couldn't stifle his joy at the prospect of seeing her on the visiting day two weeks later. Or his dismay when she stood him up for a fire again. Her letters continued to be loving throughout August, but by the first of September, his own replies had grown terse.

You asked me to be honest with you, Carly, so I will be. For the last three visitation weekends you've been off fighting fires while I've been waiting for you to come to see me. I can't do anything else to fill up my spare time. I can't catch up with you on a later day. I know the forest is burning up, but dammit, so am I. When I first wrote to you, you said you were willing to put up with all my prison roadblocks so we could be together. But what about your own?

If I'm not worth a little bit of sacrifice on your part, Carly, maybe we should forget the whole thing....

Three days later, on Saturday morning at precisely ten o'clock, a guard informed Gary he had a visitor.

Carly looked haggard. Her eyelids were puffy; half-healed blisters cloaked the left side of her face. She was dressed in the same T-shirt and blue jeans she'd worn off-duty at fire camp, and she smelled vaguely of a forest fire. She smiled apprehensively when she saw him.

Gary smiled back, too glad to see her to remember how angry he'd been. Her appearance was proof enough that she'd really been fighting fires; and her presence here, an indication that she hadn't forgotten him after all. "What kind of salve did you put on those?" was his greeting as he sat down opposite Carly at the redwood picnic table in the center of the room. Other inmates and their visitors flanked them on both sides.

Carly laughed. "Once a doctor, always a doctor. Don't worry about my face, Gary. I did everything I was supposed to do."

"Professionally, you mean." The words slipped out before he could stop them. The last thing he wanted to do was fight with Carly today. But on the other hand, he wanted a relationship with her—not a fleeting visit. That wasn't going to come about if he tried to conceal his feelings.

Carly studied him with care. "It might interest you to know that I'm still fighting a fire a hundred miles north of here. I finished night shift at seven and got special permission to leave the camp for the day. I go back on-duty at four o'clock."

Gary was humbled by the enormity of her sacrifice. She'd done more than take a long drive during her precious off-hours. She was giving up the equivalent of a whole night's sleep. She'd go back to her strenuous job with no rest at all.

"That's not safe, Carly," he said gently. "You'll be too tired to concentrate."

Carly blinked back tears...of emotion, of fatigue? "I couldn't concentrate anyway. I don't think I've ever done anything harder in my life than keep on working when I could have been here with you." She swallowed hard. "I'm committed, Gary, just like an officer who gets orders from his C.O. I don't volunteer to fight one fire at a time, you know. When I'm called, I have to go." Before he could reply, she said, "Isn't that the way it was for you at the hospital? When one of your patients was dying, did you ever say 'Gee willikers, I can't be bothered now because I've got a date?'"

Put like that, it was hard to disagree. It made him ashamed of his last letter to Carly. She never should have driven here when she was still attached to a fire.

"I'm sorry, Carly," he whispered. "It's easy to get selfish in here. I never should have sent you that awful letter. I shouldn't have bullied you into coming here."

"What letter?" Carly asked. "The last one I got was a week ago. Most of it was devoted to the ideas you had for job arrangements to clear your parole."

Gary stared at her. "When was the last time you were home?"

"Tuesday, I guess. I left Wednesday before the mail came in."

Now it was Gary's turn to swallow hard. "When you do get home again, will you do me a favor, Carly? Just tear up the letter you find there from me. Don't look at it at all."

Carly's eyes grew dark. "I don't think I like the sound of that. Have you—" fear colored her already reddened features "—changed your mind again?"

It was the first time since she'd arrived that either of them had alluded to the dark month when Gary had shut her out of his life, and the sudden pain in her eyes wounded him unbearably. Instinctively, he reached out to touch her face on the unblistered side, his fingertips reveling in the softness of her skin. "Never, Carly. I swear to you, all that is—"

"No touching!" a guard suddenly bellowed, the voice crashing through Gary's tender words.

Carly jerked back, her eyes wide with alarm, while Gary withdrew his hand, clenching his jaw in anger.

"Ignore him, Gary. Please."

Gary exhaled angrily, then tired to focus on this enchanting woman who'd come so far to spend such a brief period of time with him.

"Finish what you were saying, Gary. Please tell me... how it's going to be."

The fear in her voice surprised him. Hadn't he made his feelings clear in the flurry of letters he'd mailed her in the past month? But then he remembered the dark weeks before that, and he knew there was a lot of healing still needed between them.

"It's going to be you and me, Carly. And someday, I hope, you and me and my children."

Carly licked her lips. A few stray tears dripped over her tremulous smile. "I'm sorry. I'm just so tired. And I never know just what to expect when I see you."

"From now on—" he warmed her with a dimpled smile that came from deep within his heart "—you can expect me to be elated to see you and patient when you can't come. You can expect letters almost every day, and maybe phone calls if I can get to the phone and feel up to coping with bozos listening to our conversations." He reached out to take her hand, and ran his fingertips over her delicate wrist, marveling in the tiny sigh he heard escape from her lips. A sigh of joy. A sigh of desire. A sigh that might have been his name.

It was an exquisite moment, but short-lived. Carly had just closed her fingers over his own, interlacing them as though the two of them could somehow merge that way, when a voice cracked over them. "I said no touching!!!!"

Gary clenched his fist as he let go, doubly angry when Carly glared at the guard and stuffed both hands under the table.

"I guess I can expect that, too," she said. And then, incredibly, she found a smile, as warm as the flame of a candle in a rain-dark window. "It doesn't matter, Gary. Nothing that man says to me will change the fact that I love you." Her smile grew wider. "That's what I drove a hundred miles to say."

CHAPTER EIGHT

THE NEXT FEW weeks were hard on Carly. The fire season continued to be one of the worst in decades, and often she had to cancel her Saturday visits with Gary. What made the situation worse was that she usually couldn't warn him ahead of time because there was no way for her to call him at the prison, and even when he managed to wrest control of the communal inmate phone during calling hours, the perpetual noise and lack of privacy made conversation difficult and unrewarding.

Once, Gary suggested that Carly could leave him a specific message on her answering machine so he could at least get some information if he called her, but she'd quickly put the nix on that idea, reminding him that he wasn't the only one who called her. She didn't want the whole world to know her business. Break-ins were more likely if strangers knew she wasn't home.

At the time, it had sounded like a reasonable excuse, but the next time Carly came home to find a message from her dad on the tape, she knew it wasn't strangers she was worried about. She didn't want her father to ask her who she met on Saturdays. She didn't want to admit that she loved a man in prison.

Colonel Winston was going to be in Los Angeles in early September, his recorded voice informed her, and he hoped she could join him for a couple of days. Normally Carly greeted such news with joy—their reunions were all too rare these days—but this time she found herself apprehensive about their visit. She'd never lied to her father before, never withheld anything important from him. Sooner or later, he was bound to ask her a question she couldn't just sidestep. She'd either have to lie to him outright, or tell him the truth about Gary. Or at least as much of the truth as she was privy to. What was she supposed to say if her father asked her to explain Gary's version of why he was in prison? *I don't know, Dad, and it's driving me crazy, but I don't dare ask—for fear that he'll think I don't trust him?* That wouldn't be nearly enough for Carl Winston.

The moment of truth came a lot earlier than Carly had expected. Less than an hour, in fact, after he deplaned. She'd driven him to a cozy Italian café, where the owner spoke English with a Sicilian accent that sounded genuine. They both ordered the house special, manicotti, then munched on the finest garlic bread Carly had ever eaten while they waited for their meals.

"You look great, Dad," Carly told her father sincerely. At sixty, his black hair was peppered with gray and his face was lined, but he carried himself like a man in his prime and still considered himself middle-aged.

"I wish I could say the same for you," he replied. He wasn't teasing, and he wasn't being cruel. His eyes showed the same paternal concern she'd often read there when she'd been ill as a little girl. "I like the dress, Carly, and you're just as pretty as ever. But you've got bags under your eyes, honey, and you look run-down."

Carly swallowed hard. "It's fire season, Dad. I'm not getting much rest."

Quietly he studied her face, as though looking for some mysterious answer to a question he hadn't asked. It was his commanding-officer look, the one that always squelched rebellion and forced confessions of the most embarrassing truths. Carly knew he would pump her until he found out what he wanted to know.

"I've seen you during fire season before. You've always looked tired, but not...unhappy."

"I'm not unhappy, Dad, I'm—"

"Troubled about something. Troubled because I'm here?"

"Of course not. I'm thrilled to see you," she insisted.

"Ah," he said, as though she'd just answered his first question. "You're thrilled to see me, but you're afraid I'm going to find out something you don't want me to know."

That leveled Carly. She knew she couldn't possibly lie to him. She was ashamed that she'd even considered it. Her father deserved better from her. And so did Gary. Surely she wasn't ashamed of him, was she? She'd have to come clean.

She waited until the waitress had delivered their plates, and picked at her manicotti while her father downed his with relish. When she couldn't stand his studied silence anymore, she blurted out, "I'm in love with a man in prison."

Colonel Winston's eyes opened wide in shock, then narrowed in anger. He swallowed the food in his mouth and set down his fork. His jaw grew rigid at he stared at his only child. "Go on," he commanded her.

"His name is Gary Reid. He's a doctor. He has two little girls that he absolutely worships, who are currently living with his late wife's mother, but he's determined to regain custody of them one way or another after he gets out on parole around Christmas."

Dark brows raised; a masculine jawline grew hard as granite. At last the colonel said, "How did you meet this...criminal?"

"He is not a criminal!" Carly denied hotly. "He's done nothing at all to—"

"If he's serving time, he's been convicted of a crime. And I've never yet heard of a criminal who thinks he's guilty of anything! Good God, Carly!" he burst out, finally losing his temper altogether. "Have you lost your mind?"

She could have yelled at him; she could have told him all she'd gone through with Gary so far; how hard it was to let a relationship bloom under such tight scrutiny as the guards'. She could have told him how beautiful Gary's letters were, despite the fact that he said he was not a natural letter writer; she could have told him that no matter how horribly the visiting room depressed her each time she arrived, it only took one dimpled smile from Gary to make her whole world right. Instead, she held her ground and told him steadily, "I haven't lost my mind, Dad. I've only lost my heart."

He clenched both fists in frustration. "I can't believe I'm hearing this. At least Rodney Haywood looked like a decent guy on the surface—good job, nice manners, respectable family background. There was no way you could have predicted that he'd cheat on you the moment your back was turned. But this felon—"

"Dad, don't!" Carly burst out. "I love Gary; don't you understand? I trust him. I believe in his innocence, in his decency, in his ability to make a future for himself, in spite of all that's happened. You raised me to stand on my own, to make my own decisions. Well I have, dammit. It wasn't easy for me to give myself to Gary. I didn't do it lightly." She stopped and took a deep breath. "But it's too late for you to lecture me on propriety and family background. I'm committed to him, now."

For several moments he did not meet her eyes. At last he picked up his fork and started eating again. After three or four silent mouthfuls, Colonel Winston said, "Tell me how you met this...doctor."

Carly swallowed the lump in her throat and started to do as he asked.

GARY KNEW SOMETHING was wrong the minute he spotted Carly. They'd worked out a pattern by now, a regular place they sat together, a secret code for forbidden caresses and unspoken words of love. When he wanted to touch her face he'd touch his own; she'd clasp her hands together when she ached to hold his hand. She always greeted him with a smile, no matter how tired or uncertain she felt. The Saturday after she'd gone to L.A. to see her father, however, there wasn't even the ghost of a grin on her lovely face.

"Tell me," he said gently, rubbing one thumb along his clean-shaven jaw as soon as they'd said hello.

Carly didn't meet his eyes at first. "I told him all about you. He didn't approve."

Gary stifled a sigh. "And this surprised you?"

"Of course not. I guess I just...kept pretending, you know, that I'd be able to convince him how wonderful you were. I failed completely."

For a moment neither one of them spoke. Then Gary said, "I don't know what you want me to say."

"I don't know, either. I love him so much, Gary, and I hate it when he's disappointed in me."

He stared at her helplessly. "I'm sorry, Carly. Really I am." A few weeks ago he would have volunteered to solve her problem by bowing out of her life, but it was far too late for that now. Carly had become his sunrise and his sunset, his candle in the window, his hope of going home. They'd only known each other for three months, shared one explosive kiss and half a dozen forbidden half touches, but their bonding was more secure than that of some couples who had spent years in the same bed. Carly gave him so much and received so little. The last thing he wanted was to cause her trouble with her beloved dad.

He wondered if it would have been easier for her to face her father if she'd been able to tell him the true story of the events that had led up to Gary's arrest. He'd always been half relieved, half troubled by the fact that Carly hadn't mentioned it once during their prison visits, or even in her letters. Yet he knew that it stood between them like a filmy spiderweb. He tried to think of a subtle way to bring the subject up, but he felt trapped by the sight before him—his beautiful woman surrounded by junkies, killers and guards.

When Carly asked, "Could we talk about something else?" Gary knew that he could not deal with the cloud of her father's disapproval and the shame of his own ongoing nightmare at the same time. Struggling to think of a more cheerful subject, he suggested, "Why don't we talk about parole?"

It was, after all, his favorite subject. Even when there were roadblocks in the future, at least there *was* a future. There was Carly. And there were his two girls. With his squeaky clean record, John Henton, his lawyer, said that his parole was a sure thing. Even if the parole board believed the very worst about Gary's conviction, it was obvious that he wasn't a danger to society.

Clifford's situation was more unstable. He had a long history of convictions, but none of them involved violence, and his change in attitude since Gary had been tutoring him had not gone unnoted by the guards.

"Any news on that front?" Carly asked.

"Well, not since I wrote you last. Clifford's hearing comes up before mine, and he still doesn't have any job prospects. He's got to have something nailed down before they'll let him out."

"What does he have in mind, Gary? What can he do?"

"Well, that's the trouble. All he can do is play ball, fight fires and hustle strangers. I've worked with him night and day to get his academic skills in shape, but he still lacks confidence. Besides, he says he doesn't have any contacts who are legitimate."

"He has me," Carly said softly.

Gary smiled at her. "You're sweet, honey, but I'm not sure you want to get tangled up in Clifford's parole. In the first place, it's pretty messy, and in the second place, it could prove to be a problem for me once I get out."

"What do you mean?"

"I mean, most paroles include a provision forbidding any fraternization with other ex-cons, which means Clifford and I won't be able to go near each other for at least a year. If you're working with him, we might all end up in dutch, because I don't plan to let you out of my sight."

Carly licked her lips, apparently processing this information. "Maybe I can help him get a job somewhere else. In my line of work, you make friends up and down the state."

This time Gary nodded. "Okay, Carly, it's worth a try. I think Clifford's ready to give the straight-and-narrow a whirl this time. If he knows that some friend of yours has put himself on the line for him, he won't dare to mess up."

"Okay, Gary, I'll work on it. In the meantime, shouldn't I be working on finding a job for you?"

Instantly, he shook his head. "Not a chance. I'll take care of that myself."

"But Gary—"

"Dammit, Carly, I need to take charge of *something* while I'm in here, and there's damn little else." As he watched the hurt shadow her green eyes, he relented quickly. "I'm sorry, Carly. I don't mean to bark. It's just so hard to be locked in here. It's like living in the dark. You're my only ray of light."

"It's almost over, Gary," Carly assured him. "Just a few more months, and I'll keep coming whenever I can. This year you'll have Christmas with Shelley and Patsy—"

"Maybe." Any mention of his babies always made him feel morose.

"Not maybe. Of course! One way or another we'll get custody all arranged by then. Or at least a regular visitation schedule."

He was grateful for her enthusiasm, but he lacked her confidence. His recent news from that quarter hadn't been too promising. "My lawyer doesn't seem to be making much headway hammering out a deal. Ruth Everhard keeps digging her heels in. She says that when I killed her husband I abrogated my rights as a father, and until I'm out on parole, she's under no obligation to consider my request for visitation rights. She told John that the girls had forgotten me."

"Well, that's ridiculous! How could they forget you when you write them every week?"

"That's what I keep telling myself, Carly. I know there'll be an adjustment period of sorts. But I'm their father, dammit, and they belong with me and nobody else."

"Of course they do."

"Michelle wouldn't have wanted it any other way."

Too late, he watched Carly's face cloud over. Did it really hurt her that much whenever he mentioned Michelle? "Carly, you can't expect me to just forget her. We were married for over eight years."

"I know that, Gary."

"I loved her. She's the reason it feels right for me to believe in a woman, Carly. If I hadn't had such a good relationship with Michelle, I probably wouldn't have taken a risk on you."

"I know that, too." Her tone was stiff, her eyes dull with regret.

"So what's the problem? Why can't you accept my family? Why can't you share my love?"

"I can accept your girls, Gary. I love them already and we haven't even met. Michelle is another matter. I've already had one man beg me to marry him while his heart was otherwise engaged. I'm gun-shy about loyalty, Gary. When I fall in love I give myself completely. I don't think it's too much to expect the man I love to do the same."

Gary shook his head, recalling the letter where she'd spilled out all her remembered anguish over Rodney Haywood's clumsy two-timing. He was sure that her ongoing discomfort over Michelle was related, somehow. Now, gently, he reminded her, "Carly, Michelle is gone." Unfortunately, he couldn't say the words without pain.

"Not from your heart, Gary," Carly accused. "She's like...a ghost who haunts this room. Don't you think I know you'd rather be looking at her face than mine? Don't you think I know I'm just...an understudy filling in for the real star? I don't like coming in second place to your wife, Gary. It makes me feel as though I'm having an affair with a married man."

For a moment he didn't answer; he knew he was treading on quicksand. He loved Michelle, would always love Michelle. He'd always regret her death. But he was learning to love Carly, too, though he just couldn't bring himself to mouth the words in this hellhole. "If I could only make love to you, sweetheart," he whispered, "I could put all your fears to rest."

Her eyes flashed up to his with a rush of mirrored longing, all the hard feelings suddenly past. "Oh, Gary, I'd do anything if that could happen. Sometimes I have dreams that just won't let me rest."

"Oh, God, Carly, so do I." It took every ounce of willpower he possessed not to take her in his arms. He slid one hand toward her on the table, stopping just short of her fingertips. The guard said nothing, and neither did Carly, but she closed her eyes and shuddered in desire.

"There is a way," Gary heard himself whisper. "There is a way we could be together before I get out."

At once those green eyes flashed open. "Are you serious?"

He nodded. "I could apply for a conjugal visit. It's three days alone, in a little trailer on the grounds."

Carly looked as though she were having trouble breathing. "Why on earth didn't you ever tell me this before? Don't you *want* to be alone with me?" She sounded hurt, stunned, even angry.

His body told him one thing, his heart another. Desperately the two did battle until he blurted out, "Not like that. I don't want our first time together to be in this dungeon. I want our lovemaking to belong to us, to sunlight, only to the good times." He watched her face, still baffled, uncertain. "Besides, it's harder to clear if you're not married."

Carly answered, "And you don't want to marry me."

Now it was Gary's turn to stare open-mouthed. From the time he'd first met Carly, he'd struggled with the morality of asking her to spend the rest of her life with an ex-con. It had never been a question of *wanting* to marry her. It had been a question of right-and-wrong.

He didn't want to go into all of that, again; they'd had that fight a dozen times in the beginning. Now he asked her bluntly, "Do *you* want to marry *me*, Carly?" Before she could answer he tacked on, "For a weekend in a prison trailer?"

A dark red flush stained her face. "Make sure to word it so I'll say no, Gary. Heaven forbid you should put yourself in a situation where you'd have to make a real commitment to me."

"Carly, come on! That's not what I meant. I just want you to realize how tacky this trailer deal might be. I never brought it up before because I've got this vision of spending my first night with you in a first-class hotel. No guards, no prison. A romantic, moonlit walk along the beach first. Real food. Real clothes. Patterned sheets. I want you to make love with a *man*, not an inmate. Can't you understand?"

She didn't answer right away. She seemed to have pulled back inside her shell. Her hands were folded tightly in her lap. "I can understand why you want to wait to make love to me, Gary. I can also understand why you'd want to wait to commit yourself until you were on the outside. Right now, I'm really your only choice in the female department. Once you're free, you won't have to be stuck with me."

Despite the restraint in which he'd schooled himself, Gary leaned across the table and laid his fingertips on Carly's face. "Tell me you don't believe that, Carly. You know it's not true." In a hoarse whisper, he confessed, "Good God, sweetheart, don't you know how much I love you?"

Carly's face crumpled into tears as she tugged his hand across her lips. She kissed his palm with a tenderness that undid him completely, then ever so slowly licked his fingertips, one by one, before she sucked his smallest finger into her mouth.

He didn't think that any sensual maneuver by a woman had ever aroused him more. "*Carly!*" he groaned, unable to ignore his swelling need of her. "If you want the trailer...if you want to marry me while I'm still inside—"

"No touching!" the guard suddenly bellowed, physically tugging Gary's hand away.

Several times in his stay at Tejon, Gary had heard of somebody with a nearly perfect record blowing his shot at parole with a swing at a guard, but he'd never understood such folly until now. He wanted to blast this man, this creature. He'd lived under this guard's shadow for over a year, but suddenly he could not even recall the bastard's name.

"I'm going to leave," Carly quickly declared. "I think that's the wisest—"

"No! We have so little time together, Carly."

The guard was still standing over them, listening to every word. "We have so little time together, Carly," he mimicked in a falsetto tone.

Gary could feel the steam building up inside him. He was ready to explode.

With incredible calm, Carly began to chat about her friends and neighbors in Sespe. Her eyes willed him to silence as she prattled on about her cat, her father and how many apartments her landlord owned. Her little speech lasted almost five minutes before the guard got bored and wandered off; by then Gary had conquered the worst of his smoldering fury. When he was out of earshot, Carly's monologue came to an abrupt stop. She closed her eyes and clenched her hands into two fists.

"You're incredible," Gary whispered. "I thought I was going to kill him."

"I thought you were, too. I had to do something." She opened her eyes and stared at him with vigor. "Don't ever think you have to defend my honor, Gary, or your pride. You have one job in here to do for me. Only one. Get out as soon as you can, and in the meantime don't get hurt. Nothing else matters. Nothing. Do you understand?"

Quietly he nodded. Then he asked in a low tone, "Do you want to marry me, Carly?" It wasn't a proposal; it was an honest question. It was an issue that they hadn't really discussed before today, and he didn't want her to leave without getting a handle on her true feelings.

Carly ran her thumb down the line of her jaw in their secret non-touching code, then kissed her index finger. "I'm not sure, Gary. I'm not sure you're ready yet."

"You're not sure *I'm* ready? What about you?"

She shook her head. "It's been years since I was engaged to Rodney, Gary. There's nobody but you in my heart, no doubt in my mind that you're all I can see in my future. You're the one with your love split right down the middle."

"I love you, Carly. Surely you know that by now."

"You need me, Gary. You need me to keep your hopes up, to keep you in touch with the outside world. You may even need me to get your parole. I'm not sure that's the same as love."

He'd barely cooled off since the fiasco with the guard, and now his rage flared up again. "You've got a hell of a lot of faith in me, don't you, Carly? After the lengths I went to to protect you from this—" one angry hand gestured toward the gathering of inmates and their loved ones "—you still think I'm just using you?"

"I don't think you're using me. Not really." Slowly her green eyes met his. "But I'm not sure, Gary. Not absolutely sure."

He tried to battle down the flames of hurt, of simmering fury, but it was a losing effort. "I suppose you're not sure I'm innocent of this manslaughter rap, either." He leaned forward and braced both elbows on the table. "At least, not *absolutely* sure."

To his surprise, her gaze met his unblinkingly. "If I had the slightest doubt about that subject, Gary, I never would have set foot in this horrid place. I certainly would not have let you touch me. And I never would have—" her eyes clouded again "—risked making my father ashamed of me."

Now Gary was the one who was ashamed. He knew it wasn't Carly he was mad at. He was still aroused, physically and emotionally frustrated past all endurance, and he had no tolerance for anything today. He should have let Carly go when she'd first suggested it. He should have realized that they'd end up hollering at each other because neither one of them could holler at the guard.

"I'm sorry," he said, for what seemed like the tenth time. "You've never asked me about it. Not once since I left fire camp. I was so relieved you never pressed it, but I couldn't believe you weren't curious. I've always thought that . . . you might have been afraid to learn the truth."

Carly ran two tired hands through her sleek black hair. She sighed bitterly. "I've always been curious, Gary. But assuring you that I took your story at face value was more important than satisfying my curiosity. I always figured that you'd tell me the whole story when the time was right."

Before he could speak, he spied the guard heading back their way. "I don't want to tell you here, not with him hanging on every word. I'll have to do it by mail."

"Only if you want to, Gary." Her expression could not have been more sincere. "If you don't want to think about it, you don't ever have to tell me at all."

It was in that moment that Gary realized what a gem he'd found; not even Michelle could have given him such blind trust. Finding Carly while he was doing time in prison was an absolute miracle. Gary suddenly realized that despite the obnoxious guard, the stifling heat and the infuriating distance between them mandated by the picnic table, he was richly blessed.

He also knew that he wanted to marry Carly, and he told her so the very next time she came to see him.

"Marry me," he whispered instead of saying hello. "Marry me now."

Carly's lips relaxed in a happy grin, but she didn't answer right away. "I imagine that's probably easier said than done. Isn't there some procedure to go through or form to fill out?"

"In triplicate, no doubt. I don't care." Suddenly he felt lighthearted, almost free. "I love you, Carly Winston. I want you to be my wife. I'm absolutely sure of it."

"I thought you didn't want to make love to me in a dingy prison trailer," she reminded him. "I thought you wanted to wait till you got out."

Now he sobered. "I'm not talking about the trailer, Carly. I'm not thinking about sex. I want to know you'll be there waiting. I want to know you're mine for life."

This time Carly glanced away, and her evasiveness made him nervous. Was she really just worried about technicalities, or when push came to shove, was she not really sure she could spend the rest of her life with an ex-felon?

"We don't have to exchange vows in prison if you'd rather wait, Carly," he tried again, his voice now tense and low. "What's important is that we make the promise to each other. I want you to be my forever friend."

It was the silence, clear as day, in the hubbub of the room, that told him that something was wrong. She didn't answer right away, and when she did, her tone was awfully controlled for a would-be bride.

"I'll be waiting for you when you get out, Gary. I promise you that."

After that she changed the subject quickly, but not before he realized that she'd made no commitment beyond the first moment of his glorious freedom. Was it possible that she felt obligated to stand beside him only until he was released from his dungeon into the light of the day? Was she planning to leave him once she was sure he could stand on his own?

CHAPTER NINE

CARLY LEFT the prison trembling with frustration. Her need for some private, intimate time with Gary, almost overwhelming at times, had been bad enough when she'd assumed that there was absolutely nothing she could do about it until his release. Now that she'd discovered there was another option, logical thought on the subject was all but impossible.

Carly knew that marriage to Gary and the possibility of a pre-parole conjugal trailer visit were not synonymous, and she had not really rejected the first because of the unsavory flavor of the second. Part of her longed to marry Gary—instantaneously, if possible—but another part, rational to begin with and wary after the way Rodney had used her, knew that nothing that had happened between Gary and herself while he was in prison was indicative of what their future might bring. She'd been honest with him about her fears. When he was a free man, he would be able to see anybody and do anything. He was charming and outrageously attractive; he could make a life with any woman he wanted. She wasn't at all sure it would be her if he was free.

She'd read a letter once, in a column for the lovelorn, which advised against getting involved with a man who'd just been dumped because—despite his gratitude—once his heart had healed, he'd always associate you with the remembered time of pain. Wasn't Gary's situation similar? His "time of pain" was his sojourn in prison.

I don't want our first time together to be in this dungeon, he'd told her on Saturday. *I want our lovemaking to belong to us, to sunlight, only to the good times.* But how could he separate making love from simply loving Carly, when prison life had framed their entire relationship to date? Was it not possible, even likely, that when he was free of his legal shackles, he'd also want to be free of her?

If she ever married Gary, Carly wanted his heart given freely. She didn't want to be his only choice for a spouse. She wanted to come in first among myriad contenders. In the meantime, marriage was out of the question.

Gary didn't mention the issue in his next letter. The entire text, some twelve pages of it, longhand, was devoted to his manslaughter charge.

Dear Carly,
I know you don't like me to talk about Michelle, but I can't tell you why I'm in prison unless I mention her, so here goes.

We met in college. She was a silver-spoon kid, an only child. Daddy's little princess. I'd been born to decent, working-class stock, orphaned in my teens. We fell in love awfully fast, but at first, Michelle tried to keep her distance. She kept telling me that her parents would never accept our marriage and, of course, she was right. To make a long story short, we got married anyway, and we never fought about anything but her folks. She loved them, of course, and wanted me to put up with their constant interference, their attempts to buy my way into the "right" medical school, the "right" residency, and a snazzy house on the "right" side of town. Before the wedding, her father came to see me privately and offered me a veritable fortune and my career on a silver platter if I'd break up with Michelle and promise never to see her again. He'd even had his lawyer write up a contract. I never forgave him for that. I didn't tell Michelle because she never would have, either, and I didn't want to break her heart.

In all fairness, I ought to make clear that when I say Michelle's parents, I mainly mean her father. Before her husband's death, Ruth was a quiet soul who depended on Tom Everhard for just about everything. But she loved Michelle and came to realize that I did, too. After Shelley was born, Ruth and I got along just fine—when Tom wasn't around. That's why her stubbornness about my girls is so hard to take. She never let me explain my side of it. When the police told her what had happened, she just said, "I should have listened to Tom. He was right all along."

Michelle started feeling ill shortly after Patsy's birth. At first I put it down to postpartum depression, though she didn't seem unhappy, just tired. I was working endless hours at the hospital then, and I just wasn't paying enough attention to what was going on at home. Michelle wasn't the type to complain; I guess she got that from her mother. In any event, it wasn't until she collapsed at a family picnic that I realized something was really wrong. I couldn't diagnose her problem, though, and it took several months and a host of specialists to figure out that she had cancer of the bone spread throughout her body. By then it was way too late to save her.

I did everything I could to make those last few months bearable. I left all the household details to the housekeeper and spent every spare moment I had with Michelle and the girls. At least I got to say goodbye right, and before she died, Michelle made a farewell tape for Shelley and Patsy to hear when they were older, explaining how much she loved them, recalling all the wonderful things they'd done together. Ruth had time to say goodbye, too, and after Michelle died, she just sat there beside her body for hours, talking to her, until Tom hauled her away.

Something inside me just broke when Michelle died. I'm sorry if you don't want to hear that, Carly, but we can't have a relationship that isn't based on truth. I love you—please know that—but dammit, I loved her, too. The girls went to stay with Ruth just before Michelle died so I could devote every moment to her. But I went to see them once a day, and I told them what had happened myself. Ruth and I decided that it would be better for them to stay put until after the funeral. Aside from all the technical details and the horde of mourners, I was too disconnected to give them much support. I wanted a few days to get myself together, so that by the time they came home I'd be able to keep things bright and warm. I wanted them to be certain that we were still a family.

But when I went to pick them up as agreed, Tom told me that Ruth had taken them out somewhere and wouldn't be back for an hour. He insisted that we go have dinner, and of course he had to take his snazzy silver Jaguar. I'd always tried to be civil to him for Michelle's sake, but that went by the wayside the moment he told me that he and Ruth had decided to raise the girls. My schedule, he declared, left no room for Shelley and Patsy, and he wasn't about to have his granddaughters raised by a housekeeper. This time, he didn't bother to offer me money; he knew that was a waste of time. Instead, he told me that if I cooperated, he'd allow me to visit the girls on a regular basis. If I caused any trouble, he'd forbid me entrance to the house and destroy my career.

Suffice it to say, I went berserk, right there in the restaurant. Witnesses said I shouted, "I'll kill you before I let you take my girls." I don't recall for certain, but I don't doubt it. I'd never made a scene like that in my life, but between my fatigue, my ever-so-raw grief and my years of smoldering fury with that bastard, I lost all control. At the time, I wasn't afraid, because I knew that legally Tom didn't have a leg to stand on. I had dozens of witnesses who could corroborate my devotion as a father and husband. Anybody who knew the situation could testify that taking the girls away from me would have been anathema to Michelle.

I charged out of the restaurant without eating a bite. Tom followed me, bellowing orders. The only reason I climbed into the Jag is because I wanted to get back to the house in record time. It was suddenly imperative that I see the girls.

He always drove fast; Ruth was always begging him to slow down. I'd expressed my concern about his driving that way when the girls were in the car, but since their car seats only fit in the big Lincoln that Ruth generally drove, it hadn't been a major problem. But on that night—rainy, foggy, black as sin—he was furious when he got behind the wheel. And all the way home—at least, as far as we got— I was yelling at him.

The other car was a huge pickup driven by two drunken, joyriding kids. They walked away with bruises. But the minute I came to—I blacked out for a few minutes—I saw Tom slumped over the wheel, his neck bent sideways like a broken doll's—and I knew he was dead. Just as I started to check his pulse, the kids' truck blew up. It literally exploded into flames so close that the heat seared my face. I knew it was a matter of moments until the Jag blew up, too. All I could think of was how Ruth would feel without a casket to sit next to, a hand to hold as she said farewell. So I dragged Tom's body out as fast I could. It took me nearly a minute to disentangle him, and the whole time I was thinking, "I'm an idiot to risk getting burned alive to haul out a body. Especially the body of *this* man."

The bottom line is that for some reason the Jag never exploded, and witnesses said I couldn't possibly have had time to tell that Tom was dead before I dragged him out. As any doctor knows—most civilians, for that matter—anybody with a potential neck or spinal injury should be handled with extraordinary care. In all likelihood, the prosecution maintained, I'd broken Tom's neck and caused his death. As a physician—trained in trauma, no less—there was no question that I should have known better. My own semi-conscious shock was no excuse. When folks from the restaurant testified to the scene they'd witnessed, there was some question as to whether I'd been rational enough to deliberately take advantage of the situation to break his neck, or even grab the wheel and cause an accident, on purpose. My lawyer thinks the jury convicted me partly because I was still so disconnected—my Michelle had only been gone a few months—that I made no real effort to defend myself. And I admitted to feeling guilty about Tom's death, because I didn't think it would have happened if I hadn't been screaming at him. But that's the extent of my guilt, Carly. The jury didn't believe me, but I think the judge did. She had three possible sentences to choose from, according to the Penal Code, and she chose the lightest one.

Tom's lawyer got together with Ruth and came up with an injunction keeping me from seeing the girls before I went to prison. They were young and fragile, he maintained, and might be traumatized by an encounter with their grandfather's killer. I tried to call them—Shelley's old enough to talk on the phone—but Ruth refused to put me through, and now phone calls are added to the injunction. Not even my letters can go directly to the house. I send them to my lawyer, who sends them to Ruth's. In all this time, I've never received an answer. I know Shelley can't write, but she used to make me pictures all the time. I guess I figured she'd at least want to do that. But God alone knows what garbage Ruth's stuffed into her head in all this time.

That's it, sweetheart. No secrets left between us. I'll answer every one of your questions, if you have any. And now I have one for you. When are you going to marry me?

G.

WHEN CARLY FINISHED reading Gary's letter, she sobbed for fifteen minutes straight. Then she realized that she simply had to share her anguish with somebody. And she could only think of one somebody who might understand.

"I can't believe he never told you this before," Willard said, gently stroking Carly's shoulder as she spilled the news while they sat together in his rose-patterned kitchen. He handed Carly another tissue, then pulled two cans of cola out of his refrigerator and opened both, passing one to Carly.

Blindly she sipped the cold liquid, grateful for the comforting smile of her dear friend. "I didn't ask because I didn't want him to think I was suspicious. All this time, he's been afraid that I didn't really believe in his innocence. My dad thinks he's just feeding me a line."

Carly had not seen her father again since their awkward dinner in Los Angeles, but they'd had a long talk on the phone just a few days earlier. His disapproval—and his grief for her—was still quite evident.

"I trust your instincts, Carly," Willard maintained, "and I know for a fact that it is possible for a good man to be wrongfully imprisoned. I suspect that when your father meets Gary, he'll come around to your point of view."

"When are they ever going to meet? I don't dare ask Dad to go visit Gary in prison."

"Gary will be out soon," Willard pointed out. "By Christmas, you said. You and your dad usually get together, then."

"He may be gone by December," Carly recalled. "He's expecting orders to Japan. Besides, I can't imagine anything more awkward than sitting down to Christmas dinner between the two of them."

Again Willard smiled. "Why don't the three of you join me, Carly?" he suggested. "Willie will be here, and so will my niece, Sandra, and her three kids. And my brother Floyd, of course—Sandra's dad—who might be just the person Gary needs to see. That ought to be enough other people to defuse any family fireworks."

"Oh, Willard, you're just too good to me," Carly said sincerely.

Willard waved away her gratitude and began to talk about family holidays in the past. Carly was too deeply mired in her own thoughts to concentrate on his conversation, but she found herself warmed by his cheery tone. She still felt some jealousy of Michelle, but now it was tinged with sorrow and a new understanding of Gary's pain. As she reflected on all the circumstances of his conviction, however, she realized that his misery wasn't going to end the moment he was granted parole. She had a sneaking suspicion that his determined optimism regarding his girls was based more on paternal desperation than reality.

"Do you know anybody who's ever been granted custody of children while on parole?" she asked Willard when he came to a stop in his rambling.

Willard sobered. "No, I can't say that I have. But then again, Floyd's the only prisoner I've ever known personally, and he wasn't married till he'd been out of prison for three years. I do know," he added thoughtfully, "that it's still difficult, at times, for men to gain custody in divorce cases. About the only fellow I know who's ever gotten kids from his ex-wife is Harold Ralston." Although Carly made no comment, he gave her all the details. "You know Bonnie Ralston, who owns that garden store, Sespe Green Things, downtown? She had a stroke and was hospitalized for months. The kids were staying with Harold for the summer when it happened, so naturally they just stayed on. By the time she got out, the court ruled that the children were adjusted to their new place and there was no reason to upset them when both parents seemed equally qualified as parents, especially since Bonnie's health was still in question. It's been a year now, and she's still trying to get them back."

Carly suspected that a court would look considerably more favorably on a hospital stay than a prison sentence. Still, she pointed out, "But this isn't a divorce custody battle, Willard. Ruth's a grandmother. Gary is Shelley and Patsy's actual parent, the only one they've got. There was never any question of marital trouble between Gary and Michelle. She just died. And he's perfectly healthy, so no one can question his ability to care for them."

"He's also going to be a convicted felon on parole, Carly, which hardly commends him to fatherhood in the eyes of the court. Besides, the girls are settled in with their grandmother now. To be honest with you, I think Gary will be lucky to be granted visitation rights at all. Especially while every move he makes is at the indulgence of the court."

Carly's jaws grew stiff. "But that's not fair, Willard. When he gets his parole, he's served his time. He's free to get on with his life!"

Slowly Willard shook his round head. "I'm sorry to disappoint you, Carly, but that's not what parole is all about. It's still part of Gary's prison sentence—it's merely time served outside, to reduce overcrowding in the cells and to help gradually phase a prisoner back into civilian life. Unless things have changed a lot since Floyd was in prison, being on parole is a lot like being sixteen. You can work, drive or marry only with the parole officer's okay. He's got to approve your employer, your residence and your friends. You report to him every month, every week or even every day. It's his decision. And he can nix anything, at any time, for any reason. If you step out of line while you're on parole, it's back to prison overnight."

Carly couldn't help but shudder. Tears filled her eyes. "Oh, Willard, I thought the worst would be over soon! Gary's just counting the days till his release. His lawyer's almost certain he'll make parole."

Willard patted Carly's hand. "I'm sorry, honey, but those are the facts of life. Unless the parole officer forbids you to see Gary for some reason, it really should be much better when he gets out. For both of you. But until he's served all of his time, in jail or out of it, he won't be able to call his life his own."

CHAPTER TEN

GARY ALWAYS READ Carly's letters several times, and he'd virtually memorized the one she'd written him the day after she'd received his monumental epistle describing his journey to prison.

> I love you, Gary Reid. I loved you before I knew the truth about your tragedy and I love you even more now. I believe your version of the story with every ounce of my heart and soul, and I will do everything in my power to help you get your precious babies back. I already feel as though they're mine.

The letter he received the following week was of a different tone altogether. He read it maybe six or seven times before he handed the first page to Clifford. He was not in the habit of sharing Carly's mail, but this message had more to do with his cell mate than with him.

> Dear G.,
> I have terrific news for Clifford. After talking to everybody I could think of, I found out that Bill Lundgren—you remember, my boss when we were up at Camelback?—has an uncle who owns a sporting goods store over in Cresta. Bill called him and asked if he'd be willing to take on a parolee the next time he had an opening. At first he was pretty reluctant, even

though Bill assured him that Clifford wouldn't let him down. But when Bill mentioned Clifford's name, his uncle went crazy.

"Clifford the Clydesdale?" he hollered at Bill. "The one who used to pitch for the Eagles?" Apparently he lived in Arizona when Clifford was with the B team down there and was a great fan. This guy lives and dies for baseball, and Clifford is right at the top of his list. He told Bill to let him know Clifford's parole date, and if he doesn't have a job opening he'll make one....

When Clifford was done reading the letter, his grin was so wide that all his teeth were revealed—and a good deal of his gums, as well. "Did you read this, Doc?" he asked, even though it was perfectly obvious that Gary had just done exactly that. "This guy knows who I am. He saw me pitch! He knows I'm a convict, and he wants me, anyway!"

He grabbed Gary in a ferocious bear hug that nearly broke a rib or two, then went on to list at least three dozen reasons why working in a sporting goods store would be heaven on earth for him. "I can't believe that woman of yours! I never thought she had it in her!"

Gary grinned and thumped his buddy on the back. "I guess she figured she owed you one, Clifford. You're the one who brought us together, after all."

"Ha. A locomotive couldn't have kept you two apart. I tried, you know. I got to admit, I think I sold Carly short, at first."

Gary's smile widened. "So did I. But we all learn from our mistakes, don't we?"

At once Clifford sobered. "If you're trying to give me a message, man—"

Gary shook his head. "I'm not. I know I don't need one. Carly's stuck her neck out for you—way out—and I know you won't do anything to make her sorry." He hadn't meant to lecture, but he felt the need to say the words, for Carly's sake.

"I won't let you down, Doc," Clifford promised. "You or her. This time—" he clutched the letter to his chest "—this time it's going to work for me."

WHEN GARY CALLED Carly to thank her for finding Clifford a job, he asked her to marry him again. Once more she sidestepped his proposal. Between the blare of the TV in the background and the crude noises made by the other inmates who wanted to use the phone, the conversation was dismal and frustrating. That was, in fact, a pretty fair description of her regular visits with Gary at the prison, as well. No discussion was ever uninterrupted, no problem ever resolved. And no tender moment was allowed to remain untarnished by the ever-watchful guards.

Over time, the quality of their visits had deteriorated. The atmosphere was part of the problem, but the news they shared didn't help much, either. Gary had swallowed his pride to write to dozens of old friends and acquaintances asking for help getting any kind of a job and approved lodging so he could return to the outside world. A few had written back sympathetic "Wish I could help you, but..." letters, but most had ignored him altogether. Yet he stubbornly opposed Carly's offers to make arrangements for him in Sespe, partly because he was determined to be paroled in Vista Mar near his girls. Shelley, he'd informed her, had turned five over the summer and ought to be in kindergarten by now. He didn't want to upset her first year in school by moving her somewhere else once he got custody.

It was one Saturday in October, when Gary's eyes filled with such sadness as Carly left, that she thought she'd die if she couldn't hug him goodbye. She decided she had to do something to brighten his world. She almost broke down and promised to marry him; she almost agreed to a tawdry three days in a prison trailer. And then she decided that there was something else she could do for him that would surely splash sunshine all over his dismal cell. After a year of unconfirmed reports about his girls—condensed versions of information his lawyer got from Ruth's lawyer—Carly decided to visit the little ones herself and bring him firsthand news.

Finding Shelley's school was remarkably easy. Carly had expected to have to do some legwork, playing "Carly Winston, P.I." with the neighborhood gas-station attendants and checkout clerks. But she'd arrived at the Everhard mansion—there was no other name for the palatial, oceanfront structure—at 8:00 a.m., just as a small bus pulled up smack dab in front of her house. The driver honked the horn once. A darling blond child, dressed in bright pink pants and a matching top, skipped out to meet him, her "She-Ra Princess of Power" pack bouncing up and down on her back in sync with her bobbing ponytail. She giggled as she climbed up the steps and took her seat, then turned back to wave once at the front porch. Carly assumed that someone stood there watching, but she couldn't get a good look from her concealed spot down the road.

The bus wandered through the classy suburb of Vista Mar for over half an hour, while Carly ambled along behind it. Nobody seemed to notice her, but she was relieved when the bus finally pulled up in front of the school.

Luck was still with her when Shelley bypassed the enormous school yard and ran directly to a smaller play area that apparently was reserved for the kindergarteners. A giant classroom opened to the right of the yard, and when the bell rang, Shelley lined up with the rest of the group outside the door.

Carly knew she should have left then. "I saw her and she's fine," she could have told Gary. But she realized that he would crave more news than that. He'd want to know about Patsy; he'd want her to tell the girls how much he loved them, assure them that he'd soon be coming home.

She felt anxious and deceitful. Surely there was nothing illegal in talking to Shelley at school, but she knew that Ruth Everhard would have strongly disapproved. But Carly's loyalty was to Shelley's daddy, not her grandmother, so she pushed aside all doubts and apprehensions.

She watched the kindergarten yard until school began. Shortly thereafter, an attractive woman about her own age came outside with a clipboard and two miniature chairs. One by one, the children came out to talk to her, apparently for some kind of testing. When Shelley showed up, Carly zipped out of her car. With a few maternal smiles, she convinced both Shelley and the room mother that she had a perfectly good reason for being there. The first thing Shelley asked her, after Carly had motioned for the little girl to follow her out of earshot of the other woman, was "Whose mommy are you?"

"I'm...nobody's mommy," she admitted, surprised that the words made her sad. "I'm a friend of your daddy's, Shelley. That's why I'm here."

Shelley's ponytail whipped back and forth, as she shook her head. "My daddy's dead," she declared solemnly. Sorrow laced the terse words.

"Who told you that?" Carly burst out, suddenly awash with panic. Had something happened in the prison? Why hadn't Clifford called? And then she remembered that Clifford had just gotten out on parole. Gary had nobody to protect him anymore. Nobody to notice if he lived or died. Nobody to keep her posted.

"Nobody had to tell me," Shelley continued, her eyes tearful now. "He said he'd come back for me, and he didn't. *Never.* So he's got to be dead, just like my mama."

Carly struggled for breath, realizing that it was only Shelley's grief, not her own, that she now had to contend with. "He wanted to come back for you," she told the child softly, "more than anything in the whole world. But sometimes even grown-ups can't do what they want to, Shelley. You know that your daddy was taken away to—"

"No!" Shelley burst out, so loudly that the other woman glanced in her direction. "My grandma says they took him away to a terrible place where terrible people go. But my daddy didn't do anything wrong. Not never! He didn't come back because he's dead. If you're his friend, why do you say such bad things about him?"

The little girl was crying now. When Carly reached out to comfort her, Shelley stiffened in her arms. She knew it was just a matter of time before somebody realized she had no business being there. Desperately she pulled a small teddy bear, purchased for this occasion, out of her purse and thrust it into Shelley's arms. "This is from your daddy," she said quickly. "How could he send you a teddy bear... if he were dead?"

Distracted by the bear she clutched so tightly, Shelley's expression brightened in delight. She obviously wasn't quite sure if she could believe Carly's marvelous news, but hope caressed her cherubic features. "If Daddy's not dead, why didn't he come here with you?" the bright child wanted to know.

"Because he really is in prison, Shelley. By mistake," she hastened to add. "He didn't do anything wrong, but they won't let him out. Not yet. He wants you to know that he'll be able to leave soon, and the minute the police say he can visit you, he'll rush right over here." She didn't try to explain about lawyers and custody battles in court. But as she recalled these obstacles, a thought crystallized in Carly's mind that had been struggling to emerge for some time. "Shelley, didn't your daddy explain all this in his letters to you?"

"What letters?" She hugged the teddy tighter, as though it were her dad.

"Your daddy writes letters to you every week, honey," Carly fought her dry mouth to say. "Are you telling me that you've never heard from him? Never gotten any kind of a note from your daddy in the mail?"

Shelley put one finger to her lips, as she thought a moment. "Daddy and Mommy sent me a picture once. I still have it. They went somewhere for a vacation when it was—you know, like you get married again?"

"Wedding anniversary?" Carly ventured.

Shelley nodded. "It's a little baby seal on the beach. He's bouncing a ball on his nose."

"But that was when your mother was still alive," Carly said, thinking out loud as fury boiled within her at Ruth Everhard. And she'd worried about her own petty deceit!

"Uh-huh. It was before Patsy was born."

Carly was trembling with rage for Gary's sake, but she valiantly fought to hide her feelings from the child. Instead, she took little Shelley's hand and asked, "How is Patsy? Everything okay?"

Shelley nodded. "She's just a baby, you know. It's up to me to watch out for her. That's what Daddy told me before he left us with Grandma just before Mommy died." She looked wistfully at Carly. "Patsy doesn't remember Daddy any more. Grandma won't let me talk about him, so I just talk to him in here." She patted her tiny heart.

Abruptly the playground bell rang again, and a cacophony of hurrying and scurrying sounded in the classroom. Carly knew her time was up. Any minute now, she'd have to explain herself to the teacher, who had surely been informed that Shelley's mother was dead.

"I have to go, Shelley," she told the darling child. "But I'll see you again someday. And remember, your daddy will take you home again as soon as he can. He loves you—and Patsy, too—and he'd do anything, anything at all, to be with you."

Unable to stop herself, she gave the child a fierce hug. "From your daddy," she whispered, just before another child called out from the classroom door that the teacher wanted Shelley Everhard.

Everhard. Her mother's maiden name, not the one her parents had given her at birth. Ruth hadn't just blackened Gary's name in the hearts of his children: she'd tried to erase it altogether.

Carly knew he'd take any risk to keep that from happening, and no matter how long it took him to win the battle, she planned to keep fighting right by his side.

"WHAT THE HELL have you done?" Gary demanded the instant she joined him at the picnic table on Saturday. "Ruth Everhard's lawyer is eating John Henton alive! And John thinks I'm holding out on him because I told him I didn't put you up to it! Didn't you think the teacher would ask Shelley who you were? Don't you realize you might have delayed my custody of the girls forever? You could even have cost me my parole!"

Carly held her ground. She was still too angry with Ruth Everhard to trouble herself with the legal fallout from her surreptitious meeting with Shelley. "There's no law against giving a child a teddy bear from her daddy, Gary," she snapped back. "Or in telling her that he's alive when she thinks he's dead."

He stared at her, mouth open. "My baby thought I was dead? Just like her mother?"

"Exactly. She couldn't believe you'd break your word to her. She couldn't believe the terrible things Ruth told her about why you were in prison, and she never heard from you again, so in her five-year-old mind, she decided that you were dead."

"I've written her fifty letters since I've been in here! I even print the damned things, in case she's learned how to read!"

Slowly Carly leaned forward, hating that she had to tell him the truth, but she had no choice. "Ruth never gave her the letters, Gary. Not a one. Shelley thinks you're dead because you promised to come back and you didn't. She has total faith in your love for her, Gary. She was certain you hadn't willfully abandoned her." Carly could also have told him that Patsy didn't remember him at all, but she couldn't see how that could possibly help him, and even if it could, she just couldn't cause him any more pain.

"Oh, God." Gary slumped before her, like a man who had lost all hope. "I never dreamed Ruth would stoop so low."

Carly didn't know what to say. How could she—how could anybody—repair the damage? Instinctively she reached out to touch his hand before she remembered the guard. But a quick glance at the nearest uniform told her that the overbearing brute who usually supervised them was nowhere to be found. Today they were being watched by Smithson, a decent, gray-haired fellow whom she remembered from Camelback Ridge. He was the guard who had given Gary permission to fly to Vista Mar when Watson had been injured.

She met Smithson's eyes just as her fingers reached Gary's. Belatedly recalling the rules, she jerked her hand back. Gary didn't even seem to notice. Smithson didn't, either. He just looked away.

Desperate to think of anything to cheer Gary, Carly said, "Can't you use this information to help with the custody struggle? Surely she broke some sort of rule."

"Yeah. Common decency. I hope to God that John Henton can do something with that information in court."

For several minutes they hashed over the situation, but neither could find a silver lining in the gloomy cloud. Gary didn't want to talk about prison life without Clifford, and he reported despondently that all of his parole leads had washed out. "I guess nobody cares if I ever get out of here except for you, Carly," he finally confessed. "And even you have your doubts."

"I have no doubts." Her tone was even.

"Then why don't you marry me?"

"I told you why. I need to be sure. Sure that our love has nothing to do with your... circumstances. Sure that you don't just... need me."

Gary rolled his eyes. "How can you separate our relationship from our circumstances? Do you think I can ever forget the way you've stood by me, Carly? The risks you've taken? The devotion you've shown?"

Carly swallowed hard. "No, Gary, I'm not sure you ever can. And you want nothing more than to put this chapter of your life behind you. That's going to be kind of hard if I'm still sitting on your lap when you turn the page."

"So what do you want from me? What can I do to convince you?" He leaned forward, his frustration vibrant in his beautiful blue eyes. "What do you need to see before you'll marry me?"

Carly had given a lot of thought to this question, and she knew the answer; she just wasn't sure he could handle hearing it. Now she admitted quietly, "Ask me again when you're a free man, Gary. When you've been released from parole. When your life is your own and you know you can have any woman you want. If I'm still your first choice, then, I'll be proud to marry you."

The tension receded from his tightly pressed lips. "It's a deal, Supervisor." He held out his hand to her. "And I'll hold you to it."

Carly took his hand before she remembered where she was. She savored the warmth of his thumb pressed against her own, the power of his fingers stroking the back of her hand, then the underside of her delicate wrist. Ever so slowly he caressed her hand, arousing her as fully as if he'd been stroking the rigid nipple of her breast.

"Gary," she whispered, "Smithson will—"

"Smithson will cut me a little slack," he told her, sotto voce. "He's always been fair to me, and after Camelback, he thanked me outright for saving Watson's life. He even told me that Watson secretly admitted that the reason he's walking around right now is because I took care of him right."

It was nice to hear, but Carly wasn't about to press her luck. When Smithson strolled back toward their side of the room, she was quick to disengage her hand from Gary's. By then his eyes were starting to undress her, and she felt a curl of unbidden hunger between her legs. She hated being aroused in this crowded room that smelled of stale cigars. How desperately she wanted to press herself against the man she loved! Or, at least, to hold him while he struggled with the travesty of what had happened to his children. She ached to give him comfort, to ease his pain. What she'd give for one single moment alone with him! Or even a moment to embrace him, even in sight of a guard. Here they were discussing marriage, and they'd only shared one kiss!

It was crazy. Everything about her relationship with Gary was absurd. Except for the fact that she loved him.

"Where do things stand with your parole board?" she asked, knowing they had to concentrate on logical things. "Are they expecting any problems?"

"Everything looks good as far as my record goes. The problem is finding a job and a residence they'll approve of. I have to have a baby-sitter, you know. They won't let me live alone."

"Will they let you live with me?"

Gary eyed her quietly. "I'm not sure I want to do that just yet."

"Why? If I can get you a job in Sespe, Gary, and there's no way you can be near the girls—"

"No. This is different. You already feel used, Carly. You're not sure I'd choose you if I were free. If I have to depend on you for work and for a place to live, and answer to you in lieu of the parole officer, who'll expect you to report my every breath to him, I think it'll make it harder for our relationship to grow on its own. I think we'd be better off letting our time together be... well, just time for us. Without the legal system horning in."

Carly longed to stroke his troubled face, to take his hand again. Instead, she confessed, "You're probably right, Gary. But nothing about this situation is optimum, you know. The important thing is to get you out of here any way at all that's legal. If the only way to do that is to have you under my roof, then I don't think we have any choice." She grinned at him. "Besides, I think the advantages of living together might overcome the drawbacks."

For an instant, he shared her smile; she could see a hint of his dimples. And his eyes lit up with sensual need. But then he sobered as he pointed out, "It might be hard to clear, Carly."

"Why? I'm squeaky clean."

"You're not my wife."

Carly couldn't meet his eyes. Would it really come down to that? Oh, why did everything have to be so complicated? But Gary had warned her that it would be. He'd warned her going in. And now he was watching her so quietly, waiting... for what?

Smithson announced that visiting hours were over, before she could find out. One by one he ushered out the guests and the prisoners. Carly and Gary waited till the last moment, gazes locked.

"I'll marry you now if it's the only way you can get out," she finally whispered.

A shadow of relief, laced with pain, darkened his weary features. Slowly he shook his head. "I don't want it like that, Carly," he replied in a deep, troubled tone. "I want you to marry me because you believe in us."

Smithson cleared his throat. "Sorry, Reid, but it's time for the lady to go." His tone was straightforward, not cruel. He sounded almost reluctant to intrude.

Carly stared at Gary as he stood up and crossed the few steps which brought him to the end of the table. Quickly she did likewise. Now only air filled the space between them. Desire radiated there.

Carly ached to hold him, but she couldn't tell him how she felt in front of Smithson. She couldn't assure him of her love. And never, in all the awkward times she'd left the room, was she more certain that Gary needed it.

Without taking time to think through the consequences, Carly turned to the silent guard. "Please," she begged him, tossing her pride to the wind. "Let me say goodbye to him right."

She heard Gary gasp as Smithson replied, "I'm sorry, Supervisor, but I've got a job to do."

Desperate, she tossed her purse on the table and held up both hands. "You know I've been frisked. I've got nothing to conceal. Gary doesn't have a violent bone in his whole body, and he's leaving in a month anyway. Why on earth would he blow it now?"

"Carly, please!" Gary burst out, his tone harsh and low. "Go now. Just go." He looked terrible—like a proud, wild tiger forced to live in a cage.

Despite all of her vows that she would never let a guard see her cry, Carly's face crumpled with the injustice of it all, the misery that fate had dealt to the man she loved so much. She was sorry she'd ever shared her doubts about marriage with him. She just should have said yes and let the chips fall.

She reached for her purse, but just before her hand touched the strap, Smithson's low tone reached her. "I have to look, ma'am. But I don't have to see." Slowly, deliberately, he lowered his gaze to the floor.

It took her a moment to realize what a gift he was offering. He couldn't turn his back on a prisoner; neither common sense nor prison rules would allow it. But he knew, as well as Carly did that no harm would come to anybody if he just let her kiss Gary Reid goodbye.

Suddenly the restraints were gone: three months of steeling herself to keep her distance, three months of recalling the only kiss they'd ever shared—one searing, endless, incredibly erotic kiss that Carly ached to repeat.

Forcing herself to forget the guard's silent presence, Carly lifted both hands to Gary's face. When her fingertips brushed the white hair at his temples, the anguish in his eyes melted. His fingers found her waist and he pulled her against him, hard. Their lips met, melded, burned with mutual need.

Carly forgot all about the guard and Gary's waiting cell once she was wrapped in the majesty of his perfect touch. His warm tongue teased her lips, begging for entrance to her mouth, and her breasts tingled as she gave him what he wanted. Both nipples were instantly erect. Flames seared her lower body as she pressed against him, the hard flow of his muscles crying out for a release she could not give him.

Knowing it would only make things worse to heighten his arousal, Carly broke off the kiss and pressed her cheek against his throat. His arms wrapped around her as he kissed her forehead, then buried his face in her hair.

"I love you, Gary," she whispered. "I'm afraid of the future, but there's nothing on this earth I want more than to be your wife."

With those words she left him, and the next time they talked, she was able to share the good news that Willard's friend, Bonnie Ralston, had an opening for a salesperson at her nursery and garden supply store, Sespe Green Things. She'd had apprehensions about hiring a parolee, but Willard had persuaded her to give Gary the job.

A few weeks later, Gary went before the parole board and convinced them that he was "reformed" and no longer a threat to society. Shortly thereafter, Carly had to meet with Walt Tower, the pencil-thin parole officer assigned to his case. He never smiled, but he never frowned, either. He was a humorless individual who seemed to follow all the rules without deviation, but he gave Carly the impression that he really wanted Gary to succeed "out there."

Tower grilled her pretty thoroughly on her relationship with Gary, her concept of providing a "reliable" home for a parolee, and asked her outright if she was planning to marry him. Taken off-guard, she told him the truth about her reservations.

"I'm in love with Gary Reid, Mr. Tower," she confessed. "And I desperately hope I'll be able to marry him someday. But I don't see how we can get a realistic picture of our life together while he's in prison or even out on parole. I think it would be smarter for us to put off marriage until he's free from all his legal entanglements."

"Good for you," had been his stout reply. "Women who marry men in prison are always surprised when things don't work out later. It's wise for a lady to keep her wits about her until an ex-con proves he can make it on the outside."

"Gary's going to make it," she replied with feeling. Of this she was sure; the only question in her mind was whether or not she'd be part of his ultimate success story. "Surely you can see that he's not a criminal, Mr. Tower! He's just a man who got tangled up in bad luck."

He didn't refute her contention, but then again, he didn't agree with her, either.

There were forms to fill out, details to discuss and clothes to buy, but Gary told her repeatedly that nothing was more important than having Carly meet him the instant he was free to go. They planned everything down to the wire. He'd be released at ten o'clock on Monday morning, after Carly signed some final papers. She promised him that nothing was more important to her than his release. Nothing could possibly go wrong.

And then, on Saturday at midnight, an arsonist tossed a match into a patch of sapless chaparral and two thousand acres of southern California went up in flames.

Carly got a call from the dispatcher in Goleta about two hours later.

CHAPTER ELEVEN

THE MORNING Gary was scheduled to be released, he put on his old clothes with a strange sense of satisfaction, grateful he'd been wearing cords, not jeans, when he'd been taken into custody. Once he'd looked at denim as an old and faithful friend, but now he doubted that he'd ever voluntarily wear blue jeans again.

He gathered up his packet of letters from Carly—he didn't need the ones from fair-weather friends—but took nothing else with him. If he'd been leaving Clifford behind, he might have felt a moment's regret, but his new cell mate was a hard, vicious man, and Gary could only escape him with relief. As he passed the other cells on the way to the front gate, a few of the guards and inmates wished him well. Smithson shook his hand when he said goodbye. Neither of them mentioned Carly.

Gary was trembling when he finally spotted her, waiting in a reception area near the front gate, as far away from the cells as possible. Gary had never seen her in anything but pants, so he did a double take at the sight of the beautiful young woman clad in a saucy burgundy knit dress that showed off her shapely calves to great advantage. She wore about twice as much makeup as usual—enough to look showy, not cheap—and dramatic silver earrings. Her dark green eyes were moist with tears, but her tremulous smile confirmed his suspicion that they were tears of joy.

They did not speak or touch each other. Another guard gave them last-minute instructions about checking in with the parole officer. Gary tried to listen and nod his head at the right times, but he could only think of Carly...and the way he would greet her the moment he got out of this terrible place.

Finally, it was over. He walked outside the building, eyeing the guards by the gate. Wordlessly he followed Carly to her black truck. He didn't protest when she took the wheel.

Carly handed his papers to one of the guards at the main gate, who checked everything over as though he hadn't seen them come out of the building together. He even radioed back to the office to double check everything. Gary's breathing was labored as he prayed, *Dear God, don't let there be some kind of a foul up. I can't go back. I think I'd die.*

At last the guard nodded. Slowly Carly turned the engine back on, smiled courteously to the young man, and drove away. Gary leaned back against the seat and shuddered his relief. Carly slipped her hand in his and squeezed it hard, then let go to shift gears as she took a sharp turn that took them out of sight of the prison. A moment later she pulled up in a café parking lot, killed the engine and turned to face him.

A breathless smile wreathed her lovely face. "Oh, Gary!" she burst out, as though no other words existed.

Gary himself simply could not speak. He pulled her into his arms and hugged her so hard he thought she'd break. He felt her hands on his face, his neck, his shoulders. She kissed him urgently while he tugged her onto his lap. Instantly she wrapped her arms more tightly around him.

"I thought this day would never come," he whispered. "Even this morning, I was afraid you'd be called off to a fire."

"I was," she mumbled into the sensitive hollow of his neck. "I told the fire chief he could have me until today at dawn, no ifs, ands or buts. He called in a replacement for tonight."

He pulled back to study her face, to trace that lovely jawline he'd studied from across the table so many times at Tejon. "Does that mean you're all mine for the day?"

She grinned. "I'm all yours. You don't have to start work in Sespe for almost forty-eight hours, so we don't have to go straight home. We can do anything you want today."

A slow, hungry smile consumed his face. "Anything?"

She kissed him soundly. "Anything. Anything at all."

He brushed her smooth black hair away from her loving eyes. Gently he pressed his lips against her temple. "Carly, I want to go some place where nobody is watching us. I want to be free of walls, alone with you."

She pressed her cheek against his. "There's a snazzy resort complex south of here called Playa del Oro, that has individual suites scattered separately all over a private beach. I'm sure it costs a fortune, but—"

"Let's go." He kissed her again, slowly, lingering until he couldn't keep from kissing her again. "I'm going to have a lot of trouble keeping my hands off you today, Carly. I don't think it's safe for us to be alone together in a public parking lot."

She kissed him again, eyes shining. "I think you're right. We'd better go."

Ignoring both her warning and his own, Gary pulled her back into his arms, unable to fight either his joy or his passion. In the end it was Carly who stopped his hand as it slipped over her thigh with the breathless words, "Gary, if you do that now, I'll never be able to drive."

Somehow he managed to let her slide away from him and turn on the engine. But as soon as the truck was in fourth gear, she took his hand again, kneading it slowly as she drove. It wasn't until they pulled in front of the Playa del Oro that she let it go.

By the time they celebrated Gary's release all over again in the hotel parking lot, Carly was so aroused, so overjoyed and so relieved that she could hardly think straight when they checked in at the desk. Fortunately, Gary was eager to take charge of the details, and nobody hearing his cultured, authoritative tone would ever have guessed that he'd just completed sixteen months in prison.

He walked into the beautifully appointed suite—at the far-north end of the complex—with two lightly packed, matching suitcases before he locked the door. He didn't check through Carly's things, but he did examine the purchases she'd made for him: socks, underwear, slacks, shirts and one pair of moccasins with enough give to accommodate any errors in sizing.

"You must like red," he commented as he ran his fingers over the smooth texture of the shirt.

"I just thought you'd look good in it, with your eyes and white hair. Don't you like red?"

He grinned at her. "I like anything that isn't prison-issue. At least it's not denim."

The silence grew as he studied her face, then cupped her cheek with one hand. If he'd kissed her then, pulled her down on the bed, she would not have said no. But she would have felt rushed, and maybe a little used. She was grateful when he whispered, "I want to walk along the beach with you. Is that okay?"

"Of course," Carly replied, quickly shucking her heels in favor of a pair of walking shoes. She wished she could have traded her dress for a pair of jeans and a sweatshirt, but she knew that at the moment it would be hard for Gary to watch her undress or wait alone while she left the room. And today was one day she intended to make the sun shine for him. She would refuse him nothing.

After a quick glance around—as though he expected a guard to spring up somewhere—Gary took Carly's hand and they went outside. It was somewhat overcast, but not particularly cold considering that it was early December. Gary said very little as they walked beside the water, just out of reach of the icy waves that lapped at the shore. He watched the sea gulls, then stopped to chat with a pelican perched on a buoy. He ran his hands through the seaweed and studied the crabs. Once, he picked up a handful of sand and let it run through his fingers as though it were pure gold.

"There's no way I can tell you what all of this means to me," he confessed, so softly that a lump rose in Carly's throat. "Sun, rain, sand, sea." His eyes met hers. "Woman. Friend. Loved one." He kissed the palm of her right hand. "It's as though I was in the middle of a nightmare and suddenly woke up to discover that I was safe in my own bed."

Carly didn't answer; she just snuggled closer to him. She'd spent half of her life with military men coming home from war, and they all talked the same way. Suddenly she was grateful for that experience. She had at least an inkling of what Gary was going through, a sense of how best to help him.

He put his arm around her tenderly as they strolled back toward their room, the ocean wind starting to turn chill. "Would you like to go out to lunch, Carly?" he asked, as though they were on a typical date. "It's been a long time since we've shared a meal together."

Carly grinned. "I saw a nice spot in the main building. Does that sound okay?"

"Perfect."

When he started to steer her in that direction, Carly asked, "Could we swing by our room first? I'd like to get my sweater."

At once Gary turned around, rubbing her shoulder as they walked. "Half my time in prison, I was either too hot or too cold," he told her. "We get the same clothes all year 'round. In winter they try to save on heating bills, and in summer, we don't even have fans." He stopped and smiled self-consciously. "Am I boring you with my laments and rediscoveries?"

Carly shook her head. "You could never bore me, Gary. Besides, you need to get it out of your system. You need some time to adjust."

He eyed her uneasily. "You sound like a psychologist. Are you viewing this little holiday with me as therapy?"

Carly laughed. "I certainly am, Dr. Reid. For both of us. And as your therapist, I think it's only fair to tell you that I have a very effective technique in mind."

"Oh, you do, do you?" he asked, his blue eyes sparkling as he opened their door and ushered her inside. "And what might that be?"

"It's a form of physical therapy that's guaranteed to make ex-prisoners forget their cells and free men forget that they're parolees."

His dimples punctuated his pleasure. "Would it be appropriate to ask for a demonstration at this time? Or maybe a full therapeutic session would be in order." Lunch plans forgotten, he closed the door behind him and locked it securely, then tossed the key on the small table by the bed.

"Well, maybe a *mini*-session," Carly teased him, taking hold of both of his hands. "After all, you did say you were ready to eat."

"I said I was hungry," he corrected her, slipping her arms around his waist before he released her hands to cup her face. "I think lunch can wait."

He kissed her then; kissed her in a different way than he ever had before. It wasn't a hurried kiss or a desperate kiss or a kiss that begged for reassurance. It was a kiss that asked for her devotion and promised her his own. It was an invitation to join him in bed, an invitation to join in his life.

Her own kiss was tender, urgent, full of joy. There had been moments when Carly had despaired of ever sharing a moment like this with him, moments when she was certain that they'd forever be kept apart by her common sense or his situation or even the memory of his wife. But now, at last, it was different.

Gary pulled back just enough to speak, his lips almost touching hers. "I love you, Carly Winston," he whispered.

"And I love you, Gary Reid," she answered in the same husky tone.

He kissed her again, a long, lingering kiss that urged Carly even closer to his body. She pressed herself needfully against him, wondering if she could ever get close enough to make up for all the nights she'd been forced to stay away.

Again, he spoke. "I'm more grateful to you than you can ever know. You gave me hope when I had none. You brought back part of me that seemed to be dead."

Tears filled her eyes once more.

"I want to spend my life with you, Carly, and not just because I'm grateful. That's part of it, I know. But it wasn't the beginning of my desire for you, and it's certainly not the end."

After that, he was in no mood to give speeches, and Carly was in no mood to hear them. She cradled his head with both hands and pulled him closer, her tongue seeking the intimacy of his warm and eager mouth. He gave her what she wanted. Then, as their tongues did a dance of love, his broad, warm hands slipped up her back, fingers spreading as his palms edged toward her sides, skimming over the outer edges of her breasts as she lifted her arms to give him greater access.

Carly knew that she would never forget the first moment that Gary's fingertips circled her nipples—ever so slowly, ever so enticingly—moving in, closer and closer, until at last they closed over the taut bud at the center of each breast. She could not muffle a tiny cry of pleasure as his kiss deepened. When his pelvis pressed against hers, her whole body seemed to open up to meet him.

"I vowed not to rush you this first time," he moaned as he pulled his mouth away from hers. "I've gone over and over it in my mind. I wanted it to be slow, romantic. I was going to order flowers, and wine you and dine you before I took you to bed."

With trembling fingers he was already unzipping her dress, while Carly unbuttoned his shirt and seared his chest with a flurry of kisses. "You can wine me and dine me later, Gary," Carly murmured, her fingers tugging on the coarse black hair above his waistband. "We've waited four months for this moment. Isn't that long enough?"

Her words seemed to snap the rest of his resistance. Suddenly she was on the bed, half in, half out of her burgundy dress. Gary's cords were unzipped and on the floor, where her silky undies landed as soon as he pulled them off. He cradled her head as she wrapped her legs around his waist and pulled him toward her. She felt as though she'd waited a lifetime for this moment; she knew he had, too. They didn't need foreplay this afternoon. They'd had months of it in their minds.

She felt the warm tip of his manhood probe her soft fur, inflaming her as it pinpointed all of her desire into one intensely erotic location. She was trembling—no, shaking—with need of fulfillment, with need of him.

He kissed her throat tenderly, hungrily. She heard him groan as she pressed herself against him. "Carly, darling, are you sure you're ready for this? No matter how much I want you, it's just *got* to be right for you, too."

There wasn't a thing Gary could have said that could have made her more eager to give herself to him. But she was too moved, too impatient, too desperately aroused to answer him. Instead, she lifted her hips to envelop him, wrapping her legs yet more tightly around his waist before she slid them down over his well-muscled thighs.

The next few moments were a flame of rapture, a jungle throb of explosive desire. They rocked in perfect harmony, mouths and bodies joined, until Carly cried out her delirious relief and Gary quickly followed suit.

They stayed that way, joined, spent, joyful, until Carly caught her breath and Gary found a seductive smile. Then they started all over again.

GARY HAD SO vividly dreamed of his first day alone with Carly that he was sure the reality could not possibly live up to his expectations. Yet, miraculously, the time they spent at Playa del Oro exceeded his wildest fantasies. He could not recall any time in his life when he'd been more aroused or satisfied in bed. Not even with Michelle. Carly had acquiesced to every suggestion he'd made, and though he hardly expected, or even wanted, her to kowtow to him for the rest of her life, he was enormously grateful that she understood why, fresh out of prison, he needed her to indulge him for at least one day.

As they drove to Sespe on Tuesday night—Carly still at the wheel—Gary realized that they were about to enter a new phase of their time together. He was finally free, but not free altogether. He would no longer be watched, but he would have to report most of his activities and ask permission for all kinds of things, as though he were a child. He would be working at a job that required none of his skills, and answering to a boss who had a fraction of his education. He would be living with the woman he wanted to spend his life with, but for the next eight months she would be regularly grilled by his parole officer as to his whereabouts, his attitude and his behavior. In essence, in order to give him his freedom, Carly had been forced to agree to act as a spy.

It was hardly the best way to start off a new life together.

Worse yet, there was something vital missing from this cozy domestic scenario. He didn't care how big or small Carly's place was, the name of the city or its locale. What he held against the little town of Sespe was that Patsy and Shelley didn't live there, but an hour away in Vista Mar. One way or another, he simply *had* to see them before he lost his mind.

It was dark when they pulled into town. He noted that there had been strip development along the main road; there was a hamburger stand, a furniture store and a mom-and-pop grocery with cheery seasonal slogans painted on the front windows. Carly pulled up at a blinking red stoplight, informing him that it was the only one in town, then turned right in front of a garden shop that had rows and rows of potted trees outside.

"This is Sespe Green Things?" he asked.

She nodded. "I thought you might like to take a look at it before you report to work in the morning. It's a nice little place, Gary. Bonnie is a bit disorganized, but I think you'll get along all right."

He nodded. Anywhere that wasn't prison, he'd get along just fine. "Am I imagining things, or did somebody forget to put those trees back behind the fence?"

Carly chuckled. "There is no fence. Sespe works on the honor system."

"Nobody steals anything?"

"Nope. Though every now and then a local decides he needs something when the store's not open. But he just tacks a note on the door and walks off with a tree."

Gary shook his head in disbelief. "I must be in the Twilight Zone."

Now she laughed out loud. How he loved the sound! "No. You're in Small Town, U.S.A. Nobody in Sespe spends much time worrying about local crime."

He studied her soberly. "Has anybody here ever heard of hiring a parolee?"

Quickly she turned on the engine, her eyes now on the road. "Well, I doubt that it's common. Bonnie feels it would be better for you if nobody knows about your situation."

"Better for me, or better for her business?" He didn't mean to sound bitter, but he didn't like being treated like a leper.

"I think they're one and the same, Gary. If she loses business because of you, she'll have to let you go." Her words were straightforward, not cruel, but he still didn't like the sound of them.

"I suppose I'm going to get blamed if any of those trees gets stolen."

"I doubt it." She gave him a quick kiss, then asked, "Now, do you want to see your new home?"

He nodded, thrusting from his mind the unwanted image of the home he'd once known, sold by a realtor friend right after his conviction. The memory of the house, itself, was blurry, but the vision of Michelle and the two little girls rushing to greet him with open arms was still quite painfully clear.

FOR THE FIRST month Gary was out of prison, the sight of his dimpled smile sent Carly off to work each morning grinning like a Cheshire cat. Her coworkers at the local Forest Service office, where she was doing research on the recreational uses of a local lake, teased her daily about how she must have spent the night. She just grinned and revealed none of her secrets. As winter set in, Carly rejoiced in the brief winter rains that made a small dent in the five-year-drought conditions. As a fire fighter, she didn't want to see the land go up in smoke. As a woman, she was thrilled to go home to Gary every night, and she dreaded the spring, just a few months away, when she could expect to spend two nights out of every three away on some smoky, Gary-less hilltop.

Gary seemed happy with his new life, but not as overjoyed as Carly had expected him to be. He claimed to like Bonnie and have no major complaints about his new job. "It's not a career position," he'd said once or twice, "but anything outside of prison walls is a step in the right direction."

When Willard had dropped by to welcome Gary, he'd thanked the older man so gravely that Willard had joked, "Hey, I'm not the warden here. Just relax!" Gary didn't ask to meet any of Carly's other friends, and she didn't press him. She loved Gary; she was proud of him as a person. But his situation was just so awkward. How did you manage party talk without mentioning his parole? And Bonnie had asked him not to spread that information around town. When anybody asked him where he lived, he just said he rented from Willard Jameson, which meant he could have lived in any one of three dozen local apartments.

He was gentle with Carly, eager to help with the chores. When Gary got home before she did, he always started dinner; if not, he cleaned up instead. Often they made love in the evening...on the bed, on the couch, on the floor. They both still felt as though they were making up for lost time, and they never tired of each other's tender caresses. Sometimes, after work, they walked hand-in-hand through the landscaped neighborhood, enjoying the Christmas lights and lawn displays of Santas and snowmen. Gary talked about his past, his dreams, his future. He listened to Carly's life story of roaming the world with her dad and sang Christmas carols off-key while he helped her decorate their tiny Christmas tree. He never complained about anything except for checking in with Walt Tower, which nettled him a great deal. And almost daily he called his lawyer to check on his visitation status with the girls.

One rainy afternoon in mid-December, Carly came home early and overheard one of those conversations with John Henton. She hadn't intended to eavesdrop, but she couldn't think of any subtle way to let Gary know that she'd arrived. Not even the sound of the door slamming had broken his tense concentration.

"Now look, John," he bellowed, "I've tolerated this dillydallying for over a month now. You've put me off with one excuse after another, and you've never yet made Ruth atone for destroying my letters. Now it's been a year and a half since I've seen my children, and I'm not going to last another day. It's almost Christmas, dammit! I won't have them go through another holiday season thinking their father is dead—or just forgot them and ran away!"

Carly stood in the doorway and watched his beloved face, lined with anger and despair. She thought about all the times they'd talked about the girls while he'd been in prison and how rarely he talked about them now. The contrast seemed odd to her, important somehow. She had hoped that Gary had accepted Walt Tower's stern recommendation that he shouldn't rock the boat by threatening Ruth with a custody battle while he was on parole. The potential for trouble was just too great.

He exchanged a few more angry words with his lawyer, then slammed down the phone with such violence that Carly couldn't stifle a tiny gasp. Gary gazed at her sharply, shadows of anger still rippling across his face. But as she watched, he struggled to mask his fury. Somehow, he came up with a tense smile.

"Hi, sweetheart. How was your day?" he asked, as though everything was just fine.

Carly crossed the room quickly and snuggled up beside him. "Much better than yours, from the sound of it. What's going on with John?"

Ignoring her question, Gary kissed her hello...a long, lingering kiss that seemed out of sync with his display of fury just moments ago. Instead of telling her why he was upset, he asked, "What's new in the forest business?"

Carly studied him soberly. "Aren't you going to fill me in? What did John say about the girls?"

Gary's shoulders slumped. His tone was sheepish as he replied. "Caught the tail end of that, did you? I'm sorry. I wanted to finish before you got home."

"Why?" she asked directly. "Since when have we started keeping secrets from each other?"

Gary brushed back a lock of black hair from her forehead, then kissed the smooth skin he'd exposed. "No secrets, sweetheart. You know I'm eager to see my kids. I just don't... like to bore you with the petty details."

"Gary, nothing that has to do with your children is boring to me. I'm the one who stuck my neck out to go see Shelley at school, remember?" She knew her tone was a bit defensive, but she couldn't help herself. "It's a little late to try to shut me out now."

Gary grimaced. "I'm not trying to shut you out. I'm trying to spare you. I've been nothing but trouble to you since the day we met. You've given and given and *given* yourself to me in every way imaginable, and I've done nothing but take. About all I can do to make it up to you is keep my troubles to myself."

"Keeping your troubles to yourself is no favor to me, Gary. Anything we don't share is likely to... push us apart."

He traced her jaw with one gentle finger. "You know that's not what I have in mind. You've made my life so bright, Carly. So rich. About the only thing I can do to return the favor is try to be a helpful guest."

Carly stiffened. "I hardly think of you as a *guest*, Gary. I thought we were starting a... well, a home here."

"Without the girls?" His voice was a rasp of pain.

"Only temporarily," she assured him, helpless to provide any other balm to his misery. "Only because we have no choice. One day you will get custody, and Patsy and Shelley will settle in a lot better if you and I are adjusted to living with each other. Most families start off with two grown-ups before the little ones join them, you know."

Gary didn't reply at once; his hand dropped back into his lap as he pondered Carly's words. His lips grew tight as he stared at Homer, now meowing at his feet. He picked up the cat and stroked it for several silent moments. At last he said, "In our case it was the other way around, Carly. I had a family before I met you. I also had a home." His tone was neither warm nor cold. He was no longer touching her, but he didn't pull away. Anguish darkened his eyes as he glanced at her face.

For the first time, Carly saw through his valiant pretense—saw the pain that clouded the best of his postprison days. Had he been doing his best to act sunny because she expected it of him, because he felt he owed it to her? Now, as the reality of his false cheer struck her full in the face, she had to ask, "Has it all been an act, Gary? Are you miserable here?"

Sudden panic zigzagged across his smooth-featured face and he grabbed her hand and tugged her toward him. "No! I love living with you, Carly. It's just that...dammit, lady, something's missing. I'm not complete without my girls." He cradled her hand in both of his, then pulled her wrist to his lips for a quick, reassuring kiss before he rushed on. "Every time I talk about life before prison you act like—oh, like I'm using you, like you're just a fill-in for Michelle. I feel like I have to walk on eggshells whenever the subject of my family comes up." Now, honest sorrow darkened his eyes. Sorrow that had more to do with his future than his past. "It's the reason I don't ask you to marry me anymore, Carly. It just hurts too much when you keep saying no."

Gently, Carly kissed him, then rested her cheek against his shoulder as she slipped both arms lovingly around him. She didn't know what else to do. She couldn't tell him she was ready to throw caution to the winds. She wasn't. No matter how much she valued his honesty, the last few moments had only confirmed the fear that had gripped her from the beginning. She *did* feel like a substitute for Michelle, and she was still afraid that when Gary got his future straightened out, he'd have no vital place for her in the picture.

"Don't stop talking to me, Gary," she begged him. "And don't treat me like I'm your hostess here. If you want me to be your wife, act like you're my husband. Start thinking of us as a family, and don't shut me out when you're hurting about the girls."

She heard him exhale deeply, and then she felt his hand on her hair. For a moment she felt warmed, renewed in the wonder of their love. But then she heard him murmur, "Carly, I am *always* hurting about the girls."

She wanted to cry for him. She wanted to cry for those two precious children. She wanted to cry for herself. "Always, Gary?" she asked hopelessly, wondering if she'd ever made him happy.

Gary slipped one warm palm under her chin and tilted it toward him. A slow, sleepy smile lit up his weary face as he leaned down to give her a quiet, soul-warming kiss. Then he winked at Carly and clarified his statement. "There are times when you manage to make me forget."

She kissed him back, then hugged him closer. Unsteadily, she forced herself to ask, "Is it just your girls you miss?"

Carly felt his long fingers slip through her hair and rest at the sensitive nape of her neck; she shivered when he dropped a kiss in the hollow near her shoulder. He didn't answer her question directly, but she had to admit that she liked what he said.

"When my children come to live with us, Carly, you and I will have a real home."

Carly decided not to push for an answer to the heart of the question he'd so neatly sidestepped. She just didn't have the heart to ask him outright if he would have traded her for Michelle.

CHAPTER TWELVE

IT WAS DECEMBER twenty-first before Ruth Everhard relented, which she did only because, according to John Henton, she found Shelley weeping in her room...pouring her heart out to the little teddy bear Carly had delivered "from Daddy." She'd drawn a wonderful picture of a Christmas tree with her mommy and daddy and little Patsy underneath and was explaining to the teddy that this was what a real Christmas was like. Ruth had called her attorney the next morning.

"Damn good thing," John had told Gary. "The two of them have really taken advantage of the court's backlog to make you suffer, but once a judge finds out that she never delivered your letters to those girls, he's going to be more sympathetic. Especially when I put you and Carly on the stand."

"Carly?" he'd asked. "Why drag Carly into this?"

"You'd better believe Ruth's attorney will. For one thing, you're living with her. Out of wedlock, no less. Whenever the girls come to stay with you, temporarily or permanently, Carly will be there. The judge will want to know what kind of company this felonious father keeps." He'd gone on to say that Carly came across well with authority figures and would probably bolster his case. But then he added, "I don't know why you don't just marry her, Gary, if you can clear it with Walt Tower. It would demonstrate your stability to the court if you had a real home for the girls, with a permanent wife."

Gary hadn't told John that Carly didn't want to marry him... at least, not yet. "One thing at a time," had been his reply. "I want my daughters first, then I'll worry about marriage."

"Okay by me, Gary, but I think you're putting the cart before the horse. Why don't we talk it over with Walt Tower?"

"Tower doesn't want any trouble. He thinks I should forget the girls until I'm released from parole."

"Not a bad idea, Gary."

"Not a chance," he'd replied.

So Ruth had stalled and the court had delayed, and eventually Walt Tower had given his permission for Gary to see his children—only if he had a signed statement from Ruth Everhard saying that she voluntarily gave her consent. Custody was out of the question while Gary was still being "supervised" in Carly's home. The most he could hope for was periodic visits at Ruth's estate.

Gary's mood had grown increasingly black as the holidays neared and the stack of Christmas presents for the girls mounted under the tree. Compared to his previous Christmas in prison, Gary loved every minute of the celebration with Carly, but he found it hard to refrain from telling her about the customs Michelle had instituted in his first married home. Carly's father was flying in on Christmas Eve to join them for dinner at Willard's, and Gary couldn't say he was looking forward to being grilled by the man. He anticipated a very difficult couple of days, but he was going to do his damnedest to make it a happy time for Carly.

And then the phone call came. "You've got an hour on Christmas Eve at 10:00 a.m.," John told him. "Ruth will be there. In the same room."

Like a damn prison guard watching me, he wanted to shout out loud. *When I reach out to hug my babies, she'll probably scream, "No touching!"*

"Is she afraid I'll steal them? Or just tell them the truth?"

"Either. Probably both. But it's the best I can do, Gary, and it's a hell of a lot better than Christmas without seeing them at all. Hold your temper, keep your cool. Don't even speak to Ruth if you think either one of you will have trouble being civil. If you handle this right, it could be a big breakthrough in our long-term negotiations. If you blow it, we're back to square one."

"I'll be perfect," Gary promised, spitting out every word.

The next few days were very hard for Gary. Somehow, he managed to carry on at work, which grew harder as he grew increasingly bored with his daily routine. The problem, he knew, was that it was not the job he wanted. In all fairness, his job at Sespe Green Things was not particularly demanding. All he had to do was water the plants, keep the shelves stocked with garden supplies, help the customers and ring up their purchases. Being around the plants was uplifting compared to prison life, and the customers were generally friendly. His boss, Bonnie Ralston, had appeared a bit edgy the first week he was on the job, but nowadays she acted relaxed and happy whenever he was working.

Bonnie was a chatterbox, and though her conversation sometimes grated on Gary, he always dreaded the times she left him alone. He triple checked every credit card and every check, and stayed alert for short-change artists. He glanced out the window at the unguarded trees every half hour. Sooner or later, he was certain that something would happen when Bonnie was gone. And no matter what it was—no matter what the circumstances—he knew he'd end up taking the blame. One false step, Walt Tower had warned him, and any paroled employee was out of a job and back behind bars.

By the rainy morning of the twenty-fourth, he was more afraid of a false step with Ruth Everhard than with Bonnie Ralston. Over and over again, he rehearsed what he might say to her and what he should desperately try *not* to say. He and Carly had discussed every possibility, even role-played a few. He knew he'd been acting selfish, ignoring all of Carly's other interests while he focused single-mindedly on his kids, but he just couldn't help himself. He'd waited too long for this reunion, this hour of incredible relief. By the time he was ready to leave for Vista Mar, he was checking his watch every other minute.

Although he and Carly had purchased a second car, mainly so he wouldn't feel so housebound, Gary let her drive him up to Ruth's house. They'd both decided that it would be best if she waited in the truck, but they arrived in the middle of a thunderstorm.

"Maybe you should come in, honey. You're likely to catch cold if you sit outside in this weather for long."

Carly shook her head. "Things are going to be touchy enough in there without you trying to introduce a new wife to your ex-mother-in-law."

"Ah, the Christmas spirit must be getting to you, Carly. Are you feeling like my wife today?"

Carly stroked his smooth jaw. "I always feel like I'm your wife, Gary. It's a feeling I like very much."

He almost asked her then. She might have said yes, and if he'd told her what John Henton had said about his custody troubles, it might just have been the nudge she needed. But the one thing Gary was sure of, was that he wouldn't ask Carly to marry him again until *he* had something to offer *her*, instead of the other way around.

As he kissed her goodbye and gathered up his pile of red-and-green-ribboned boxes, Gary looked out the rain-splattered window at the showplace where Michelle had grown up, the house which he now viewed as a prison which kept his girls inside. Once more, he checked his watch. Yes, he was right on time.

As he opened the truck door, Carly laid one quiet hand on his arm. He turned to meet her eyes, those beautiful green eyes that always glistened with so much love.

"I want you to remember, Gary," she whispered against the drumbeat of the rain, "that no matter what happens inside that house, there'll be somebody out here waiting for you with open arms, eager to go home with you tonight."

He swallowed hard, profoundly moved by her tenderness, her loyalty, her strength. He reached out to trace her full lower lip with one gentle finger, then braved the storm outside. It was nothing, after all, compared to the storm in his heart.

He rang the doorbell and waited. He rang a second time. He began to think it had all been an elaborate hoax when the third ring brought no answer. He was about to put the packages back in the truck and confer with Carly when a woman he had never seen before opened the door. She had short blond hair, a thick waist and tired hazel eyes that showed just a trace of apprehension as she studied Gary. By her plain clothes and servile demeanor, he assumed she kept house for Ruth. The Everhards had always had a knack for making honest working people feel like scum.

The woman studied him warily but did not speak as she motioned for him to follow her through the immaculate living room toward the back of the house. Nothing seemed to have changed. The presence of children had not affected the white carpet, the delicate Japanese watercolor wallpaper, or the shimmering silk-and-velvet furniture that the girls had never been allowed to touch. Gary had once tartly told Michelle that Tom and Ruth might as well have papered the walls with hundred-dollar bills; it would have been more subtle. Now, he wondered where Ruth kept the kids bottled up. All of the bedrooms were on the second floor, but his guide was leading him toward Tom's study, off to the left of the massive kitchen.

He came on them suddenly, surprised to find them right before his eyes, playing with dollies on the floor just inches from an enormous, glittering silver tree. Shelley was wearing a red velvet dress with a matching ribbon in her fine golden hair—three times as long as he remembered it—and Patsy's chubby little knees were half covered by a vivid green jumper tied over a white embroidered blouse with an enormous bow. Ruth sat ramrod-straight in a stiff wooden chair behind them, clad in a formal, beige gabardine suit. Her gray hair was coiled in a tight bun and her lips were frozen in a grimace. If Gary hadn't known she'd never seen a gun in her life, he would have sworn that she was armed. He was glad that he'd had the foresight to don a three-piece suit in deference to the occasion—though a coat of mail might have been more appropriate.

He tried to recall the civil words he'd rehearsed to say to Ruth, but all he could think of now was "Hello" and "Thanks for taking care of the children." After all, with Gary in prison, there had been no other good place for them to go. But the venom in her eyes—or was it fear?—chilled him to utter silence. He stopped in the doorway, arrested by her unspoken fury, almost afraid to enter the room.

And then, Shelley saw him. She shrieked. It was a little girl's shriek, high-pitched and delighted, and he knew in an instant that Ruth had not told her to expect him today.

"*Daddy!* Daddy, Daddy, Daddy, Daddy, *Daddy!*" she cried out, her ponytails flying as she sailed across the room to slam her tiny body against his chest.

He picked her up and gathered her into his arms, as though he'd left her only yesterday, rejoicing in the soft warmth of her small body as her legs wrapped around his chest. "Oh, baby," he whispered fiercely to his firstborn child in a voice thick with a year's worth of unshed tears. "I've missed you so terribly much!"

He didn't know what he said after that. He could hear Shelley crying, begging him to tell her why he'd been gone so long, pleading for his promise that he'd never go away again. She smelled like bubble bath, the kind Michelle had always used. Her skin was silky soft, her eyes huge and blue. She dropped tiny wet kisses on his cheek and neck, sobbing, "Daddy, Daddy!" over and over again.

Eventually he loosened his hold on her, not because she was heavy—how she'd grown!—and not because he could ever get enough of her love. But he had another precious child to greet, a baby who'd grown into an active toddler while he'd been gone. Patsy hadn't been walking or talking when he'd been imprisoned; now she wobbled toward him muttering disjointed syllables that sounded something like, "Who-you? Who-you?"

Still holding Shelley with one arm, he knelt to reach the tiny child who wavered in the center of the room. "I'm your Daddy, Patsy," he coaxed her. "We used to play pat-a-cake while I gave you your bath."

"Baf?" she repeated, trying to repeat the familiar word, as she continued to eye him with wariness.

Gary knew she was two, the most volatile of ages; he also knew there had been no one but Shelley to keep his memory green. He knew, too, that Ruth was watching, silently *willing* the little girl to reject him, but he had to ignore her vituperative glare. Nothing was more important than reclaiming his place in Patsy's little heart. Certainly not his pride or his unwelcome position in the Everhard house.

He got down on his knees and started to crawl toward her, still holding Shelley with one hand. Patsy giggled as he approached and made no move to run away. He made silly faces the way he used to do, trying to stifle the beating of his heart. And then, at last, he reached her, and touched her precious, pudgy little hand. Unable to bear the distance a second longer, he pulled her into his arms.

Or, at least, he tried to. But the moment Gary tried to embrace his baby girl, she screamed as though he'd brutalized her. "Patsy, honey!" he pleaded, wounded beyond all logic, beyond all words.

But he was talking to Patsy's back, by then. She was running for her grandmother as fast she could, stumbling as she went. When she got to her, she clung to the woman's skirt, still screaming as Ruth pulled her up on her lap, pressed the tiny face against her bosom, and glared at Gary while she shielded his baby from him with two gnarled, protective hands.

GARY DIDN'T SPEAK when he got back in the truck, so Carly said nothing, either. She hadn't expected the visit to be easy for him, but she had hoped that any time with his girls would be cause for celebration. Now his silence—and the terrible pain in his eyes—destroyed that hopeful vision.

She took his hand as they drove away, and he clung to it like a lifeline. For fifteen minutes he said absolutely nothing, and when he finally spoke, his voice was so low she could hardly hear him.

"I'm not shutting you out, Carly. I want to tell you everything. I just can't talk about it now."

"I understand," was her only answer, but she tightened her grip on his hand.

They'd been home an hour before he told her what had happened, how long it had taken for Patsy to tolerate his touch. She never had warmed up to him. Shelley, on the other hand, had sobbed when he'd left and begged Gary to take her with him. By the time Gary was done sharing his anguish, Carly was in tears herself.

Still, after several hours of Gary's morose silence, Carly had to remind him that her father was due at the airport in Los Angeles in less than two hours. Over the previous week, they'd discussed Colonel Winston's arrival in great detail; both had agreed it was imperative that Gary make a good impression right off the bat.

Yet when she mentioned the time, he said nothing for several moments, and when he did speak, his words offered no awareness of her need for his support.

"Carly," he said with a heavy sigh, "I want you to go get him by yourself."

It wasn't an order, exactly, but it wasn't a request. It was the opposite of what Carly needed to hear. Despite her great sympathy for his situation, she wished that Gary could have realized that Christmas posed a delicate family situation for her, too. She couldn't squelch her resentment that from the time they'd first met, his needs—his agonies, his fears, his heartaches—had always taken precedence over her own. In prison, of course, his selfishness had been inevitable. But there were times, she had to admit, when she thought it was time for him to rise above the lousy hand life had dealt him and be grateful for what he now had.

While Carly silently fumed, Gary's solemn gaze flitted up to meet hers. His snow-white hair looked rough and wild from all the times he'd run nervous fingers through it. His loosened tie and half-buttoned shirt gave him a reckless look. She had a sudden flashback of their first meeting in the county jail, and she knew that in his present state, Gary was going to make a terrible impression on her father.

"I'm sorry," he whispered. "I know tonight is really important to you, but I've just got to have a little more time." He stood up. Tenderly he cupped her face with both hands. "I'll get myself together before you two get back here. I promise, sweetheart. Trust me. I'll put on the right show for your dad."

Before Carly could answer, Gary pulled her into his arms and gave her a beautiful, intimate kiss. Two warm hands massaged her back. To her surprise, he said with feeling, "I love you, Carly Winston. I love you so very much."

Carly hugged him, suddenly overcome with her love for him, determined that she'd find a way to banish his sadness.

"Someday I'm going to make this up to you," he promised her. "Someday I'll have a chance to prove that when the chips are down, I'll be there for you, too."

Carly forced herself to believe him, but it took all the strength she had.

GARY PREPARED FOR Christmas Eve at Willard's as though he were an actor in a play. He had a job to do, one he likened to being forced to perform surgery when he was sick or exhausted or out of sorts. His mission was to convince Colonel Winston that he brought joy to his daughter, not trouble or grief. In the process, he'd be giving Carly the Christmas gift she most deserved: her own holiday family joy.

Carly and her father arrived around six. She looked tired, uncertain. Colonel Winston looked possessive, intimidating, morally tenacious. Even though he was wearing a civilian suit, he carried himself like a man in dress blues.

"This is Gary, Dad," she said in lieu of greeting. She sucked on her lower lip. "Colonel Carl Winston, my father."

Somehow Gary found a smile as he shook the other man's hand, a gesture he'd initiated when the colonel had failed to do so. "It's a pleasure, Colonel. I feel as though I ought to salute when I say that. It's been a long time, but I guess there are some things you never forget."

Dark brows were raised in obvious surprise. "You were in the service?"

Gary nodded. "Army medic, sir. Vietnam." And then, unable to help himself, he added truthfully, "Two tours of duty."

Out of the corner of his eye he saw Carly's eyes light up with approval. He'd managed to bring up an act of valor of which no career military man could fail to approve. But he didn't try to milk the moment. Instead, he produced a tray of cheese and crackers that he'd arranged in Carly's absence.

"We're not due at Willard's for another hour," he pointed out. "I thought you might like a snack in the interim."

"Thank you, but I ate on the plane," said Colonel Winston. His tone was perfectly civil, but on his face there was no trace of warmth.

But Carly shot Gary a look of supreme gratitude. "I'm starving, Gary. Thank you," was her eager reply.

And then he smiled at Carly. For just a moment he forgot her father's fierce scrutiny and the morning's pain. She grinned back at him with all the quiet joy he always saw in this woman he so deeply loved, and for the first time all day, he wondered if he might be able to enjoy this Christmas after all.

AFTER A FINE dinner of ham and scalloped potatoes—a joint project assembled by Willard and his niece Sandra—the group drifted toward the living room, forming clusters around the punch bowl and plates of Santa-shaped cookies and holiday fudge. Willard's widowed brother, Floyd, entertained everyone by playing Christmas carols on the piano. Colonel Winston spent a good deal of the evening reading *The Night Before Christmas* to Sandra's three children—two boys and a girl—and reminiscing about the years when he'd read it to Carly. Sandra monopolized Carly's ear with ex-husband problems, while Gary became involved in doctor talk with Willard and his son. He seemed to glow as the three of them analyzed surgical procedures and recent developments in state-of-the-art antibiotics. Willie, on the other hand, simply glowed whenever his successes were mentioned.

"Willie was a track star in high school," Willard proudly informed Gary during the course of the conversation. "When he's home we still go jogging every day."

Willie colored slightly. "Well, actually, Dad, I haven't had time to do much running lately. This neuro training has been a bit overwhelming."

"Can you believe that our little town is actually going to have a trained neurologist, Gary?" Willard bragged. Before Gary could answer, the older doctor turned back to his son. "Gary's a trauma specialist, Willie. Used to work out of St. Paul's in Vista Mar."

"Really?" Willie looked impressed. Though Gary's earlier display of medical knowledge had revealed professional training, the younger man hadn't bothered to ask about Gary's present status. "I've got a friend up there. Chuck Holton. You know him?"

Gary nodded. His eyes were bleak, but his smile stayed in place. Carly remembered the name. Chuck was one of Gary's fair-weather friends who'd made no effort whatsoever to help him land on his feet when he left prison. "We did our residency together," was all Gary said.

Willie asked a few questions about Chuck, then posed the question that Carly had dreaded. "So where are you working now, Gary?"

The silence in the room seemed to overwhelm Carly as she waited for his answer. His determined smile grew so stiff she thought his face would crack. "Sespe Green Things," he said truthfully.

"You've got to be—"

"It's a long story, Willie. Let me get some more cookies and I'll be right back."

But Gary didn't return at once. He headed for the plate of cookies next to Carly's father and ended up sitting down beside him for the better part of an hour. Carly couldn't catch much of their conversation, but once or twice she saw her father smile. It was easier to follow Willard's conversation with Willie, who brayed in laughter as he bragged about his women and his work, managing to mention surgeries he'd performed on two famous actors, a politician, and a popular rock deejay. Carly found his pompous remarks irritating and his graphic descriptions of the operations lacking in couth. It seemed to her that he might have found a better topic to discuss on Christmas Eve, with three children in the room.

Gary didn't interact much with Sandra's children, though he was kind whenever they spoke to him and did his best to hide the pain in his eyes as he watched the darling little girl. Though he seemed to have trouble staying in one place for very long, he'd often glance at Carly or toss her a reassuring, holiday smile. Once he pulled her under the mistletoe for a discreet kiss, and for half an hour, he sat down beside her and held her hand. Eventually he retired to a quiet corner with Floyd, and there he seemed to have found his place. He stayed with the former prisoner for hours. The only time Carly got close enough to overhear their conversation, she picked up words like "parolee" and "home."

All evening, Gary played his role to perfection—he was happy, courteous and helpful to the host—but Carly sensed his pain. After he admitted that he worked for Sespe Green Things, he didn't mention medicine again.

It was after midnight when the dinner party broke up and Colonel Winston suggested that Carly drive him back to his motel. At once, Gary intervened. "You've done a lot of driving today, sweetheart," he pointed out. "Why don't you let me run him over? You two can chat all day tomorrow."

Carly gave him a worried glance, but he dropped a quick kiss on her cheek and grabbed the keys to his own middle-aged sedan. He didn't give her father a chance to overrule him. He knew they needed to talk man-to-man, and they might not get another chance.

Gary made amiable conversation of no importance as he drove through the silent little town. The streets were so full of blinking holiday bulbs that he could have turned off his headlights and still seen everything just fine. Christmas carols hummed on the car radio, brightening the uneasy mood in the car.

When Gary pulled up in front of the motel, Colonel Winston made no move to get out of the sedan. He sat stiffly, as though he were prepared to fire questions at his prospective son-in-law like rounds of ammunition.

"I love her, Colonel," Gary proclaimed, before the other man could start. During the evening they'd talked about everything else but Carly. Now it was time to roll up their shirt sleeves and get down to work. "That's the bottom line. Now—" he turned to face Carly's father squarely "—what else do you want to know?"

The colonel didn't hesitate. "I want to know how you tricked a sensible girl like Carly into taking an ex-con into her home. I want to know how a man of your obvious intelligence and education managed to get locked up in a cell. I want to know how my daughter fits into your long-range plans."

Gary ignored the first two questions altogether. What difference did they make now? To the third he said, "All my long-range plans center around your daughter. I have very few choices while I'm on parole. But when it's over— and this chapter of my life *will* soon be over, sir—whatever I do and wherever I go, I want Carly right beside me."

"Will you ever be able to make a decent living again? With your record?"

"I intend to."

"Doing what?"

"To be honest with you, I don't know yet. I was trained for a career in medicine. Any other profession isn't even a second choice. But once I'm free to start my own business or move freely from place to place, I intend to make a good living, Colonel Winston. I think Carly's too modern a woman to expect me to earn our total income, but I certainly intend to carry my own weight, and then some." When the other man didn't answer, he added, "Besides, I'm the one coming to our marriage with heavy expenses. I suppose she's told you that I already have two girls."

The colonel's eyebrows rose. "Do you intend to have other children? With Carly?"

"I imagine so, but to be perfectly honest with you, sir—and I drove you over here precisely so you could hear the truth—I can't give much thought to a new baby until I reclaim the two I already have. There's no question of some new child replacing the old."

"Is that true with wives, too?"

Gary took a deep breath before he answered that loaded question. "My first wife died, Colonel Winston. She was a wonderful woman and I loved her very much. We had a terrific marriage. Before I met Carly, I didn't think anybody could ever take her place."

"And now?"

He chose his words with care. "Carly doesn't need to replace Michelle, sir. Carly has carved out a place in my heart that's all her own."

Their eyes met, questioned, held. And then the colonel said, "If that's true, then why haven't you asked my daughter to marry you, young man?"

"I have. Three dozen times."

"And she says no?"

"She says not yet."

The colonel nodded. "Levelheaded girl, my Carly. I'm damn proud of her."

So was Gary, but not because she refused to marry him. Deciding that he'd given his honesty to Colonel Winston but he didn't owe him his life's blood, he asked, "Any more questions, sir? Or do I pass the test?"

Carly's father studied his face. "I don't like my daughter living with a felon," he said bluntly, but without rancor. "You seem like a decent man, but your legal situation makes me very unhappy."

"Believe me, sir," Gary confessed, "it makes me considerably more unhappy than it makes you."

A change came over the colonel's face, as though it had occurred to him for the very first time that Gary's time in prison hadn't just hurt Carly; it had hurt Gary, too. Now he said, almost apologetically, "She believes in you, young man, and I believe in her. I suppose that means I ought to trust you, too."

Gary wasn't sure how to respond to that left-handed vote of confidence. "You might consider giving it a try, Colonel."

"I'll think about it." His voice was still stony, but Gary, glancing at the older man's face, thought he detected the tiniest hint of a grin.

GARY WAS GLAD when Christmas was over. He'd found it hard pretending that all was sweetness-and-light with Carly's father, and he was ashamed of the intense envy he felt toward Willie Jameson, who now stood exactly where he had just two years ago: at the tail end of a residency, waiting to be launched in private practice. Ready to find the pot of gold at the end of the rainbow.

Willard seemed to realize that meeting his successful son had been hard on Gary. Two days after Willie left, Willard dropped by to ask if Gary might like to try his hand at a daily morning jog. Feeling the need for exercise, Gary had accepted, and on the first morning, Willard apologized for having made such a fuss over Willie's medical achievements on Christmas Eve.

"I was just thinking like a proud papa, son. I never gave a thought to your feelings until the next day."

"It's okay, Willard," Gary assured him, certain that Willie would have done just as much bragging without his father's help. "I know how it is. I'm a father, too."

Most of the time he didn't *feel* like a father, though, not with Ruth Everhard doing everything in her power to shut him out of his children's lives. It was for Shelley's sake, he knew, that Ruth ultimately decided to let him come back again. However, she wouldn't agree to a regular schedule. Gary had to beg, by way of his lawyer and hers, each and every time. By March he'd seen the girls three times, and Patsy was beginning to welcome him as a gift-bearing, grown-up friend. But she had no idea that he was her father, and he couldn't get her to call him "Daddy." Her world centered around her grandmother, her sister and the housekeeper. The man who'd cradled her just seconds after her birth meant almost nothing to her.

Less than an inch of rain had fallen over the winter, so Carly started taking off to fight fires weeks before fire season was officially declared in California. Gary couldn't help but resent the time she spent away from him. He knew that under some other circumstances, he'd be glad to have such an independent woman; he'd spend the time pursuing interests of his own. But he wasn't able to socialize—he couldn't explain his situation without jeopardizing Bonnie Ralston's business—and he couldn't keep his mind off the girls when he spent so much time alone. His nursery job was growing increasingly boring, but he hated to complain. As time went on, it seemed as though his conversation with Carly consisted of platitudes or complaints, neither one of which brought much emotional depth to their relationship. *Her* conversation, of course, was peppered with the joy of well-earned promotions and doing the job she'd been trained to do. Of course, there were moments when everything was wonderful between them—funny times, tender times, times when her double bed rocked and spun and made him feel as though he were seventeen again—but sometimes he wondered if those magic moments were just an illusion. Carly was a winner in life. He was still a paroled ex-con, with his personal and professional life in tatters. How long was it going to last?

And then one day, everything changed for Gary. It started out to be a perfectly ordinary spring morning. He'd eaten a solitary breakfast because Carly was fighting a fire somewhere, then jogged two miles with Willard, as had become his habit. When he'd gotten to work, bright-eyed, brown-haired Bonnie had told him that she had a dental appointment at ten o'clock, and he'd have to man the shop by himself for an hour.

She'd been gone about ten minutes when a wizened old woman walked slowly into the shop on the arm of a very attractive redhead wearing skintight pink pants and a huge white sweatshirt. A black panther with glittering rhinestone eyes covered most of the front. Upon settling on Gary, the woman's own eyes took on a flirtatious challenging look.

She was about twenty-two, he figured; old enough to know how to put the make on a man, but too young to realize that some men just weren't interested. Gary's indifference could not have been more complete. As Paul Newman had once said, "Why bother with hamburger when you've got steak waiting for you at home?" Of course, Carly wasn't at home much these days, but that had no effect whatsoever on Gary's loyalty.

Gary spent about half an hour helping the elderly lady pick out some African violets for her house, learning, in the process, that the redhead was her granddaughter and was as outspoken as her grandmother was polite.

"I don't know why you want African violets, Grandma," the redhead complained. "They're so...dreary. So old-fashioned. Why don't you collect plants that are bright?"

The elderly woman smiled apologetically at Gary, ignoring the young woman's complaint. "I'd like all of these, young man," she told him, one trembling hand pointing to the cluster of small pots she'd laboriously gathered at one end of the counter. Gary began arranging them in a box for her. There were twenty-five of them altogether, at $4.95 a piece. "It takes me a while to get out to the car, so I'll start while Sheila signs the tag, if that's all right."

"Of course. That will be fine," Gary assured her.

"Thanks so much for all your help."

"My pleasure, ma'am." She was a kindly soul and he had enjoyed talking violets with her. What did not please him, however, was that she'd left him with one of those nebulous small-town credit promises that he was sure would get him into trouble someday. Bonnie, who knew everyone in town, never asked for identification, and often recorded house-credit purchases on the back of cash-register receipts, which she taped to the wall until the customer returned to pay another day. Those who preferred to mail in a check once a month usually signed a store form that listed their purchases, and these forms were actually filed in a businesslike fashion. Gary's problem, of course, was that he didn't know any of these people, and had to take their word for who they were or risk offending them, something Bonnie had expressly forbidden.

Now, tugging out the proper form, he had to ask the redhead, "Under what name is the account?"

He got a sultry smile in reply. "Genevieve Harmon. I didn't think there was a soul in this town who didn't know my grandma. You must be new here."

"New enough, I guess," he agreed. "They say anybody who's been here less than twenty years is an outsider, and I've been here a lot less than that."

She giggled as though he'd told a terrific joke. "Do you live here in Sespe, or commute from out of town?"

"I live here. With my fiancée," he added pointedly, softening the information with a smile.

Her full lips drooped into a deliberate pout as she picked up the box of violets.

Gary, undaunted, asked her in his most even tone, "Would you mind signing the tag before you go?"

She laughed. "My, my, you really are new. I don't think any Harmon has ever been asked to sign for a purchase in Sespe."

Steadfastly, Gary slid the form and a pen in her direction, then reached for the box in her hand. "Here, let me hold that for you," he offered, hoping he wouldn't have to be any more blunt about the necessity of her signing for the plants.

Her seductive smile widened, and she handed him the box as though it contained precious jewels. "Who is your fiancée?" she asked.

"Carly Winston," he answered proudly. It was none of her business, but in Sespe, he knew, everybody felt free to poke their noses into their acquaintances' affairs. It was considered neighborly, not rude.

"Ah, the fire girl," Sheila replied, her tone dismissing Carly altogether. "I hear she's... out of town a lot."

Still holding the violets—and still waiting for her to sign the damn tag—Gary struggled for a reply that would successfully remove the irritating woman from the store but wouldn't have any backlash that might later get back to Bonnie. He was toying with "She's home a lot, too," as a possibility, when a loud crash drew his attention to the front of the store. Actually, there were two sounds in quick succession. The first was the noise of a large pot shattering on concrete. The second was the dull thud of a human body collapsing on the floor.

CHAPTER THIRTEEN

CARLY HEADED STRAIGHT home after the Orange County fire. It had been a quick one, so they hadn't set up a fire camp. That meant she had to wait till she got home to shower. With any luck at all, she thought, she'd have time for a little nap before she made a quick run to the grocery store. She always felt the need to do something special for Gary when she'd been gone, and after all those months of tasteless prison food, she knew that nothing pleased him more than a gourmet dinner.

But notions of rest and food fled when Carly pulled up in front of the Jameson house. It was in turmoil. Half a dozen cars filled the driveway; she couldn't get back to her apartment and had to park down the street near a giant van emblazoned with KQVN, a local TV station's call letters, on the side. From Willard's living room came the loud buzz of conversation. Carly was dying of curiosity, but she decided that she'd better sneak up to her own place to wash off the soot before she made an appearance at the gathering.

And then, as she slipped past the front porch, she heard a reporter drone into a microphone, "...but all that came to an end for Dr. Gary Reid today in the little town of Sespe, California. How do you think things will change for you now that the whole town knows you're on parole?"

Carly's stomach flip-flopped with dread. If Gary's parole was common knowledge, Bonnie might feel that she had to let him go. And if he lost his job, he'd surely lose his parole. Unless some sort of miracle happened.

The miracle, she realized, as Bonnie's voice answered the newsman, had already occurred.

"I don't think it will change a thing," she declared with great enthusiasm, as though she'd never once warned Gary that if her customers found out he'd been a convict she'd have to let him go. "Everybody in Sespe who knows Gary can see what a fine man he is. His unhesitating rescue of Genevieve Harmon only confirms that fact. I hired him because Dr. Willard Jameson said he was a man I could trust. I don't think anybody in Sespe has ever questioned Willard's judgment or good sense."

"Rescue?" Carly murmured to herself, rushing through the front door as Bonnie went on to explain about Gary's "bogus" conviction and express faith in his absolute innocence.

Nobody noticed her at first. The reporter, a handsome man in his forties, was watching Gary, who sat sandwiched between Bonnie and a redhead whom Carly recognized as Sheila Harmon. To Carly's knowledge the Harmons were not special friends of Willard's, so what, she wondered, was Sheila doing there? And why was she sitting so close to Gary, with such a possessive look on her face?

She told herself that Sheila's presence undoubtedly had something to do with "the rescue of Genevieve Harmon," which Gary had apparently performed. She wasn't sure which Harmon Genevieve was, or what Gary had done. All she knew, for certain, was that when he first spotted her by the door, a wash of red swept over his face.

She knew in an instant that Gary was ashamed of something he had done in Sespe today.

LATER, when the chaos was over and the news crews were gone, Gary explained everything to Carly. While he talked, she worked on a very late dinner.

"It was a mild myocardial infarction. Heart attack. I gave her CPR and ordered Sheila to call Willard and an ambulance. By the time Bonnie showed up, half the town had gathered around. To tell you the truth, I think it was Bonnie who told them I was really a doctor on parole. By making me a local hero, she got some of the glory for 'spotting' me as a diamond in the rough, so to speak. As far as I can tell, my job's not in danger. In fact, she expects her business to improve because people are going to stream in just to meet me." His eyes met Carly's glumly. "Sort of like they stare at a monkey in the zoo."

Carly listened to all the details and waited while he reported the whole event to both his lawyer and his parole officer and declared that, for the time being, his parole situation remained stable. Then she asked, "Why was Sheila Harmon there? With you on the couch, I mean?"

Gary looked baffled. "I think she gave a statement to the reporter before you got there. She was the only one besides me who saw the whole thing."

"She didn't look like her mind was on her grandmother," Carly couldn't help but say.

Gary sat down on a kitchen chair and pulled Carly into his lap. His dimples deepened as he grinned at her and nuzzled her hair. "If I didn't know better, I'd think you were jealous, sweetheart."

Carly met his eyes and saw no deceit written there. "Should I be?"

His reply was a kiss.

Carly snuggled close to him, feeling silly and relieved as she pointed out, "She looked like she wanted to jump on top of you."

"She probably did, based on her performance before her grandmother collapsed," Gary answered nonchalantly. Then he nibbled on Carly's right ear. "But it takes two to tango, after all, and I do all my dancing in this apartment."

Relaxing against him, Carly confessed, "I guess I was just...taken aback by the way you looked when I came in the door down there, Gary. You looked so...ashamed."

Gary didn't loosen his hold on her, but she felt a new heaviness in his limbs. "I had a lot of moments of shame today, Carly, but none of them had anything to do with you."

Carly ran a gentle hand through his thick snowy hair. "What do you mean?"

He shook his head, then turned miserable eyes on her. "First, there was Sheila, coming on to me when I had to act polite—because of my job and parole. I never really appreciated a woman's point of view regarding sexual harassment on the job before."

"And?" Carly prodded, certain there was more.

"Then there was the patient, lying there on the floor. I should have had one thought, and one thought only—what's the soundest medical maneuver available to me that can save this woman's life?"

"But you did save her, Gary! You must have done the right thing."

"Yeah, I managed to. But all the time I was thinking, 'What if I blow it? Will they haul me away again?' Before I realized how serious it was, I even had a moment where I considered playing dumb, just calling for help, because I was afraid that if the truth about my background came out, I'd lose my parole." He looked pale as he pressed his face against her neck. "No doctor should ever think thoughts like those, Carly."

"Nobody's perfect, Gary," she tried to console him. "You're still in a period of adjustment here. In time you'll get it all sorted out. I'm sure of it."

"How can I get it all sorted out if I never practice medicine again? Do you know how it felt to act like a doctor today? I mean, to actually *be* a physician? It felt so good, so right, for those few moments. I was doing what I was trained to do, what I've dreamed of doing for half of my life." He turned bleak eyes on Carly. "And then it was all over. I was just another felon again."

Carly kissed him gently. She grieved for him during his dark moments, and she worried about her future with a man who was so clearly frustrated by all the broken dreams he held in the palm of his hand. She'd done everything she could for him, but between his aborted career and his children, she was beginning to wonder if he could ever be happy again.

TO GARY'S AMAZEMENT, he became an overnight celebrity in Sespe. Business tripled for a week. All sorts of new faces drifted by his cash register. There seemed to be a sudden rush on the newly arrived spring bedding plants, and Bonnie ran out of a season's petunias in three days.

Sheila Harmon claimed to be an avid gardener. At least, that was her excuse for dropping by the nursery almost every morning. Sometimes she "ran out" of something vital—fertilizer, plant food or gardening gloves—and sometimes she needed advice. Gary had only an average backyard gardener's knowledge of plants, but she hung on his every word. He continued to grit his teeth and be amiable, until the day Carly showed up just as Sheila was leaving.

"Thank you *so* much, Gary," she oozed, wriggling enough to make sure he noticed her free-swinging breasts through the tight red T-shirt. "I'll see you soon."

"Have a good day, Sheila," he called back noncommittally. He bid all of his customers farewell that way.

"I suspect her day is all downhill from here," Carly greeted him dryly once Sheila had departed.

Gary turned to greet her, his expression wary. After her comments regarding Sheila on the night of the rescue, he was afraid she might take offense at Sheila's style. But when she didn't push the issue, neither did he.

"Hi, sweetheart. What's up?" He would have kissed her if they'd been alone, but there were customers in the store and Bonnie was close enough to see.

"I dropped by to tell you I'm on my way to a fire. Big one up the coast. I suspect I'll be gone for three or four days."

He couldn't hide his frustration. "Carly, they call you all the time! Isn't there anybody else who can do it?"

"Gary, it's my job," she reminded him a bit tersely.

"No, it's not. You're a resource technician. You're supposed to be as concerned about recreation areas as you are about forest preservation. You're also supposed to be involved in long-term planning. This fire stuff is extra. You volunteer for that."

"Sort of like you used to volunteer for emergency-room work?"

"That was different," he protested. "It was a mandatory part of my work. People's lives depended on it."

"People's lives depend on fire fighting, too, Gary."

"I know that. I just don't know why it always has to be you."

"I imagine Michelle used to say the same thing late at night, while you were gone."

Gary was surprised by the cruelty of her comment. She'd always handled the subject of Michelle with kid gloves before. "You fight dirty, lady," he said softly, hoping Bonnie had moved out of earshot.

Carly glanced down at her hands. "I'm sorry. I guess I feel guilty leaving you alone so much."

"I don't want you to feel guilty. I'm sorry I brought the subject up. It's just that I miss you, Carly. Even now that I'm out."

Her eyes narrowed. "That's really why it bothers you so much, isn't it? You've never forgiven me for missing visits at the prison because I was fighting fires."

Slowly he shook his head. "You have your own life to lead. You gave me more than I had any right to hope for when I was behind bars."

Before Carly could reply, a customer arrived with a bundle of bachelor's buttons and white-faced pansies. "Will that be all?" Gary asked her courteously.

"I guess so," Carly answered, although she realized that he hadn't been speaking to her. "I'll call you later to see how things are going."

Her tone was casual, offhand. He knew she didn't want to get him in trouble by acting mushy in public, but if she was really going to be gone for several days, he would have preferred a more tender goodbye.

Even a smile might have warmed him up inside.

CARLY WAS AWAY from home fifteen out of the next twenty-three days. But she called Gary every afternoon, before she went on her shift, and since she'd been sent to a fire that was only an hour from Sespe, she drove home to sleep when she could. Though her schedule was bizarre, they had an arrangement worked out to make maximum use of their time together. Gary checked in at six o'clock every day, just in case she'd come home while he was at work. His plans for the evening were always put on hold until he knew if she'd be free. It seemed like a good system to Gary, until the third time Walt Tower called for Carly in the same week and expressed his considerable displeasure that she was so often away.

"I realize that you've been a model parolee, Gary," the other man had conceded, "but I think Bonnie Ralston knows more about your whereabouts than Carly does. I'm pleased with Carly's reports, but it sounds to me like she's taking your good behavior for granted. Fire or no fire, you're supposed to check in with her every day. Is there someone else who lives nearby who might take over that responsibility?"

Reluctantly, Gary mentioned Willard—who also saw him daily since they jogged together, whether Carly was home or not. Tower promised to think over the situation, after he talked to Carly, but he didn't sound too happy when he hung up the phone.

Neither was Gary. How he hated having to report his whereabouts to everyone, as though he were a child! At the moment, Willard Jameson was the only person in his life who regarded him as a peer. The older doctor frequently loaned Gary his medical journals and shared his ideas on new surgical techniques. Which was why it would have killed Gary to ask Willard to baby-sit for him in lieu of Carly. Just knowing that Tower expected *her* to keep a close tab on his whereabouts was hard enough to take.

That afternoon, when Carly called him, he couldn't help but ask, "Did Walt Tower give you specific directions about calling me when you were fighting a fire?"

"What?" she asked. She was calling from a phone booth on the highway, and he could hear the sound of trucks rushing by.

"I said, are you under orders to check up on me every day?"

"Check up on you? Is that what you think I'm doing?"

She sounded so hurt that Gary was ashamed of his suspicions. "Look, sweetheart, forget it. Just call Walt Tower as soon as you get home, okay?"

"Okay," she replied, still sounding puzzled. "By the way, I've got some good news."

"Good news?" Just the sound of the two words made him feel brighter. "You've decided not to volunteer for the fire crew this season?"

Silence greeted him. Then she said, "I was serious, Gary." When he didn't reply, she reported that Bill Lundgren was her fire chief at the moment and had reported that his uncle was just tickled pink with Clifford's work in his sporting-goods store. "He runs the store alone at night. It's actually a promotion of sorts."

Rich pride filled Gary's chest at the news. He missed his old friend, and he deeply resented the parole rules that made it impossible for them to visit. After all, they had even more in common now than they'd had in prison—both of them were struggling to come to terms with life on the outside as ex-convicts. Since his release, the only person Gary had talked to who really understood how he felt was Willard's brother. But Floyd had only come to Sespe for Christmas; after a week, he'd returned to his own life in L.A.

After they talked about Clifford, Carly asked about Homer and Willard, and Gary reported that Willie was coming home for the weekend to finalize plans for his joint practice with his father, scheduled to begin in June. After that, Gary realized that he didn't have any more news—at least none that he could share with Carly. He'd met a fascinating woman at work that morning whom he really wanted to get to know better... as a friend. But after Carly's response to Sheila's bold flirtation, he knew he'd have trouble explaining his innocent interest in Theresa Longman, so he didn't mention her at all.

Instead, he admitted, "Carly, I miss you like the devil. The nights are so long when you're not home."

"They're long for me, too, Gary," she confessed. "Just pretend that I'm right there in bed beside you. And that's where I'll be, just as soon as I get home."

That night he did as she suggested, pretended that she was home. And then he realized that on the few days she *had* come home lately, Carly had been so tired from fire duty that she'd zonked out on the couch or fallen asleep in bed curled up at his side, unaware that he ached to feel her close beside him, ached to reclaim her as his own.

With a jolt, he realized that the last few times he'd tried to make love to her, she'd begged off. At the time, he'd believed her excuse—acute fatigue—but now, as he lay awake listening to the clock tick, he started to wonder.

Had her feelings for him changed since he'd been released from prison? If so, why? And what on earth could he do about it?

THE MORNING AFTER Carly reported Clifford's news to Gary, Wade Haley, her division counterpart on this fire, sat down beside her at breakfast and studied her weary face. They'd joined forces on half a dozen fires since Camelback Ridge, and each time Wade had studiously refrained from making irritating personal comments, which had improved their relationship enormously.

Now he reflected her own thoughts as he pointed out, "This one isn't going well, Carly. I wish we weren't dependent on so many convict crews."

Carly always treated the con crews with inordinate courtesy, a fact that had not gone unnoticed by the grateful men... or Wade Haley.

"You're still too easy on those guys," he now observed, "but at least you're not being suckered by any of those felons this time around."

"I beg your pardon?"

Wade rolled his eyes. "You know what I mean. You never admitted it, but you had a thing for one of those guys during that fire we fought on Camelback Ridge."

With a wash of shame, Carly realized that she'd never once admitted to Wade or any other fire-fighting friend that she was involved with a former member of one of their convict crews. She'd never even told the people in her own office that she was living with Gary—seriously contemplating marriage—and now she had to ask herself why. Did she just want to spare herself from any of Wade's barbed comments, or was she ashamed of the man she loved?

A third possibility nagged at her subconscious mind: was she afraid to let people know that she'd given her heart to Gary because she was still afraid that he might leave her once he was released from parole? She gave some thought to her flicker of jealousy over Sheila Harmon, triggered by... well, nothing, really. Nothing but the lingering scars left by Rodney Haywood... and the uneasy thought of all the reasons Gary needed Carly's continued goodwill. They had nothing whatsoever to do with love....

She suddenly realized that Gary might also be afraid that the end of his parole would drastically alter their relationship. What had he asked her on the phone? If she only called home to check up on him for Walt Tower? He'd warned her that if he lived with her while he was on parole, the mandatory supervision might harm their flowering love. He'd been right, of course. His legal situation filled their lives with heaps of emotional debris. And there was no point in adding to it with her own old baggage of hurt and distrust. Time and time again, Gary had told her that he loved her; either she believed him or she did not. It was as simple as that.

Deciding to take a brave step toward the future, Carly squared her shoulders and confessed to her fellow fire fighter, "As a matter of fact, I'm planning to marry one of 'those guys,' Wade. Probably before the end of the year." *As soon as his parole is over*, she promised herself. *As soon as I'm sure that even though he's free to go, he still wants to stay.*

Wade stared at Carly, a half grin on his face. "You're pulling my leg, Carly. It's not nice to tease an old friend."

Carly's lips tightened. "I'm not kidding, Wade. I fell in love with Gary Reid during the Camelback fire. I went to see him in prison every chance I could get. I helped arrange for his parole."

Wade's mouth went slack. "He's out? That doctor con?"

Carly bristled at his terminology. "He got out in December, Wade." She raised her head, ever so proudly, as she confessed, "And now he's living with me."

GARY WAITED HOPEFULLY for the phone to ring when he got home after work, but at six o'clock, he resigned himself to another night alone. If Carly didn't call by then, he knew by long experience, she was off fighting a fire somewhere and wouldn't be back for at least another day.

As he stuck a frozen meal in the microwave, Gary mentally replayed his last several weeks with Carly. He was lonely, tired of spending night after night by himself, tired of watching her sleep on the rare occasions she did spend some time at home. He knew that he'd subjected Michelle to exactly this kind of torture for years, but that didn't change the fact that now he knew better. A loving relationship needed time and energy to grow. At the moment, Carly had neither to spare for him, and he hated the fact that the debt of gratitude he owed her for deigning to love him at all prevented him from telling her exactly how he felt about that.

His resentment vanished the instant the phone began to ring. Granted, it was too late for it to be Carly, but still... he couldn't help but hope.

But the voice on the other end of the phone did not belong to Carly. It was a voice that filled him with conflict, a voice that triggered old memories of great affection, new memories of fear.

"Doc?" Incredibly, it was Clifford—Clifford gasping for breath, his voice racked with pain in a way Gary remembered only too well. His friend had sounded almost the same way the night the prison guard had worked him over and Gary, brand new to the prison and to Clifford's cell, had managed to save his life.

"Clifford, what's wrong?" he burst out, discarding everything he'd been warned about associating with an ex-convict.

"You gotta get up here. To Cresta."

There were a dozen replies Gary could have made, and three dozen rationales why he could not, should not, *would* not break parole by roaring up to Cresta Mar. But when the man who'd kept him sane in prison gasped, "I'm gun shot, Doc," all Gary said was, "Give me your address, Clifford. I'm on my way."

CHAPTER FOURTEEN

AFTER A FITFUL day's sleep in fire camp following her chat with Wade, Carly woke up at three to hear some excellent news. The day shift had brought the fire under control and she would probably be able to go home in the morning. Under any circumstances it would have been a relief, but ever since she'd confessed her relationship with Gary to Wade—roughly the equivalent of announcing it to everybody she'd ever known with a bullhorn—she'd felt uneasy about their future. Her last few days at home with Gary had not been particularly reassuring, and their most recent chat on the phone had been even worse. He was clearly frustrated with her demanding work schedule, and though he tried to refrain from harassing her about it, he was starting to bring the subject up entirely too often.

She told herself that a few spats were inevitable, and she shouldn't let a harsh word or two bring her down. When she got back to Sespe, she'd see Gary's beautiful blue eyes light up with the joy of seeing her, and she'd know that everything was all right between them.

As it turned out, Carly was released just a few hours after her shift began, and she managed to get home by nine o'clock. Only Homer was there to greet her, however, imperiously demanding food. Gary normally kept the cat's bowl full to the brim, but he must have forgotten to check it tonight, because it was empty.

Carly was disappointed to find that Gary was gone, but since she hadn't called him by six to say she was coming home, she wasn't particularly surprised to find that he'd left for the evening. Tired and hungry, she decided to eat and take a shower, then nap until Gary got home.

But when she opened the microwave to put in a frozen dinner, she found that one was already there. At least, it had been a frozen dinner, at one time. Now it was thoroughly thawed and, apparently, already cooked. Yet it hadn't been left out long enough to spoil.

While Carly tried to figure out why Gary would have left a microwaved dinner uneaten and Homer's bowl unfilled, she noticed some other unusual things about the kitchen. It was always spotless when she got home, but this evening it was littered with unwashed dishes. The empty frozen-dinner package lay on the floor, as though it had fallen there and nobody had bothered to pick it up, and a half-empty Coke can on the table was starting to attract ants. Next to the can was a newspaper—today's paper—still rolled up. The sight of the unread newspaper was jarring to Carly, because in all the time Gary had lived with her, she couldn't remember a single night when he hadn't read the paper from cover to cover the first instant he'd gotten home.

Obviously he'd planned to eat dinner while he read the paper, so why hadn't he done so? The only person he ever palled around with in the evening was Willard, and Willard wasn't known for spur-of-the-moment plans. Postponing her own meal, Carly decided to see if Willard was home, but nobody answered her knock on his door. Since Gary parked his car in Willard's garage, Carly decided to check there, too, but it was empty. If both cars were gone, she realized quickly, then Willard and Gary weren't likely to be together, unless one of them had had car trouble and called the other for help.

It wasn't a good theory, but it was the only one Carly could come up with at the moment. She grew increasingly uneasy as she ate dinner, showered, and crawled into bed. Despite her fatigue, her sleep was uneasy and colored with a miserable dream about Rodney and his hateful blonde. In it, the two illicit lovers were discovered making love in the bed where she now slept, and Rodney, a blond, had snow-white hair in the dream.

When Carly awoke, she lay restlessly in the darkness, feeling guilty about her unfounded suspicions of Gary revealed by the dream. She strained to hear every sound on the street until the screech of a car pulling into Willard's garage suddenly snapped her upright with relief.

One car. Not two.

Pulling on a bathrobe, Carly bolted down the stairs and knocked again on Willard's door. He appeared a moment later, dressed casually in a blue shirt and matching slacks, looking perfectly contented.

"Hey, Carly," he greeted her cheerfully, "what are you doing here?"

"I live here, remember?" She tried to keep her tone light, but knew she sounded testy. After all, it was almost midnight and Gary had neither arrived nor phoned. She was uneasy—maybe even a bit suspicious—but she was starting to get frightened, too. Could something have happened to him? Did she dare call the police to find out?

"I know that. But I thought you were meeting Gary somewhere." He winked at her. "Not that he spelled it out quite like that, but I sure had the feeling that you two lovebirds had something special planned."

Relief and dread swelled Carly's heart in equal proportions. "He told you where he was going? You know where he is?"

Willard shrugged. "Well, not exactly. We just pulled out of the garage about the same time this evening. I was on my way to Sandra's for dinner and Gary was... well, off someplace. I sure thought he was going to meet up with you."

"Why did you think he was meeting me, Willard?" she asked. How could Gary possibly have hoped to find her on the line? And why would he even try to do so unless there was something terribly, terribly wrong?

"Well, it was just a guess, actually. We didn't get to talk much. He was in an awful hurry, but he told me he wouldn't be free to run with me tomorrow morning. When I asked why not, he looked all embarrassed and said he had special plans for the evening and he wasn't sure when he'd be back. I started to tease him about it because I figured the two of you had some secret rendezvous planned. I mean, why else would he plan to be gone overnight? But he wouldn't tell me another thing. He just waved me off and zipped away in the Chevy." Now Willard peered at her closely. "Does that help you any?"

A wave of nausea all but felled Carly where she stood. Everything in her system was clamoring déjà vu. She'd tried so hard not to tar Gary with Rodney's brush, not to saddle him with her ex-fiancé's shiftless ways! Oh, they weren't identical. Gary would put his life back together, all right; she'd never doubted it. But obviously he had no more patience with Carly's schedule and priorities than Rodney had had. He'd been complaining for weeks now, and she hadn't done a thing to modify the situation. Clearly he'd come up with a solution on his own.

The only question was whether the solution was a brunette, a redhead or a blonde.

GARY FOUND CLIFFORD in the "mother-in-law" suite of his employer's house in Cresta. Apparently Bill Lundgren's uncle had taken his wife and kids to Florida on vacation. No one would be home for the next five days.

"Check everywhere for blood, Doc," Clifford begged him. "Did you hide your car?"

"It's down the block, and I didn't see any blood when I came in. Now let me look at you."

There was a pile of bloody clothes in the metal wastebasket by the bathroom, which Clifford explained was the result of his efforts to staunch the bleeding. He didn't dare use any towels or sheets the lady of the house might notice. Nobody, but nobody, could find out that he'd been shot, or all his dreams would vanish. With his record, he maintained, no parole officer or cop would ever believe that he'd been playing it straight when he got shot, and any doctor but Gary would be required by law to report a gunshot wound. Of course, Gary had a legal obligation to do the same, but the debts he owed to Clifford were too great to be measured by any law. If he could fix up Clifford without any authorities finding out about the incident, maybe, just maybe, Clifford could continue to live out his dream as an employee of a sporting-goods shop. Otherwise, it was back to prison. Perhaps forever.

Gary was too concerned about his friend's physical condition to worry unduly about the legal ramifications of his own role in the incident. Since Carly hadn't called him by six, she wouldn't be home for at least another day, and Willard hadn't questioned his excuse for missing one morning's jog. All Gary had to do was get back to Sespe by the time Bonnie opened Sespe Green Things in the morning, and he probably wouldn't get caught. He wasn't looking forward to explaining the whole thing to Carly once she got home, but under the circumstances he was certain that she'd understand why he'd taken the risk of breaking parole. He just hoped she wouldn't have to lie to Walt Tower for him.

Gary was relieved to see Clifford's wound. It was serious, but not fatal—at least, it wouldn't be fatal now that Clifford was going to get medical attention.

While Gary fished out the bullet and cleaned the wound, Clifford got the story out in bits and pieces.

"About a week ago, I stopped for a drink after work at a neighborhood bar. I've been there lots of times. I never had any trouble. But while I was there, three guys came in, and I recognized one of them from Tejon. He wasn't there when you served with me, Doc—it was a long time ago. But he knew me, you know, and came over to talk. I didn't want to talk to him, because it's a breach of parole to see any ex-con, and this guy and I were never close." He gasped as Gary cleaned the wound, but otherwise offered no protest to his friend's ministrations. "I told him I was on parole, but he still got his feathers ruffled when I suggested that it would be nice if he'd keep his distance. But he went back to his table, I left the bar, and I thought that was the end of it.

"But a few days later, he shows up again. Tells me he's got a sweet deal—just the kind I'm best at. Nobody knows me up in Cresta—on the street, I mean—so I'm perfect for the job. I told him to forget it." His eyes met Gary's in a moment of desperate pleading. "I *swear* to you, Doc! Even if I didn't care about my own future, I'd never do it to my new boss or Carly, after all they've both done for me."

Gary kept on cleaning the wound. "I believe you, Clifford. Don't waste your strength convincing me." And he did believe him. But he also knew that nobody in the legal system ever would. From what he'd heard so far, any number of people at the bar could probably give the police evidence that Clifford had been "fraternizing" with an ex-con, which not only was a parole violation but would lay the groundwork for a criminal case if anybody pointed a finger at Clifford during any sort of investigation.

"He got really upset with me that time. Said I thought I was too good for my old friends. I walked out on him because he was about to start a ruckus, and if anybody called the cops, there I'd be, associating with a known felon."

Gary nodded. He could almost guess the rest.

"So two nights ago, he shows up at the store. Tries to convince me to fake a holdup and split the dough. I refused. He got testy, but he finally took off and I hoped that was the end of it. I was wrong."

He explained how he'd come to work alone in the evenings, how he was up for a promotion to assistant manager. His boss had even asked him to consider coaching a kids' ball team sponsored by the store. The man had faith in him, which to Clifford was worth pure gold. He loved everything about his life in Cresta. For the first time in thirty years, he'd actually started to believe that he was going to be able to forge a worthwhile life for himself outside of prison.

"Last night, he comes in with another guy and tries to rob me straight out. I had to get rough, but a customer showed up during the scuffle and I managed to hold onto the cash while they split out the back door. So tonight, I kept a real close eye on everything, but nothing happened at the store. I thought everything was cool until I got into my car and found a .38 pointed at my head. Turned out that the guy I knew from Tejon wasn't free-lancing, and his partner, the guy I'd roughed up during the attempted robbery, was the son of the guy who owns the streets up here. My old 'pal' wanted to make sure I understood that his boss doesn't take no for an answer."

While Gary stitched up the ragged edges of his friend's flesh, he listened soberly to the sordid details of Clifford's fight for his life with a crew of hoodlums. No wonder recidivism was so high among ex-convicts! Even when they tried to go straight, life never gave them a chance.

"So there's been nothing stolen yet? No damage to the store?" he asked when Clifford started talking about his obligation to the store again.

"No. But it's just a matter of time before they come back." His face was ashen. "The day manager is a good kid, a real straight-arrow. He'd be scared to death, if I told him what went down. I know he'd call the cops. He likes me okay, but he doesn't have the guts to back me up." Clifford was trembling now. "If the boss was here, I might lay it all out for him. He might be able to report it without getting me canned. If he believed me, that is. And that's a pretty big 'if.'" Clifford was shaking violently now. The wound was bleeding again. "Tell me what to do, Doc," he pleaded. "I don't want to blow it here. I owe this guy so much! Besides—" his voice dropped shakily "—it's my last chance."

AT TEN TO nine the next morning, Gary still hadn't come home. Carly wasn't sure whether she decided to go to the nursery to tell Bonnie he wouldn't be in—with God knows what excuse—or to see if he had shown up on his own. Just because he'd forgotten his responsibilities to *her* didn't mean he'd forgotten that Sespe Green Things was his current ticket to freedom.

He might have a perfectly good reason for staying out all night, Carly tried to convince herself. *Don't crucify him, until he's had a chance to explain.* It was the same speech she'd been giving herself all night long, but it had done little to brighten her heart or smooth the heavy bags from under her eyes. It was a battle between her deep-down belief that Gary Reid was an honest man worthy of her trust and the knowledge that he was, after all, an ex-felon convicted of killing a man.

Carly was waiting outside the nursery when Bonnie arrived. By the time Carly darted out of her truck and greeted the other woman, Bonnie's eyes were studying the far side of the street. "You and Gary in separate cars this morning?" she asked.

Carly was about to explain her reason for being there, when she heard Gary's voice, tired but cheerful, calling out a greeting to Bonnie.

"Good morning! Beautiful day, isn't it?"

Carly froze. For one joyful minute she closed her eyes in relief. He'd come back; he was okay. And surely, the moment he saw her worried face, his eyes would light up with love and he'd rush to reassure her, to explain why he'd had to spend the night away from home. But when she turned to face the man she loved, he didn't return her tentative smile. He didn't greet her at all.

Gary looked like something the cat had dragged in—unshaven, his eyes bloodshot and his shirt slightly wrinkled, as though he'd slept in it. He might look good enough to the casual eye—certainly Bonnie didn't seem to notice anything amiss—but to the woman who loved him, who'd shared his life and his bed, the sorry state of his condition was blatantly clear. So was the way he dodged her piercing glare.

Suddenly Carly knew that she was done making excuses for him, even in her head. As Bonnie sauntered off to open the back door, Carly whispered angrily, "Where the hell have you been?"

Fire flared in Gary's eyes as he finally looked at her directly. "You sound like a damn prison guard! Don't we start the day with hellos and kisses anymore?"

"I was ready for hello and a kiss last night when I got off the line," she snapped back. "But I guess you couldn't wait for that, could you? How often do you spend the night at home when I'm fighting a fire?"

Before he could answer, Bonnie had joined them again, commenting on the rich color of the blooming petunias. Gary answered noncommittally; Carly remained silent. When Bonnie greeted the first customer, Gary whispered, "I've got to get to work, Carly. We'll talk about this when I get home."

"We'll talk about it *now*!"

Gary's face turned dark. "I've got half a dozen people pulling the strings in my life, Carly. I'll be damned if I'll let you order me around, too!"

Before she could come up with a retort, Gary had turned his back on her and marched over to the cash register. And just like that, Carly realized, he could walk out of her life the instant he was released from parole.

THE NEXT THREE days were sheer hell for Gary. Carly had already taken off for another fire by the time he got home for lunch, desperate to apologize for his harsh words to her at the nursery. When he'd arrived at work—making the drive from Cresta in record time, without a moment's sleep—the last person he'd expected to see there was Carly. It wasn't until she'd roared off, in fact, that he'd fully realized what hell he'd put her through the night before.

Had she been terrified that something had happened to him? Or had she—God forbid—thought he'd strayed, as Rodney Haywood had? Was she now wondering if he really had been using her all along? That her feelings meant nothing to him and he planned to take off for greener pastures as soon as his parole was over?

Desperately he wished that he could have talked to her alone that morning, or had been able to transcend his own private hell at the time. He'd been exhausted, still very afraid for Clifford, and worried about his own serious breaches of state law and parole. Under other circumstances, he'd have been relieved to unburden himself to Carly. But he'd been afraid that if he tried to explain anything in front of Bonnie, his own job, not to mention Clifford's, would have been put in jeopardy.

He'd also been taken off guard to find Carly in Sespe, let alone at his store, first thing in the morning. If he'd guessed for a minute that she'd end up worrying about him all night, he'd have left her a note. But how on earth was he to have known she'd show up a whole day early? Or that the first words out of her mouth would be blind accusations about all the terrible things he might have done? He'd needed comfort and understanding, or at the very least, patience until he'd had a chance to explain! Her unfounded suspicions had made him see red.

In hindsight, Gary knew he couldn't have handled the situation much worse, but fatigue, fear and resentment had obliterated his common sense. Even now, he was off kilter, counting the minutes until Carly called or came home.

For the first time since he'd moved in, she didn't check in with him once a day. He was accustomed to being in the apartment without her, but previously, the memory of her warmth had kept him company; now he felt abysmally alone. He even felt lonely at the crowded store and found it difficult to concentrate on his duties there. Once he even made a ten-dollar error making change, which Bonnie caught at the end of the day.

Gary checked on Clifford daily, until the night Clifford's boss was due home. He cleaned Carly's apartment to perfection and planned a week's worth of exotic meals. He talked to his lawyer about the girls, but did not mention how strained things were with Carly. John Henton still thought that a quick marriage would help him get regular access to them, or even legal custody, but Gary had no intention of asking Carly to marry him again. Not until he was sure there was something in it for her as well as for himself. Not until he was sure she'd feel good about saying yes. That possibility had never seemed less likely.

Gary was afraid that Willard would notice how distracted he was when they went jogging, but Willard made no comment. In fact, Willard was so morose that Gary decided that something was bothering his elderly friend. When they stopped in Willard's kitchen for some orange juice after the run, Gary asked him outright, "Did you get a call from my parole officer?" He wanted to find out if Willard knew he'd stayed out all night, but that was a can of worms he didn't dare open.

Willard's shaggy eyebrows rose. "Parole officer? No. What would he want with me?"

Gary was forced to admit, "He's worried about Carly being gone so much during fire season. I think he's going to need another watchdog, or he'll have to move me."

Willard gazed at Gary as though his mind were elsewhere, or possibly deep in thought regarding the matter at hand. "How much longer are you on parole, Gary?" he finally asked.

"Another six months, more or less."

"You're not counting the days?"

"I did enough of that in prison. That was hell. This is purgatory. Better, but a long way from heaven."

Willard looked slightly offended. "You're not happy in our little town? You're not happy with our Carly?"

Gary shook his head. "I love your little town and I adore Carly. But a man in irons is chained wherever he goes, Willard. The rattle haunts my every step."

Willard's eyes met his with unveiled sympathy. "I wish I could help you, son."

"You have helped me, Willard. More than you possibly know." He didn't explain that nobody but Willard really treated him as equal, made him feel like a man. He knew his friend would understand.

It's funny, Gary mused. *This dear old fellow couldn't be much more different from Clifford, but they both did the same thing for me. Cheered me up when the chips were down.*

At the moment, it seemed to Gary that Willard was the one who needed some bucking up, but before he could offer a shoulder to lean on, Willard asked, "What do you plan to do when your parole is over? Keep working at the nursery?"

Knowing that Bonnie was Willard's friend, Gary chose his words with care. "It's possible. Bonnie's been very good to me, and I have no quarrel with my job. But—" there was just no way around it "—I'm a doctor, Willard. Even if I can't ever practice medicine again, there ought to be some way I can get back on the fringes. Maybe I could start an ambulance company, or sell medical supplies. I don't know."

Willard shook his head. "What a waste."

When Gary didn't reply, Willard said nothing, either. In fact, he was quiet for so long that Gary finally felt that the time was right to ask, "So what's got you so down today?"

Willard released a long, miserable sigh, then met Gary's eyes with unmasked pain. "I got a letter from Willie yesterday. He's got an offer to go into private practice with one of the most highly respected neurologists in L.A. He says he's got to think about it. He hopes I understand."

"Oh, Willard," Gary murmured with genuine grief, knowing how much his son's return to Sespe meant to the older man. It was, in fact, the one bright star in his future, as vital to Willard as Gary's own hope of reclaiming his children. He had assumed that all the details had been nailed down on Willie's last trip to town. "I'm sure he'll decide to come back, once he thinks it over. It's got to be a flattering offer, but—"

"He's already decided," Willard cut him off. "I know my boy. He would never have mentioned it unless he meant to follow through. He just wants to give me time to get used to it."

As his sad, tired eyes focused on Thelma's picture on the wall, he whispered, "I guess I don't need to tell you, Gary, that there are some things a man never gets used to."

Gary squeezed the old man's shoulder, but he couldn't think of a single word to say.

THE APARTMENT WAS empty when Carly came home that night. There was Homer, of course, who purred and demanded to be fed. Once that would have been enough for her. Now the place echoed with ghostly memories of Gary.

She'd had a speech all prepared. "You've got one last chance to tell me I'm just imagining all this," she'd planned to tell him. "If you've got a good excuse for being out all night, this is the time to let me know."

But Gary wasn't there, and by eleven o'clock she decided to accept the fact that he wasn't planning to spend the night at home. *Home.* Was that how he thought of her apartment? Or was it just a pit stop on his way to real life once he was free of her?

At least there's no messy divorce to go through, she tried to console herself. *Just I-told-you-so from my father and Wade and... everybody else who knows.*

On the fire line she'd been too busy to indulge in much grief. Her fury had kept her going. Now, however, in the privacy of her room—in the empty bed she'd so joyfully shared with the man she'd given every ounce of her love— she hugged the huge orange cat close to her chest and let the waterfall of tears spill over.

She was still weeping when Gary arrived an hour later. She didn't hear the front door open; she didn't realize he'd returned until he strolled into the room, slipped both arms around her shoulders and leaned down to kiss her hello. Carly stiffened and turned her face so his lips only grazed her cheek. She couldn't look at him directly, but from the corner of her eye she saw him recoil in shock. It was a remarkably convincing display.

"I'm glad you're home," he said, standing perfectly still beside the bed. "I wasn't expecting you back tonight."

"I wasn't expecting you, either," she said bluntly. "Did you drop by to pick up your things?"

His eyes widened in shock, but he did not speak.

"Makes it kind of messy with Walt Tower watching your every step, doesn't it? Maybe it'll be easier to explain to him if you explain it to me now. Sort of like a dress rehearsal. After all, I'm used to being an understudy for your real life by now."

Gary's lips tightened; still he did not speak. The silence that gripped the room was terrible. So was the gray pain that colored his face. The agony in his eyes did battle with her anger.

Could anybody really fake that much feeling? Carly wondered.

Homer meowed, then hopped down to greet Gary, who ignored the cat as it rubbed against his leg. His eyes never left Carly's. The tension in his mouth never once abated.

It was Carly who finally had to look away.

Only then did he ask, "When did we give up trying to talk out our troubles, Carly? Did you just wake up one morning and find that your love for me was gone?"

"No," she snapped. "I stayed up all night waiting for you to come home and found out that *your* love for me was only a ruse. For eighteen hours I lied to myself, swore that you had some justifiable reason for staying out all night! If only I could see you, you'd explain it all to me! And when I finally saw you face-to-face, you kicked me in the teeth!"

"Carly—"

"I may be slow, but I'm not stupid." She turned wet green eyes upon him. "I don't really think you faked it all the way, Gary. I think you probably did feel something for me in the beginning. Maybe you still do. And I can't turn my feelings off and on like a spigot, so you don't have to worry about how this will affect your parole. I'll never be angry enough to send you back to prison. I'll cover for you officially until you can clear your new arrangements with Walt Tower, assuming that you...do have...new living arrangements in mind." By now she was crying again, her tears begging him to tell her that she was wrong. Surely it was all a terrible misunderstanding!

He didn't reply at once, but his eyes darkened with such pain that she knew she'd wounded him deeply. In fact, he looked afraid to speak, afraid he'd say the wrong thing and anger her even more. At last, very quietly, he said, "I'm profoundly sorry for the way I talked to you at the nursery, Carly. I have no excuses, but...I do have an explanation, I guess. You caught me at a terrible time. I was exhausted. I was scared. And Bonnie was there. I'd gone out on a limb the night before, but I'd...I'd counted on your support. Maybe I'd started taking it for granted. When you started hurtling accusations around, I guess I went berserk."

Carly tried futilely to wipe away her tears with already wet hands. A tiny glimmer, ever so small but there nonetheless, had begun to glow in her heart. "Are you telling me that...there might be an explanation for why you were out all night that I could forgive you for?" she whispered.

Gary ran a weary hand through his thick, snowy hair, before he answered. "Carly, the only thing I've done that begs forgiveness is treat you so shabbily at the store. I never doubted that you'd understand why I did what I did; and I would have left you a note, but I was certain you wouldn't be coming home. I didn't leave until after six, and you always call by then to let me know if you're coming back."

Unable to let him pace his own confession, Carly asked outright, "Where did you spend the night, Gary?"

This time, he looked her straight in the eye and said, "With Clifford, up in Cresta. He was shot in the abdomen. If I hadn't gone to him, he would have died."

A tiny cry—of guilt, of dismay, of fear for the kindly black man—escaped Carly's lips. She was ashamed of her suspicions, afraid of what harm they'd done. But she was still uneasy, uncertain. Gary's eyes remained utterly grave.

"Sit down and tell me about it, Gary," she said softly, gesturing toward the foot of the bed.

Gingerly, he did so, but he did not touch her while he talked. His expression was wooden as he reported, "Clifford was shot as a result of trying to protect his store from a holdup. He called me so it wouldn't be reported to the cops. I didn't know how bad it was. All I knew was that my friend was in trouble. I was afraid he was dying. As a physician, I broke the law by not reporting the wound. I also fraternized with an ex-convict and failed to sleep at my assigned residence, so I broke parole, too." His voice was tired, broken, absolutely devoid of heart. "I never intended to keep it from you, Carly, even though I knew it might cause you trouble if Tower ever found out. But I couldn't tell you in front of Bonnie, and when I realized that you thought the worst, something in me just snapped. Right now, I feel just like a marionette. John, Walt, even Bonnie—all of them are pulling my strings. You have no idea what you mean to me, Carly. I just couldn't stand it when you started acting like another puppeteer."

Carly had held her breath the whole time he was speaking. Now, belatedly, she asked, "Is Clifford all right?"

Gary nodded. "He calls me every day. His boss came home last night, and I hope Clifford laid it all out for him. I think the guy will go to bat for him. After all, nothing's stolen yet and Clifford honestly did nothing wrong." His eyes bored into hers. "He seems to think that no civilian ever completely believes the word of an ex-con. Maybe he's right."

Carly pulled her legs up and wrapped both hands around her knees. She had one more question she had to ask.

"Where have you been this evening?" She did her best to state the question in a straightforward tone.

He sighed, clearly resentful of the continued grilling. "I've been to dinner and a movie with Willard. He just found out that Willie has decided to go into practice in L.A. and it's just about broken his heart. I had to do something to cheer him up."

"Oh, Gary," Carly murmured. Her eyes met his, and read there genuine sympathy for his older friend. She couldn't stay angry, not when she thought about him trying to fix up Clifford, and attempting to cheer up such a dear old man. Still, there were things yet to be resolved between them, and she tightened her grip on her knees.

"You thought I was with a woman; didn't you?" Gary suddenly asked.

Carly bit her lower lip. "I...thought it might have been a possibility."

To her surprise, Gary snapped, *"It was not."*

Their eyes met. Hers were haunted, afraid, regretful. Gary's were downright furious.

"From the day we met, you've been accusing me of one damn thing or another, Carly. You've saddled me with all of Rodney's shortcomings, covered yourself for every way I might fall off the wagon. Have you ever really believed in me? In us? In my love for you?"

Bravely she met his eyes. "Sometimes I believe it. Sometimes I'm sure of it. Until Willard let me know you'd planned to be out all night, I was only afraid for you, Gary. Even when all the facts seemed to indicate that you were with somebody else, I told myself you must have a good excuse. If you hadn't hollered at me, I don't think I would have thought the worst."

"You already thought the worst. My behavior just confirmed it."

Carly glanced down at her interlaced fingers. She truly didn't know what to say.

"Dammit, Carly, what do you want from me? You know what prison was like for me, but I risked going back to stand by an old friend. Don't you think I'd do the same for you?"

Tears welled up in her eyes again, then spilled over altogether when Gary ran one thumb along his jaw the way he'd so often done in prison when he'd been forbidden to touch her. She knew that in his mind right now there was a voice calling out, "No touching!" But this time that voice was hers.

She couldn't look at him while she slid her trembling fingers over his. His grip was tight, desperate. "I love you, Carly," he whispered in an anguished tone. "I can't imagine why you think I'd want any other woman when I have you."

Carly started to cry again. "You keep saying you don't have me. You complain because I'm gone so much. And when I'm here, I'm too tired to give you what you need."

Gary ran a gentle hand through her hair, then leaned down until his cheek brushed hers. "All I need from you is your faith in me, Carly. I used to think that was a sure bet. What happened? How did I let you down?"

His tone was confused, tender; his touch infinitely gentle as he pressed his lips against her temple and whispered, "Tell me what you want me to do, sweetheart. What can I do to make things right?"

There were a thousand things Carly could have told him, some realistic, some purely make-believe. There were more accusations she might have made, demands, pleas, questions he might or might not have been able to answer. But suddenly none of them seemed too important. Or maybe too important to probe with so much darkness in her heart.

Her voice was thick with three days and nights of mental torture as she begged him, "Just hold me, Gary. Hold me while I cry."

She wrapped her arms around him as he crushed her to his chest.

CHAPTER FIFTEEN

GARY WOKE UP at five o'clock and soon gave up trying to go back to sleep. Carly lay beside him, still huddled against his side. He felt more hopeful than he had in that terrible moment when she'd all but ordered him out of her life the previous night, but his stomach still wobbled with fear.

Gently he stroked her hair, trying not to awaken her. How had he ever botched things up so badly? He'd done everything he possibly could to be perfect for Bonnie, for Willard, for Carly. What had gone wrong?

When Carly's eyes opened, she didn't speak at once. She was eyeing him warily, as though she recalled that they'd fought but not that they'd made up. For one terrible moment he was afraid that she might be thinking of ordering him out of her apartment again.

"Good morning," she said. "Are you in the mood to talk?"

Cautiously, he nodded. Then he rolled over to brace himself on one elbow, keeping his other arm loosely draped around her. He knew that his touch always melted her anger. Somehow—no matter how thorny were the issues they discussed—he had to keep her calm this morning. He couldn't bear to have her order him out of her life.

"You know that I love you, Gary," was her opening line. "But something's not right between us. Something that goes far deeper than the fact that I was scared and suspicious when you stayed out all night. I should have been able to trust you, and I didn't. You should have been able to assure me instead of making things worse, and you didn't. We need to find out why." She paused, her beautiful green eyes gazing with great longing at his face. "Assuming we both still think it's worth the effort."

Gary swallowed hard. "There's no doubt in my mind, Carly," he confessed. Then he held his breath, until he heard her whispered answer.

"No doubt in mine, either." She leaned over quickly to kiss him—a quick kiss, not one of passion but of promise.

He wanted to take her in his arms, to wash all the hurt away. But Carly pulled back, the set of her jaw quite serious. "Twice I've heard you compare my concern to an accusation made by a prison guard. You said you'd had 'all of that you could handle.' What exactly did you mean by that?"

Gary battled the tightness in his chest. "Please, Carly. Forget what I said. Can't we just—" he cupped her cheek with a beseeching hand "—try to put things back together now?"

Carly covered his pleading fingers with her own as she insisted, "I don't think we can fix what's wrong between us just by wishing everything was all right. Let's get to the bottom of things—lovingly—" she turned to kiss his palm "—so it never sneaks up on us again. Deal?"

Still uneasy, he leaned forward to kiss her, and her lips were soft, yearning, full of the tenderness he'd always savored. "You promise not to get mad again?"

"No," she replied, but this time honored him with a pixie grin. "But I promise not to order you out of our home. Unless I ever find out that you've betrayed me."

"Never." The word stuck in his throat. He could never tell her how much it hurt him that she even had to ask. Instead, he decided to explain some of the feelings that had been building up inside him for months. It wasn't going to be easy, but he knew he had to try. "I think maybe the trouble is that I've been bending over backward *not* to betray you, Carly. Not to let you down. I've done my damnedest to be perfect all the time. I thought I could do it. I thought anything would be easier than life in prison." He closed his eyes as the memory wounded him again. "But at least when I lived with Clifford, I could be myself."

Carly looked as though he'd slapped her in the face, but she didn't pull away. "And you're not...yourself...now? You don't feel at home here?"

Slowly, honestly, he shook his head. "At heart I'm a terribly sloppy person, Carly. If I lived alone, I'd let the dishes pile up in the sink for days and always have heaps of clothes lying around the house. But every day I scramble around here trying to keep everything neat and tidy. I tell myself that I'm just trying to be courteous. But deep down I've always known my motivation is deeper than that. I do it because I'm afraid."

Her eyes widened, but she did not interrupt.

"Every time you ask me where I've been or how I spent my lunch hour, or call me when you're fighting a fire, my hackles rise. I try to tell myself you just want to make sure I'm happy, but deep down I'm afraid you're spying for Tower. For my own good, I know—" he hurried to say before she could deny it "—but I feel watched, invaded, all the same."

For a moment the room was filled with painful silence. Homer jumped up on the bed and started to purr, demanding to be petted. Unable to bear the strain of waiting for Carly's reply, Gary stroked the cat. To his surprise, so did Carly. When their fingers met under the big cat's chin, she lifted her eyes to meet his sober consideration. Then she gripped his hand tightly and elbowed the cat off the bed.

Quietly she asked, "Is there more? Get it all out, Gary. No more secrets now."

He took a deep breath before he faced her. "I feel caged when I can't get out, do things, make friends. Before I rescued Genevieve Harmon, I wasn't supposed to get close to anybody because I wasn't supposed to reveal that I was on parole. Afterward, you got so jealous about Sheila that I didn't feel free to pursue any other friendships that happened to be female. And the one person in this town I'd really like to get to know better—besides Willard, I mean—is another customer you don't even know. She's about forty, a super lady who's asked me to join her for lunch a couple of times. She's involved with a man who lives in L.A. and I'm sure she only wants to be friends. We've got a lot in common, intellectually and emotionally, and we're both lonely a good deal of the week because our 'significant others' are so often gone. But I feel obliged to cut her off as coolly as I do Sheila, because of you." He tightened his grip on her hand, afraid she'd pull away. But she didn't. She just watched him, her eyes careful, assessing. He decided to get the rest of it over with.

"I think that's one reason your accusation made me so angry. Here I'd been working double-time to make sure you didn't misinterpret anything I did, and you nailed my hide to the wall anyway." He met her eyes unhappily before he concluded, "I think that's about it."

Carly took several moments to digest his words before she replied in an even tone, "It sounds as though you've put a lot of effort into putting on a show. I wonder where we'd be if you'd given up trying to be perfect and just acted like yourself."

"Back in prison," he replied without thinking. "With bars again between you and me."

Suddenly she kissed him. Her hands slipped around his neck and pulled him closer. He heard her murmur an anguished, "No, Gary, no."

Gary closed his arms around her, the woman he so deeply cherished, and buried his face in her beautiful black hair. He'd never been so keenly aware of how much he needed her love, how completely it would break him if she ever tossed him out of her life. "I was so afraid of losing you, Carly. Right from the beginning, I couldn't imagine that a woman like you would want to give up her future for a prisoner like me."

"You're not a sacrifice, Gary. You're all that I want," she whispered in his ear. Then, in a shaky voice, she confessed, "You're not the only one who's been acting here. After all you'd been through, I couldn't bear to do anything to make you unhappy. I never felt free to snap at you, or complain about anything, or contradict any of your wishes. I've always tried to cheer you up, to bolster you, no matter how I felt. How tired or down. Or sick, sometimes, of listening to your miseries." She kissed him quickly to soften the blow. "I know I'll never fully understand what you've been through. But you're free now, and even if you don't have the girls back yet, you do have *me*. I just wish you could be grateful for that. Or happier. When I look at what you've got now, compared to what you had when we met, it makes me feel...as if I'm unimportant to you. You worry so much about the future."

"Oh, Carly," he whispered, "don't you understand that *you're* the reason my future troubles me so? I want to be able to support you in style. At least adequately! I want to make you proud of me...willing to introduce me to your friends! Do you realize you've never invited anybody over, never taken me to a party, never—"

"Gary, I never see anybody during fire season! I'm exhausted when I come back. I don't want to waste my time on anybody but you!"

Gary sighed, half relieved, half angry for all the hurtful moments they'd both endured because they'd refused to trust each other. He didn't point out that it wasn't yet fire season, and if she didn't quit fire fighting, things could only get worse. "Carly," he confessed, "from the moment I asked you to marry me in prison—and you said no—I've been trying to live up to some majestical image, achieve some mythical goal. You made it clear that you were afraid I'd discard you once I had everything I wanted—my freedom, my career, my children. That's the main reason I've pushed so hard for all of them. The pot of gold at the end of my rainbow is *you*."

He didn't know if she believed him, but he knew he'd finally told her the truth. And he knew that when fresh tears filled her eyes, they were tears of joy, of hope, and that the time for conversation was over.

He savored the feel of her fingernails against his scalp as she slowly pulled his head yet closer, lifting her mouth to his. With infinite tenderness he kissed her lips, then slid his hands over her shoulders, across her back, and slowly down to her shapely backside, naked where the pink satin nightgown had ridden up.

Carly rolled slightly to press herself against him, and he felt a turgid physical need for her spring to life. "Carly, sweetheart," he murmured. "I love you so much. I'd never hurt you on purpose. Never in a thousand years."

Her answer was a kiss that started with quiet assurance and ended with a fiery thrust of her tongue between his parted lips. He savored the moist warmth of her tender flesh against his own, relished the feel of her ever so feminine curves against his own urgent hardness. As one fingertip traced the line of her hip, then circled back to insinuate itself between her thighs, Carly's legs parted to give him access. He felt her knee slip over his own. A moment later, a confident female hand locked around his own swelling hunger, and he made no effort to stifle his urgent moan.

Gary gloried in the haze of his own hunger, echoed in Carly's purr of rising pleasure as his fingers deftly heightened her woman's need of him. This morning it was time for a slow siege of loving, time for healing and celebrating the love they shared. Gary took her to the edge of pleasure as tenderly as she led him toward the same mountaintop. By the time she rolled over flat on her back and beckoned for him to join her, he was more than ready to fill her with his love.

As their bodies merged, in love and forgiveness and tender desire, Gary cradled Carly tightly against him. As he felt her rock with waves of passion that carried him in on the same high tide, she whispered against his tingling throat, "I'll always love you, Gary. We've got a thousand tomorrows to make up for last night."

WHEN GARY LEFT for work, Carly lay in bed, humming, deciding how to spend her day. There was laundry to do, of course, and a letter to write to her father. She wanted to check in on Willard, then pick up a present for a dear college friend whose birthday was just a few days away. The evening—the image that came to her mind produced an embarrassed grin—she would save for Gary.

She tried to remember when the last time was that they'd spent a whole evening together, but she couldn't recall. As she tried to piece together the exhausting weeks since Christmas, it occurred to Carly that she didn't see Gary now all that much more than she had when he was in prison. Then, as now, she'd put fire fighting first. For years it had been the most important thing in her life.

But was it now? *Of course not.* Gary was the center of her world; on that issue, her heart and mind had no debate. So why did she keep fighting fires? Why did she insist on compounding their difficult domestic situation? Of all their problems, Carly's work schedule was the only thing either of them could do anything about.

But was it also her badge of honor, of independence? A way of denying how terribly important Gary really was to her, so that if he ever left her, she wouldn't look like such a chump? Would fighting fires keep her days and nights full until the anguish went away, as it had when Rodney had betrayed her?

But suddenly she realized that if she ever lost Gary, the anguish *wouldn't* go away. Her love for him was a thousandfold what she'd felt for Rodney. And there were times when she was certain that Gary's love—oh, why couldn't she believe it with all her heart?—was a thousandfold what Rodney had ever felt for her. How long was she going to keep him on trial, waiting for him to prove it? *Maybe I could just take a season off,* she told herself. *Just till he's free of parole.* But once he was free of parole, he'd probably have a better shot at getting his children back. As a mother, how could she be gone such terrible hours? Would she hold on to the job if she had a baby of her own? And if she couldn't think of Gary's children as her own, what kind of a mother would she be?

She had no good answers for any of her questions, no way to soothe the sudden realization that she, not Gary, was the one who hadn't yielded all of her heart. It was a stunning discovery, one she decided to share with Gary the moment he came home. But less than an hour later, the telephone rang with news preventing that move.

"We need a night-shift supervisor for a fire in the Sierra Nevada," the Goleta dispatcher informed her grimly. "How long will it take you to get across the state line?"

Gary was crawling the walls by the fourth day of the Nevada fire Carly had bolted off to the morning after they'd made their peace. She'd stopped by the nursery to kiss him goodbye, her eyes assuring him that all was forgiven. But she'd also told him she would no longer be calling to check in, and she hoped he'd enjoy having lunch with his new female friend. At the time he'd been honored, assured, too relieved to worry a great deal about how much he'd miss her. Now he was not only lonely, but increasingly worried about the woman he treasured. He also knew that he had nobody but himself to blame for Carly's failure to contact him. Hadn't he told her how much he resented those calls? But he'd also looked forward to them, ached to hear her voice and rejoiced in the opportunity to get caught up with her, however briefly, almost every day. It was the reason he thought she had been calling that troubled him, not the calls themselves.

Despite Carly's magnanimous offer for him to have lunch with his new friend, he hadn't been able to set anything up until the following week. On Saturday he went to see the girls, acutely aware, as always, of Ruth's eyes on him. She was speaking to him now—hello, goodbye, brief snippets of news about his children—and once she'd shown him Shelley's report card. But things were still so guarded between them that he didn't know how to say, "I'm sorry for your grief, Ruth. I had my troubles with your husband, but I never wanted to see him dead."

On Sunday, Gary had lots of time to think about his latest fight with Carly. He tried to determine what was worth holding onto and what was not. Reluctantly he realized that his obsession with proving himself to her, career-wise, was counterproductive. For the time being, he needed to set medicine aside. He could live without it. He didn't want to, but he could. What he couldn't live without was Carly and his children. Like half the rest of the men in the world, he'd have to take whatever job best provided for his family. He had to celebrate the miracles in his life—Carly and his freedom—and do his best to be grateful for his precious moments with his girls. In time, he vowed, he'd bring them home. The trick was not to let the waiting destroy him. He couldn't afford to lose Carly in the meantime.

Gary was pleased with his decisions and mentally preparing for his regular meeting with Walt Tower in the morning when he heard a brisk knock at the door. He peeked out the curtains, found Willard on the steps, and cheerfully invited him in.

"Carly's still gone?" the older man asked.

"Yep. Real dry this year."

Willard's eyes looked bright, downright eager compared to the last time Gary had seen him; the old doctor had remained depressed ever since he'd received news that Willie had decided to stay in L.A. But now a huge smile lifted the wrinkles of his face. Certain that Willie must have had a change of heart, Gary said, "Don't keep me in suspense, Willard! Looks like somebody's got good news."

Willard laughed out loud. "You're a shrewd one, Dr. Reid. If you'll invite me in, I'll tell you all about it."

Gary stood aside as Willard came in, then found him a cold soda in the refrigerator. It occurred to him that a few months ago, he would have felt awkward about inviting a friend into this apartment, serving him food from Carly's refrigerator. But now this was his home. His income was decent, if not enormous, and it was an honest living earned in a friendly little town. He knew half of his customers; folks waved to him as he walked downtown. And Carly loved him. She'd given him another chance to make things right. Granted, she was gone a lot, and he still desperately missed the girls. But all in all, life was a million times better than he'd ever imagined it might be on that terrible night when Michelle had died. He had a dozen reasons to rejoice, not the least of which was that Willard was happy again.

"So, what's the good word?" he asked, his curiosity truly piqued by now. "Willie's seen the light, right?"

When silent denial shadowed the old man's face, Gary backpedaled quickly. "Hey, I'm really sorry. I didn't mean to rub salt in your wounds. I was just so sure he'd turn around!"

"So was I."

"Dammit, Willard! Some day he'll regret it. He just doesn't understand what he's giving up. Any doctor in his right mind would give up his eyeteeth to go into practice with you."

"Even you?" Willard lifted his bushy eyebrows dramatically. "Even if it meant you had to endure some pretty pointed questions from the Board of Medical Quality Assurance before you got your license back?"

"I beg your pardon?" Gary sputtered, taken off guard by the unexpected mention of the official state board in charge of licensing.

Willard was smiling now. Broadly. "I've got a buddy on the Board, you know. Did I ever mention that?" Before Gary could reply he continued, "We went to med school together. Fought over the same girl before I fell in love with Thelma. Haven't seen him in thirty, forty years, of course. But I'm pretty sure he'd remember me."

This time Gary said nothing. He wasn't sure where Willard was heading, but he was sure—wasn't he?—that Willard understood how much his lost career meant to him. The other man would never use that knowledge to jest.

"For thirty years I've waited for my only son to become a doctor here in Sespe, Gary. To share my business and my life." Willard took a long, dramatic swallow, then looked Gary straight in the eye. "You spent most of your adult life sweating over textbooks and operating tables. Living without sleep. Living on dreams. I know what it's like to live on dreams. I know what it's like to have them snatched away." He was no longer smiling. He was deadly serious now. "I like you, Gary. I believe in you as a doctor. I believe in you as a man. If you want to become my partner—part-time at first, more as the practice requires it—then I'm willing to take you on."

Gary was sure that his breathing had stopped. He struggled for words, but absolutely nothing came out of his mouth.

Mercifully, Willard saved him. "I know we're going to have to jump through a lot of legal hoops. Before you saved Genevieve Harmon, I don't think this town would have taken a risk on a former prisoner. But now, if we let them get used to you gradually, I think we can make it work. You may have to start off in the background—not exactly emptying bedpans, mind you, but prescribing penicillin for strep throat. It's not going to be easy. For either one of us. But if you're willing to give it your best shot, I'm willing to take a chance on you."

Again Gary tried to speak, but his joy was beyond words.

THE INSTANT CARLY had surveyed the Nevada side of the Sierra country by plane, she'd known it was going to be the worst fire she'd ever fought. It had been fifteen years since they'd had a blaze in this part of the high mountains, which meant that the ground was blanketed with tinder-dry pine needles and a host of other forms of instant kindling. Wade, her divisional counterpart on this mission, had taken one look below him on their overview flight and shaken his head. Carly had done the same.

She sorely resented this out-of-state call for her services. She knew that the Nevada fire-fighting crews were desperate, depleted partly because a number of people were on loan to Oregon. Normally she'd have rushed to help a neighboring state without a moment's hesitation, but this time she'd realized from the moment that she got the call—less than hour after Gary had left her basking in the afterglow of their morning loving—that she simply didn't want to leave him to fight another fire. She'd spent forty-five of the past sixty-seven days covered with soot, battling blisters and inhaling acrid smoke, but her resistance now stemmed from more than fatigue. She desperately needed to spend some time with Gary. For a dozen years now she'd given all of her free time to the Forest Service. Now it was time to give it to him.

High winds had tripled the flames the first night Carly spent on the ridge. The second night things had started to look better, but by the next evening, an inversion once again made the crews lose control. It was well into the fourth day of the fire—around midnight, in fact—when she was reflagging a line through a dense part of a ridge, wishing that she could talk to Gary, that the wind switched directions and started pushing the fire directly toward her.

The smoke was suddenly overpowering; she gagged as she went down.

"I'M TRYING TO reach Dr. Gary Reid," declared the brusque male voice on the phone.

"Speaking." Gary squinted at the clock by the bed. It was three o'clock on a Sunday morning—the one day that Sespe Green Things was closed—and Gary had planned on sleeping in. Whoever was calling at this hour couldn't be bringing good news; it was the time of day when doctors are awakened to hurry to the emergency room. The possibilities filled him with dread.

"This is Wade Haley, a colleague of Carly's. We've met before, but I doubt if you remember me."

"I remember." *As if I could ever forget,* Gary mumbled to himself. But the remembered resentment vanished in an instant as he realized that there was only one reason that burly Wade Haley could possibly be calling him in the middle of the night. Fear clawed at his belly as he asked, "Is Carly all right?"

It seemed to take forever for Wade to reply, though Gary's rational mind realized that his reply was quick and sharp. "Yes, but I'm sorry to say that she's been injured. She's got serious smoke-inhalation problems. Poison-oak smoke, which complicates the situation considerably."

Considerably? Gary repeated to himself, marveling at the understatement. Half of him was thrilled that she was alive and not suffering from terrible burns. But he knew how serious poison oak in the lungs could be for anybody, and because this patient was his Carly, his whole body flushed with alarm.

"What kind of medical care is she getting?" Gary asked at once. "May I talk to her attending physician?"

"I'm sorry, he's not here and I don't know the answers. All I know is that they put her on a respirator and promised me she'd be all right. I'm going to stay right here until I'm sure she's out of the woods, but she once told me that you are—" he paused for a moment, as though searching for the right word "—family to her, so I thought you ought to know."

Gary took only a moment to decide what to do. He'd have to call Walt Tower and somehow get permission to cross the state line, even though it was prohibited under the regular terms of his parole. But Tower could legally approve almost anything, and Gary was reasonably sure that the man would see his point of view. After all, Gary had a spotless record and a crucial reason for going to Nevada, which the parole officer could easily check out. Surely Tower would understand!

Quickly he dialed Tower's number, but at this hour of the night, all he got was a recording telling him that the office opened at eight o'clock. Five long hours from now! Any emergencies were referred to the sheriff's office.

Gary felt ill as he considered his options. Even if he could bear to sit still for five hours waiting for the parole officer to come to work, Tower might conceivably say no. And if Gary left a message for Tower with the cops, they'd probably ignore his good intentions and pick him up before he crossed the state line. But if Gary left California before he talked to Tower, he'd be breaking parole. If he got caught, he'd be sent back to prison.

As he hurriedly dressed in the dark, Gary realized that he could probably reach the Nevada border by the time the parole office opened if he left right away; with any luck at all, he could reach Walt Tower from a phone booth on the California side of the line. If Tower gave his permission, Gary would be free to go straight to Carly. In the meantime, he wouldn't have broken any rules or wasted any time.

It was a great plan. The only question that plagued Gary was what he'd do if Walt Tower came in late to work today.

IT WAS A question that Gary had to answer when he pulled into a gas station just off the road at eight-fifteen, as the Mojave desert was shaking off the last of the night's brief chill. He was relieved when a secretary answered—a real person instead of a recording—but sickened when she told him that Mr. Tower would not be in until later that day.

"May I take a message?" she asked politely. "He should be able to get back to you this afternoon."

For Gary, even an hour's wait was intolerable. His woman was in peril! Yet his freedom was also on the line. He had to rely on his instincts to make this emergency decision. He thought of Willard's life-changing offer; he thought about his children. He thought about all the months of kowtowing to Walt Tower, pleading with Ruth. He thought about the sheer hell of spending another six months in prison. And then he thought about Carly, and all she'd risked for him.

"Yes, I'd like to leave a message for Mr. Tower," he finally decided, trying to quell the tremor in his voice. "This is one of his parolees, Gary Reid. Will you please tell him I won't be able to keep our appointment at three o'clock today?"

"Certainly, Mr. Reid. Will that be all?"

He hesitated, then remembered his advice to Clifford: take a chance on trusting the people who'd taken the chance of trusting you. Tower had allowed him to live with Carly even though the officer knew that Gary was often on his own at night. He had been fair and kind and given Gary slack whenever he could. He deserved better than deception now.

And so did Carly.

"Please tell Mr. Tower that I need his permission to go to Nevada because Carly Winston has been badly injured." He gave her the name of the hospital and his exact route... even the phone number and address of his current location. "Tell him I just found out at three o'clock this morning and I tried to reach him then. I was hoping to talk to him personally before I left the state, but I... I think he'll understand why I couldn't wait."

He also hoped that Tower would give him retroactive permission to cross the state line, because, like the night he'd gone to Clifford, Gary knew what he had to do.

CHAPTER SIXTEEN

WHEN CARLY WOKE up again, she was gagging on the horrible pipe stuffed down her throat and her hands were tied down to the bed. She couldn't move and she couldn't think clearly, but her momentary panic faded when she recognized the frightened blue eyes in the loving face beside her.

As she slowly focused on Gary, he offered her a tremulous smile. "You're going to be okay, Carly," he whispered, his voice unsteady. He laid one infinitely gentle hand on the top of her head. "You'll have to put up with this apparatus for a couple of days, but if you don't fight it, it won't hurt so much. And I'm going to be right here every minute."

She couldn't talk and she couldn't touch him, so Gary had to do all the loving for both of them. "I called your dad in Japan, and he asked me to take care of you until he got here. I told him I'd stay here whether he came or not, but I figure it never hurts to have your whole family around you, does it?"

Carly started to cry. She wanted to see her father, but she knew she needed Gary more. She needed him and he had come to her, even though she hadn't asked, even though there was absolutely nothing he could do but sit beside her... and even though he'd broken parole to do it. He'd risked prison; he'd risked losing touch with his girls. No sane man did that out of guilt or gratitude. He did that for the woman he truly loved.

As he stroked her hair with trembling fingers, Carly studied his anguished face and realized that even if she hadn't known about the risks he'd undertaken by breaking parole, one look at his frightened eyes would have been enough to tell her everything she'd always longed to know. Gary loved her. Just as his pain had been her pain, now her pain was his.

For the very first time, she was certain that he loved her as much as he had once loved Michelle.

With that joyous realization, she faded back into semiconsciousness while he held her; when she woke up hours later, he was still at her side. For two days and nights she floundered between consciousness and sleep. Every time she came to, she saw Gary's face, felt Gary's hands, drew strength from the way Gary's love surrounded her. Later she saw Gary and her father chatting like two comrades who'd fought a long, hard battle together side by side. Once she thought she saw Wade with his hand on Gary's shoulder; another time she was sure she heard her dad tell Gary he must get some sleep. But Gary never left her side. She felt his presence, his love, his eternal devotion surrounding her, uplifting her, willing her back to health. On the third day, they removed the respirator, and Carly was finally able to speak.

"What can I do for you?" Gary asked her, his weary eyes still full of love, now flooded with relief.

Her throat hurt terribly, and it was hard to speak. But now that she knew that Gary loved her, all doubt had vanished and nothing was too great to bear.

"Marry me," she begged him.

A joyful smile stole over his unshaven features. His eyes grew wide and puzzled. "Carly? Am I hearing things or are you hallucinating?"

Carly grinned. "Neither. Both. Will you marry me?"

He bent to kiss her cheek. It was a gentle kiss, a slow kiss, a kiss that answered her question without words. He pulled back to study her face, tracing her eyebrow with one gentle finger. "Are you sure, Carly? Are you truly sure of me now?"

She lifted her fingertips to caress his lips, wishing she had the strength to pull him down beside her. "My life is yours," she said simply.

Gary closed his eyes as he pressed his lips against the palm of her hand. For a moment, he could not speak. Then he promised softly, "I'll ask Walt Tower for permission the minute we get back. No matter what."

Deliriously happy, Carly drifted back to sleep. It wasn't until the next time she woke up that she realized what Gary meant by that last phrase. Under the circumstances, "No matter what" might easily translate into "Even if I'm back in prison."

The possibility filled her with dread, but Carly knew that even if Gary was locked away the next day, she'd marry him, anyway.

"NOW LET'S GO over this whole scenario again," bony Walt Tower proclaimed sternly as Gary faced him in the tiny office three days after Carly was released from the hospital. "At three in the morning you received word from Wade Haley that Carly had been injured. You tried to reach me, but got a recording at that hour. Before you crossed the state line, you called back from a ghost town, more or less, with one pay phone. This time you spoke to the department secretary and were informed that I would not be available until after lunch. You left a message for me with her, spelling out the precise information about your destination and rationale for—" Gary waited for him to say "breaking parole," but instead, he finished with "—rescheduling our appointment at the last minute." He studied Gary for a moment, then tacked on, "You were reasonably certain that I would approve of your actions."

"Yes, sir," Gary said politely, still trembling as he waited for the verdict. Some parole officers, he knew, would already have sent the black-and-whites to pick him up by now. Tower, who'd talked to him long-distance at least four times during Carly's stay in Nevada, had not mentioned that as an option, though he had ordered Gary to check in with the local law enforcement people in Nevada every day. It had been his impression that they'd been informed that Gary's trip had been authorized before he'd crossed the state line, not after. They'd been quite courteous to him, all things considered, when it became obvious that he was making no effort whatsoever to run away.

"You called back to talk to me personally at one o'clock, shortly after I received your message from the secretary. You explained the situation in detail. I arranged for temporary supervision in Nevada, and according to my records, you called or appeared as ordered every time."

"Yes, sir," Gary said again.

Tower studied the window for a moment, his back to Gary. "Bonnie Ralston says she has no complaints with your performance on the job. Since you'd never missed work or come in late for any reason in all the time you've worked for her, she was understanding when you phoned her from Nevada to explain why you would be away a few days."

"I'm glad to hear that, sir. I do my best."

"Do you plan to continue working there when you finish your parole?"

Certain that Walt Tower knew or could find out absolutely everything about him, Gary declared, "I've had an offer to go into practice with an elderly physician who will be partially retiring soon. Carly's landlord, Willard

Jameson. He's willing to help me try to get clearance from the proper authorities to practice medicine, again. If that pans out, sir, I'll be staying in Sespe, but not at the nursery. All of this is on hold until my parole ends, of course, and I'll give Bonnie plenty of time to replace me."

Tower turned around now, his eyes narrowing as he faced Gary in a way that made it clear that somebody had already told him everything about Willard's offer.

"And your living arrangements. Are they still satisfactory?"

Gary nodded. "More than satisfactory, sir. Carly has consented to marry me as soon as... you give your permission."

It killed him to ask another man for permission to marry Carly. He hadn't even asked her dad, though Colonel Winston had given Carly his blessing before he'd flown back to Japan. And under the circumstances, Gary knew he might well be going back to prison before he could clear the legal hurdles for a wedding, but at least he'd have his request on the record. It was a little step, but an important one. From the moment Carly had mentioned marriage in the hospital, everything between them had changed. They were a couple now in a way they had never been before. And while Carly had rejoiced in his good news about Willard's offer, it was important to Gary that she'd consented to marry him before she knew there was any hope at all that he'd have a decent future. It was, strangely enough, the discovery that he'd be willing to go back to prison just to be with her when the chips were down that had convinced her of the depth of his love. If it really came down to that, he thought, it would be a terrible price to pay. But worth it, if that was what it would take to keep Carly in his life.

Walt Tower did not reply to Gary's request for permission to marry Carly. He stood perfectly still as he faced his supplicant. "How much longer is your period of parole, Gary?"

"Five and a half months, sir. One hundred and seventy-six days."

"I take it these five and a half months are... slowing down all of your plans? Not just your custody problems with your children, but your medical career and your marriage, as well?"

"Yes, sir." Gary's hopes were dying with every minute. Tower looked like a man who was enjoying playing cat-and-mouse. Gary was reasonably sure that his parole period—in or out of prison—couldn't actually be extended, but Tower had it in his power to make it as difficult as it could possibly be.

Tower sat down opposite Gary and steepled his hands. Then, incredibly, he smiled. "You know what, Gary? You're just a lot of trouble for me. Parole is supposed to help rehabilitate a felon, readjust him to the outside world. You're so squeaky clean now I can hardly stand it, and as far as I can see, being on parole isn't doing you any good. It's just making it harder for you to fit back into civilian life."

Terrified that the next sentence was going to sound something like "You're going back to Tejon," Gary leaned forward in his stiff wooden chair, begging for a heavenly reprieve.

"Are you aware, Gary, that as your parole officer it's my prerogative to keep you on the outside, send you back to prison or grant you early release from parole?"

"Early release from parole?" Gary muttered, not at all certain what that entailed, but once more willing to hope. "You mean you can grant me a *pardon*?"

Tower's eyes narrowed. "Not a pardon. That's the Governor's department. It would wash your conviction off your record completely, and I sure wouldn't waste any time hoping for that."

Gary did not reply.

"An early release, on the other hand, simply shortens your total conviction time. It means that I don't think your continued parole is of any help to you or necessary to protect the public. In other words, you've cleaned up your own act, Gary. I'm just getting in your way, and—" for the second time since Gary had known him, the man actually cracked a smile "—you're wasting my time."

Gary couldn't breathe. "Are you serious? Are you going to set me free?"

"I am." The grin grew wider. "I am, indeed."

ALMOST A MONTH later, Carly joined Gary at an appointment with his attorney, the purpose of which was to initiate legal action regarding custody of the girls. His first act as a free man had been to marry Carly in a private civil ceremony with only Bonnie and Willard in attendance. His second act had been to apply for his license to the California Medical Board of Quality Assurance. Now, with a bright gold ring on his left hand, he slipped one arm possessively around his new wife and said, "I'm tired of waiting, John. I'm tired of court decrees and delays and Ruth's petty restrictions. By law, I am the sole parent of Patsy and Shelley Reid. There's no reason on earth that they shouldn't be living with me."

Quietly Carly added, "And no reason on earth why I shouldn't be allowed to adopt them."

She felt Gary's loving gaze embrace her. She'd only met Shelley once, and she'd never laid eyes on little Patsy at all, but it made no difference to the place Gary's children held in her heart. She had already decided that it was time to back off from her overwhelming schedule, time to devote herself to her marriage, time to give some thought to when she could give birth to babies of her own. But for now—while she worked nine-to-five for the Forest Service and spent every joyous night at home—she was determined to join Gary in his fight for his children. If they belonged to Gary, then they now belonged to her. The issue of their custody was a battle they were going to fight together.

"Look, folks," John declared with a touch of asperity, "I'm not the one you need to convince. It's the court that will need to be persuaded."

He began to outline the procedure, attack and counterattack that would likely occur as he and Ruth Everhard's attorney slugged it out in court, using poor little Shelley and Patsy as weapons. From everything Gary had told her, Carly was sure that they loved their grandmother and needed her, too. In spite of everything the woman had done to Gary, Carly understood her passionate loyalty to her late husband and daughter. If anything ever happened to Gary, Carly knew she'd have been hard pressed to listen to any sort of logic that might have cleared the allegedly guilty party. Her love for him surpassed all common sense. So did his love for her... and for his little girls.

For two hours, Carly listened to the men chew on strategy, argue over details. And then, just as she and Gary were leaving, an idea came to her, as clear as sunlight after a dark winter's night, and she decided to enlighten them with a woman's point of view.

"I think you're wrong, John, when you say that it's the court that needs to be convinced of Gary's fitness as a parent," she told the attorney bluntly. "His parenting skills have never been called into question by anybody. Not before the accident, not after. The claim that needs to be proven is that *he did not kill Tom Everhard*, accidentally or on purpose, and the only person he needs to convince now is Ruth."

AT ELEVEN O'CLOCK on Monday morning—the housekeeper's day off—Gary left Carly waiting in the truck and rang Ruth Everhard's doorbell. Half an hour after Patsy usually took her nap and an hour before the bus brought Shelley home, it was the only time Gary was sure he could talk to Ruth without being interrupted. He'd considered making an appointment, but that would have given her time to confer with her lawyer and build up a whole new wall of defenses before he got there. So far she'd had every advantage in their battle for the girls. Just this once, he longed to have the upper hand.

He did. Ruth was clad in a pair of stained and sloppy slacks when she opened the door. Her hair was not yet trapped in its daily bun. She blinked and let out a tiny gasp when she saw Gary standing on the porch. But she recovered herself before he could speak. "This isn't your day to see the girls," she said bluntly.

"I didn't come to see them. I came to talk to you."

One white hand fluttered to Ruth's throat. "We don't... have an appointment," she said.

"We have an *obligation*," Gary countered, "to settle this out of court."

"I owe you nothing!" Ruth burst out, her face contorting in pain. "You killed my husband! You—"

Gary took a quick step toward her and grabbed hold of her waist with both hands. "Look at me!" he ordered. "Dammit, Ruth, look me in the face and say that!"

She tried to wriggle out of his grasp, but Gary wouldn't let her go. "I'm going to say this once more. I tried to tell you the night it happened, but you were hysterical. You couldn't hear me. You couldn't listen. I understand that. I went crazy when Michelle died." He loosened his grip on her, but did not release her. He waited until she tremulously met his fierce gaze. "Ruth, I didn't like your husband. But I adored his daughter. For that reason alone, I never would have hurt him. You know that. You know how many times I swallowed the hard words he deserved. You know how he goaded me, insulted me, tried to buy me off. I protected Michelle from all of it, or as much as I possibly could. You can't deny that; can you?"

He took her wide-eyed silence as assent.

"My wife was dead and he tried to steal my children. Yes, I was angry. Yes, I hollered horrible things at him. Yes, I would have fought him tooth-and-toenail to keep custody of Shelley and Patsy, just as I'm willing to fight you, if need be. But I never touched him while he was driving that Jag, Ruth—" he lifted her chin with one trembling hand "—and when I came to and found him slumped over the steering wheel, there was *absolutely no doubt in my mind that he was dead*." She tried to look away, but she couldn't. She stood perfectly still, rooted to the spot as he concluded softly, "I only pulled his body out so you'd be able to say goodbye. I know how much it meant to you to sit beside Michelle before we buried her."

Ruth's wrinkled face collapsed in a spasm of tears. With trembling, bony hands she pushed him away and ran into the house. He didn't have the heart to fight her, to holler at her, to make her stay. But when he realized that she hadn't slammed the door behind her, he decided to follow her inside.

He found her at the kitchen table, sobbing into her hands. He didn't try to comfort her, nor did he try to hide his presence. He walked over to the cupboard where the coffee was kept and brewed her some, just the way she'd always liked it. For three minutes, the automatic coffee maker burbled and hummed as a backdrop to her sobs. No other sound intruded on the silence.

She said nothing as Gary handed Ruth her favorite cup—at least, it had been her favorite once—and took a chair beside her. She still didn't meet his eyes, but she didn't order him out of the house, either.

"I've been released from parole, Ruth," he said calmly, even though he was sure that she already knew it. "I'm going back into medicine. I got married last week to a wonderful woman who stood by me in prison as loyally as Michelle would have. Carly is as eager for the girls as I am."

At last Ruth met his eyes. "It didn't take you very long to get over my daughter," she said accusingly.

Gary shook his head. "You're mixing apples and oranges, Ruth. I adore Carly. I'd give my life for her. But I will never stop loving Michelle."

He didn't try to explain any more to Ruth. After all, she was Michelle's mother, and she didn't want to hear about his passion for her ex-son-in-law's second wife. But Michelle lived in one part of his heart; Carly lived in another. Michelle was an untarnished memory, but Carly was now the very fabric of his life.

It was an awkward hour, but Gary felt that they were finally making headway. He reminded Ruth that, despite Tom, he and she had once been friends. He even admitted how much he regretted his long hospital hours and his failure to realize that Michelle was in grave danger until it was too late. Ruth confessed that she was often haunted by the possibility that she had misjudged him, that she'd punished him because it was the only way she could cope with her grievous double loss. But she also informed him that the only reason she'd backed Tom's original decision to take the girls was because, with Gary's hours, she was afraid that her granddaughters would be raised by a series of housekeepers instead of a father. Gary was quick to assure her that he'd learned so much in the past two years, he would never put his work before his family again.

As gently as possible, he told her, "You're sixty-seven, Ruth. You must be exhausted trying to raise two active little girls, even with a housekeeper to help you out. This is the home where they're going to end up being raised by a stranger. You'll admit that if you'll be honest with yourself."

Again her eyes flashed open. "What about that woman you picked up? She's a stranger! Why should she raise them instead of me?"

"Because she's my *wife*," Gary answered levelly. "And she loves them, too. Besides, I'm not planning to leave the childrearing to Carly. Don't you think I learned anything from Michelle? I'm dying to make up for lost time with my children, Ruth, and I've found a way to earn a living and spend time with them, as well."

"How?"

"The fellow who's taking me into his practice only needs part-time help right now. I probably won't go full-time till he retires. In the meantime, he's perfectly willing to arrange my time so I can work while Shelley's in school. Between Carly's hours and mine, I doubt that Patsy will spend more than ten hours a week with a baby-sitter." His eyes met hers gravely. "It could even be you, if we work together and plan it right."

Ruth licked her lips. "You're saying you'd let me see them all the time if you had custody? After all I've done to you?"

Gary nodded, but honesty compelled him to say, "I wouldn't be doing it for you, Ruth. My babies have been through more than any little girls should have to bear. I won't cut out a single loving family member from their lives. Their happiness means a lot more to me than my pride." He let the words sink in before he added quietly, "If you really love them, the same should be true for you."

His words seemed to clatter through the empty house; they echoed on the lonely air. Ruth stared at Gary, then at the floor. Several moments of awkward silence passed before she said, "Are you hungry, Gary? I was just about to make a sandwich. I've got some roast beef left over from last night."

Stunned but delighted, Gary acquiesced. "That would be very nice, Ruth. Thank you." He had no appetite at all, but somehow, he vowed, he'd choke down whatever she prepared.

Ruth stood up and started tugging things out of the cupboards, assembling two roast-beef sandwiches and a bowl of fruit in a leisurely fashion. He had the feeling she was stalling for time, but he wasn't sure why.

At last, after she'd served him and taken a bite herself, she murmured, "If I admit that you're not guilty, then I have a terrible burden to bear." The tone in her voice made it clear that this morning wasn't the first time she'd ever considered the possibility.

Determined not to lose his advantage by gloating, Gary told her, "It doesn't matter, Ruth. I mean—it does matter. Of course it matters. I've been through a hellish couple of years, and you've been a big part of my misery. But we can't do it over now, not any of it. I'm happy now, and that's all that matters. I probably wouldn't have met Carly if I hadn't gone to prison."

"She's your silver lining?" Ruth asked, with only a trace of resentment in her voice.

"Yes, she is." His voice throbbed with conviction. "And she can be a source of happiness for my children, too, Ruth. She knows she can't ever replace Michelle, but she really *wants* to be a mother to my girls."

Ruth studied him warily. "What do you propose?"

"Let me have them for a year. Six months, at the very least. Give them a chance to get adjusted, then we'll talk again. No lawyers in the meantime. No injunctions, no orders, no battlefield. You can see them whenever you want, as long as you promise to stop poisoning their minds with lies about me. I promise not to speak ill of—"

He broke off as Ruth began to cough. No, gag. A choking sound. At first he thought she was protesting his suggestion, but as he watched her, he realized that she was having trouble getting down a bite of her roast beef sandwich. "Should I get you some water?" he asked, when the coughing went on and on. She nodded, but when he handed her the glass a moment later, she couldn't seem to hold it. It flew wildly out of her grasp and shattered on the tile.

By now he realized that she was truly choking, and in order to help her, he'd have to risk her wrath. "Stand up, Ruth!" he ordered, grabbing her from behind to execute the Heimlich maneuver. He crossed his wrists to pummel both fists into her flesh just below the rib cage, but she continued to flail wildly. Her eyes bulged in terror, and her lips were turning blue.

CARLY TOOK HOPE from the amount of time Gary stayed inside. He'd been so hesitant, so unsure when they'd discussed this plan. They'd role-played possible scenarios a dozen times. When an hour passed, she began to believe he and Ruth were hammering out a plan.

Carly was surprised to see the yellow school bus pull up outside the house. She and Gary had agreed that Shelley should not overhear what he said to Ruth, but neither of them had expected the conversation to go on this long. Instantly she bolted out of the truck, trying to head off the sweet-smiling little blonde before she reached the front door.

"Hi, Shelley, remember me?" she greeted the child, almost breathless from her gallop up the street.

Shelley stared at her for a moment. "Oh, you're my daddy's friend!"

"Yes, I am." She smiled warmly, but Shelley's bright eyes dimmed.

"Are you here to tell me that Daddy's back in jail?"

Quickly Carly shook her head. "No, honey. Your daddy's just fine. He just came by to chat with your grandma, and I think we should let them talk alone for a while."

Shelley's lips puckered. "My grandma won't like that. I heard her tell the lady who cleans the house that she wanted her to work special on the days when Daddy comes." Her expression grew troubled as she confessed, "I think she's afraid of him."

Before Carly could answer, a piercing scream echoed from the house clear out to the street. The scream of a baby or a very small child.

"That's Patsy!" cried her big sister, bolting into the house.

Carly would have stayed outside, but the frenzied wail went on and on, spiraling into hysteria. Worse yet, a moment later it was echoed by Shelley's frantic yelp: "Don't you hurt my grandma!"

Unable to stop herself, Carly ran full-speed toward the sound of the screaming little ones. Red-faced, diapered Patsy had blood dripping from her feet, and Shelley was pummeling Gary's back.

"Trust me!" Gary yelled at his child. "Stay back!"

Stunned by the violence of his tone, Shelley froze, her eyes enormous as she stared at her grandmother, now lying limply on the kitchen table amidst scattered cups and dishes. Gary leaned over Ruth's body, gripping her throat with his left hand. In his right, he clutched a paring knife.

Despite the terrifying, surreal quality of the scene before her, Carly knew with every fiber of her being that

Gary was trying desperately to save Ruth Everhard's life. She also knew that—with his legal history—if his emergency kitchen tracheotomy failed, no jury in the state would fail to convict him of murder.

EPILOGUE

THE CHRISTMAS LIGHTS still glistened all over the yard of Willard Jameson's house at the tail end of December. But nowadays Willard lived in the tiny apartment where Carly and Gary had started out; he agreed that the three-bedroom house in the front was a better size for a family of four, with one on the way. The Reids had purchased it outright from Willard a month ago, determined to own their own home before the baby came.

While Carly cleaned up the dinner dishes, Gary walked Ruth out to her car, loading up the back seat with presents from the girls—and one from Carly and himself—before she drove away. Gary was proud of the fact that the scar on her throat was so small that it barely showed. Her gratitude for his lifesaving maneuver still flowed forth from her very smile, and her Christmas present to him had been a legal document relinquishing all claim to the girls. Carly's father's present had been just as vital. He'd arranged for leave to spend the holidays with them, and had asked the girls to call him Grandpa. Both of them had cried when he'd returned to his post the day before.

It had been quite a holiday, the house full to bursting with joyous sounds of Christmas, delectable aromas of holiday cooking, new traditions mixed with old. A Christmas card from Clifford had assured Gary that his future in Cresta was secure, and Willie spent his whole winter vacation in Mexico with his father, which went a long way toward healing Willard's emotional wounds. The practice itself was going extremely well. Once Gary had battled his way through the state requirements for reinstatement, his partnership with Willard had been a dream.

As Ruth drove away, she called back warmly, "You be sure to give me a call if you need help with that baby."

"I'll do that!" Gary promised as he waved goodbye. "It'll be a comfort to know there's somewhere I can go for good advice."

He didn't think he'd need a lot of help this time around, but Ruth would be the only grandmother his third child would have, and what baby could have too much family love?

It was Gary, not Carly, who'd be staying home part-time to take care of the little one due next summer. Although Carly worked only reasonable hours for the Forest Service these days, they had both agreed that for the time being, Gary should be the one to run the house, even after she had the baby.

He picked up Patsy and tossed her on his broad shoulders as he headed back up the walk. "Daddy, Daddy!" she squealed with delight. Shelley took her father's hand, hopping up and down as she tugged him back toward the house.

As they reached the front porch, Shelley stopped to point through the parted kitchen windows. Behind Carly, a crackling fire was burning in the grate, casting her Madonna's silhouette on the far wall.

"Look at Mama!" Shelley burst out, using the new name she'd adopted for the second loving mother in her life. "She looks just like a candle in the window."

As if she'd heard her name, Carly turned to face the three of them, her eyes meeting Gary's through the December fog. Her loving smile radiated through the window with more warmth than the sizzling blaze behind her. It seemed to Gary that he had never been surrounded by this much joy, never been so certain that his world was all in order, never felt more fully enveloped by everyone he loved.

As he opened the front door and slipped his free arm around his pregnant wife, Patsy tugged on his snow-white hair and Shelley squeezed his hand a little more tightly. Carly slipped an arm around his waist, then took hold of Patsy's little foot as though to close the circle. Catching on quickly, Shelley reached out for Carly's free hand.

And then, right on cue, the baby started kicking.

Harlequin American Romance

Gull Cottage

SUMMER.

The sun, the surf, the sand...

One relaxing month by the sea was all Zoe, Diana and Gracie ever expected from their four-week stays at Gull Cottage, the luxurious East Hampton mansion. They never thought they'd soon be sharing those long summer days—or hot summer nights—with a special man. They never thought that what they found at the beach would change their lives forever. But as Boris, Gull Cottage's resident mynah bird said: "Beware of summer romances...."

Join Zoe, Diana and Gracie for the summer of their lives. Don't miss the GULL COTTAGE trilogy in American Romance: #301 *Charmed Circle* by Robin Francis (July 1989), #305 *Mother Knows Best* by Barbara Bretton (August 1989) and #309 *Saving Grace* by Anne McAllister (September 1989).

GULL COTTAGE—because a month can be the start of forever...

If you missed #301 *Charmed Circle*, #305 *Mother Knows Best* or #309 *Saving Grace* and would like to order it, send your name, address, zip or postal code along with a check or money order for $2.75 plus 75¢ postage and handling ($1.00 in Canada) for *each book ordered*, payable to Harlequin Reader Service, to

In the U.S.
Harlequin Reader Service
901 Fuhrmann Blvd.
Box 1325
Buffalo, NY 14269-1325

In Canada
Harlequin Reader Service
P.O. Box 609
Fort Erie, Ontario
L2A 5X3

GULLG-1R

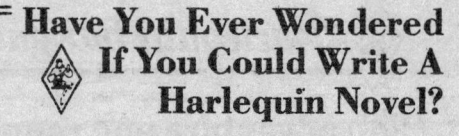

Have You Ever Wondered If You Could Write A Harlequin Novel?

Here's great news—Harlequin is offering a series of cassette tapes to help you do just that. Written by Harlequin editors, these tapes give practical advice on how to make your characters—and your story—come alive. There's a tape for each contemporary romance series Harlequin publishes.

Mail order only

All sales final

TO: *Harlequin Reader Service*
Audiocassette Tape Offer
P.O. Box 1396
Buffalo, NY 14269-1396

I enclose a check/money order payable to HARLEQUIN READER SERVICE® for $9.70 ($8.95 plus 75¢ postage and handling) for EACH tape ordered for the total sum of $_____*
Please send:

- ☐ Romance and Presents
- ☐ American Romance
- ☐ Superromance
- ☐ Intrigue
- ☐ Temptation
- ☐ All five tapes ($38.80 total)

Signature_____
(please print clearly)
Name:_____
Address:_____
State:_____ Zip:_____

*Iowa and New York residents add appropriate sales tax.

AUDIO-H

Harlequin Intrigue®

High adventure and romance—
with three sisters on a search...

Linsey Deane uses clues left by their father to search the Colorado Rockies for a legendary wagonload of Confederate gold, in #120 *Treasure Hunt* by Leona Karr (August 1989).

Kate Deane picks up the trail in a mad chase to the Deep South and glitzy Las Vegas, with menace and romance at her heels, in #122 *Hide and Seek* by Cassie Miles (September 1989).

Abigail Deane matches wits with a murderer and hunts for the people behind the threat to the Deane family fortune, in #124 *Charades* by Jasmine Cresswell (October 1989).

Don't miss Harlequin Intrigue's three-book series The Deane Trilogy. Available where Harlequin books are sold.

DEA-G